Summer 2022

Dear Friends,

Here's a bit of surprising news. No author is an island. We don't publish alone. Yes, the words are mine, and I personally wrote this book, but I have several teams of talented experts who strive to bring out the very best in me as an author. It starts with my own personal team who support me here at my office, along with my wonderful agent. And, of course, my publishing team. They each guided me through the many manifestations of this book. To them I owe a debt of gratitude. My attorney friend Lillian Schauer read through the courtroom scene so all the details align with reality. Thanks, Lillian! And my assistant, Shawna, read through multiple versions of this story.

I actually thought *The Best Is Yet to Come* would be my last book and that I would ease into retirement. But then I had a really good idea for another story. Writing is such a big part of who I am that I doubt I'll ever give it up entirely. The best for me is yet to come it seems, as Wayne and I travel. We bought an RV this summer and adventure awaits us.

Debbie
MACOMBER

The Best is
Yet to Come

SPHERE

SPHERE

First published in the United States in 2022 by Ballantine Books,
an imprint of Random House, a division of Penguin Random House LLC, New York
First published in Great Britain in 2022 by Sphere
This paperback edition published by Sphere in 2023

1 3 5 7 9 10 8 6 4 2

A CIP catalogue record for this book
is available from the British Library.

ISBN 978-0-7515-8092-1

Printed and bound in Great Britain by Clays Ltd, Elcograf S.p.A.

Papers used by Sphere are from well-managed forests
and other responsible sources.

Sphere
An imprint of
Little, Brown Book Group
Carmelite House
50 Victoria Embankment
London EC4Y 0DZ

An Hachette UK Company
www.hachette.co.uk

www.littlebrown.co.uk

To

Jennifer Hershey

and

Shauna Summers

Thank you for your faith in me.

The Best is Yet to Come

Prologue

"All rise," the bailiff announced, as the judge stepped into the courtroom. "Judge Walters presiding."

John Cade Lincoln Jr. rose to his feet next to his court-appointed attorney. He'd met the woman only once and had agreed to plead guilty. He faltered as he stood. His balance was off, as his leg had never properly healed from the shrapnel wound he'd suffered in Afghanistan. He caught himself by grabbing hold of the edge of the table where he sat as a defendant.

His attorney, Ms. Newman, a young woman who appeared to be fresh out of law school, leaned close to whisper, "The judge altered the agenda from the clerk's office so you would be the last case of the afternoon," she whispered.

"What does that mean?"

"I . . . don't know."

It didn't sound like it was good news. With the way his life was spiraling downward, he didn't expect anything less.

The silver-haired judge with piercing blue eyes took her seat, and everyone in the courtroom followed. Cade watched as she picked up his case file, and silently observed as the prosecutor read through the list of charges against him. Judge Walters slowly raised her head and looked directly at him. Her eyes narrowed at the long list, as she closely studied him. Cade met her gaze and squared his shoulders, as if standing before his commanding officer.

Disorderly conduct.

Assault and battery.

Destruction of private property.

Resisting arrest.

What captured his attention was a gasp that came from the back of the courtroom. He knew that voice. Knew the woman who'd made it. His mother. Groaning inwardly, he dropped his head, humiliated and humbled that she would turn up on the second-worst day of his life. He sank, grateful to take the weight off his leg, back into his chair as shock waves rolled over his shoulders because his mother sat in this very courtroom.

Sara Lincoln, his mother, was the last person he expected or wanted to see. The last communication, if it could even be defined as communication, had been nearly six years ago. The conversation consisted of his infuriated father yelling, his face red with anger, as he lambasted Cade. After calling him spoiled and ungrateful, he made sure Cade knew he was a major disappointment, a disgrace to the family name. And that had only been what Cade heard before he slammed out of the house. He had never gone back.

Maybe enlisting in the army had been a mistake, but it was his to make. As far as he was concerned, the choice between serving his country and attending law school following graduation had been a no-brainer. From the time he could remember, his father, John Senior, had expected his son to follow in his footsteps and join the family law firm.

From the moment he was born, it was assumed Cade would become an attorney. No one had bothered to ask him what he wanted. His job was to fall blindly into his family's expectations. He'd been given no choice in the matter. It had all been arranged. Set in place as soon as he'd drawn in his first breath.

Unable to resist, he looked over his shoulder. It was indeed his mother, and she was alone, which relieved him but at the same time hurt. He knew better than to hope his father cared enough to support him when he'd hit rock bottom. What he did notice was the love emanating from his mother's gaze. He quickly returned his attention to the front of the courtroom. If she was sorry for that final scene, it was too late now to make amends. If she'd said one word, one single word, in his defense, he could forgive her. Instead, she'd remained silent, and her silence had said everything.

He could only guess how his mother had learned he'd been arrested. He hadn't spoken to anyone in his family since the day he left for basic training in California. He hadn't even listed their names as next of kin on his enlistment papers, and he'd never looked back.

Six long years.

It went without saying: His parents would have nothing to do with him until he was willing to admit how terribly wrong he'd been. Once he realized his mistake, his parents would then be willing to welcome him back into the family fold.

Judge Walters looked up from the papers and again met his gaze, holding it for a long moment, as if gauging his character.

"Mr. Lincoln, have you been informed of your rights?" she asked.

Cade rose to his feet with the same awkwardness as earlier, gripping the table to maintain his balance. "Yes, Your Honor," he said, keeping his voice flat. His attorney had given him a rundown on what to expect. He had no defense. He'd been drunk and stupid. He deserved whatever punishment he had coming to him. He'd take it like a man without offering excuses or justifications.

"The court hereby accepts your guilty plea."

Cade assumed that was all that would be required of him. His attorney said the judge would accept his plea and then read his sentence. When silence followed, his gaze returned to Judge Walters, unsure and wary of what would happen next.

The judge glanced up from her file. "It says here you served in the military."

"Yes, Your Honor."

"And were awarded a Purple Heart."

He nodded and looked away. Like he cared. He survived, while Jeremy and Luke, his two best friends, had died. It would have been easier if he'd died that night, too. With every fiber of his being, he wished he had.

"What were the extent of your injuries?"

The last thing he wanted to do was provide a detailed list of the physical and emotional scars he carried. "I'm alive."

"Are you sure about that?" the judge asked, with arched brows.

The question shook him, and he raised his gaze to meet hers, offended by what she implied.

"Are you continuing with your schedule of physical therapy, Soldier?"

If she asked the question, she clearly knew he hadn't.

"No, Your Honor."

"Can you tell me why not?" she demanded.

"No, Your Honor." What was the use? His leg would never be the same. He would walk with a limp for the rest of his life. A limp that was a constant reminder that he had survived, while two of the best friends a man could ever want rotted in graves at Arlington Cemetery.

"I see," Judge Walters said slowly. "The same holds true for the mental counseling as well, it seems."

"I don't have PTSD," Cade insisted. What good would it do to sit and cry about what had happened? Grief was grief. You learned to live with it and move on. No way was he going to spill his guts to some VA counselor who likely didn't have a clue of what it was like to engage the enemy in a firefight and watch your friends be blown to bits. It wasn't no, it was hell no!

"According to the list of charges, it appears to me you are dealing with a lot of anger issues."

Cade was willing to admit that. Truth be told, he was downright furious with the world. The memories of that last battle engagement clawed at him like an eagle's talons, his sleep peppered with nightmares that his mind insisted on tossing at him like a hundred-mile-an-hour hardball pitch. He drank to forget. To sleep. To escape.

Alcohol had become his only friend.

"I am hereby sentencing you to three hundred and sixty-five days in jail with three hundred and sixty days suspended, giving you credit for the five days already served."

Cade heard the soft weeping sounds of his mother in the background. He refused to turn around and look at her. It was bad enough knowing she was here to see how low he'd sunk. He doubted his father knew she'd come. He would have forbidden her to ever speak to him again.

His attorney grasped hold of his arm. "Do you understand what that means?" she whispered.

No jail time. This wasn't what he deserved or had expected with a sense of dread and inevitability.

"That said, in light of your service to our country, I'm ordering two years' probation with mandatory participation in both physical therapy and counseling. You will make full restitution for damages and serve five hundred hours of community service."

Silence fell over the courtroom at the leniency of the sentence. The prosecutor stood as if to protest, but one look from the judge and he took his seat.

"Soldier, do you agree to these terms?" the judge asked.

"He does, Your Honor," the young woman standing at his side said quickly.

"I didn't ask you, Ms. Newman. Mr. Lincoln?"

Ms. Newman leaned close and urgently whispered, "This

is better than we could have hoped for. Agree with her before she changes her mind."

"Soldier?" the judge said, staring him down.

"Yes, Your Honor."

She pounded the gavel, and everyone stood as she left the courtroom.

"What happens if I don't comply?" Cade asked his lawyer, hoping there was a way to avoid mandatory counseling and physical therapy.

"Then you serve out the three hundred and sixty days in jail. It's your choice. It seems to me Judge Walters has taken a personal interest in your case. My advice is not to disappoint her."

Cade muffled his distress. He should be grateful. If the prosecutor had his way, he'd be wearing an orange suit and led away in handcuffs.

"You'll need to collect the Judgment and Sentence paperwork," his attorney said.

The courtroom had cleared. Before he could reply, he heard movement behind him.

"Cade." His mother reached out and touched his arm.

He pretended he didn't hear her soft voice and, without another word, followed his attorney to the clerk, who was preparing the paperwork.

When he looked back, he saw that his mother had left. He was sorry she'd come, and even sorrier that they had nothing to say to each other.

Chapter 1

A teacher really shouldn't have a favorite student.

Yet Hope Goodwin did. She was consistently blown away by Spencer Brown, the awkward young man in her Introduction to Computer Science class. He was miles ahead of everyone else. Hope feared his ability would quickly shoot past anything she could teach him. When he first showed up for class, she was surprised. He was by far the smartest kid in school and destined to be class valedictorian. He didn't need the credits. Every other class in his schedule was at AP level. The gossip she'd overheard in the teachers' lounge was that both Stanford and Yale were looking at him. The kid was going places. Sure as anything, Spencer didn't need a basic computer class.

It didn't take Hope long to discover the reason Spencer was in her classroom.

Callie Rhodes, another senior, a member of the dance team and senior class royalty. She was far and away out of Spencer's league.

Hope hated that Spencer was setting himself up for a major disappointment. Every class, the kid gave himself away. Hope was convinced she wasn't the only one who noticed, either. Spencer seemed unable to take his eyes off Callie.

Hope wondered if he'd heard a single word of anything she'd said the entire class period. His entire focus remained on Callie, and the pretty teenage girl seemed completely oblivious to him.

Callie was popular, pretty, and smart. From what Hope had been able to determine, she was dating Scott Pender, the school's star athlete and quarterback. She'd heard Scott played key positions on the basketball and baseball teams as well. Compared to Scott, Spencer didn't stand a chance.

Hope's last period of the day was AP U.S. History, and both Spencer and Callie were in that class. Oceanside High was a small school with fewer than three hundred students. The size suited Hope. She'd been looking to make a significant change in her life. Living in California, being alone in the world, she'd badly needed to get away, to forget and move forward.

No state income tax was only one of the reasons Washington State appealed to her. It was beautiful and she felt sure she could find a good job there in a charming and friendly community. So she applied for teaching positions in several small towns that dotted the western half of the state. With her two degrees—a master's in education and another in counseling—she wasn't surprised to be hired by Oceanside High School. She knew she was a good candidate. In addition to teaching computer science and U.S. history, she also worked as a counselor in the afternoons, which wasn't an opportunity afforded her at other schools. It made Oceanside an even better fit. Students came to her with a variety of issues. Mostly they needed someone willing to listen.

Moving to Oceanside had been the right move. Living close to the ocean had always been important to her. Any home or rental within ten miles of the Pacific in California was way out of her limited budget. It astonished her that the small rental cottage she found in Oceanside was well within walking distance of the ocean and, best of all, affordable.

Her landlords, Preston and Mellie Young, were great. Preston operated the local animal shelter, and Mellie was a full-time mother to their two toddlers. For the most part they kept to themselves. Hope exchanged pleasantries whenever they met. Mellie stayed indoors a lot, so Hope didn't see her often, but that was fine.

The cottage was older, probably built sometime in the 1960s or '70s. Mellie had mentioned that it had once been a summer rental. Only in the last few years had it been rented out full-time. Given how old the house was, it was only natural that it needed a few minor repairs. The kitchen could use a new paint job. One of the faucet handles was loose in the bathroom; the railing on the step was held together by a single nail. All minor details that would be easy fixes. Hope wasn't complaining, though, seeing how reasonable her rent was. Determined to be a good tenant, Hope would gladly fix whatever needed to be done herself. No need to give her landlords a reason to raise the rent.

Oceanside was the perfect place for her to escape, put down

roots, and get a fresh start at life. Her desire was to let go of the pains of the past and move forward, breathing in the new and exhaling the past.

Following the last class of the day, Hope left the classroom and headed toward the office where she had been assigned a small space. Glancing out the window, she saw the football team was on the practice field. She noticed Callie on the sidelines with a few of her friends from the dance team watching the boys do their drills on the grassy field.

Spencer sat on the bleachers with an open book in his lap, surreptitiously watching Callie. The poor kid was setting himself up for nothing but heartache. Hope hated to have to witness what was sure to follow. She knew there was nothing more she could do unless Spencer sought out her advice.

After an hour of meeting and talking with a number of students, Hope left for the day. The football team was still on the field. One thing Hope had learned early on was the pride the entire community took in the success of the high school football team.

One advantage of renting the cottage from Preston and Mellie was that the school was a close walk from home. Because she had errands to run, Hope had driven that morning. These errands were admittedly a delay tactic for what awaited her at the cottage.

After stopping off at the grocery store and the cleaner, she headed back. The two-bedroom house had come furnished but was small. Still, it had far more space than the studio apartment she'd rented in Los Angeles. Although the functional furniture was outdated, for the most part, it wasn't an eyesore. Whoever had lived here previously had taken good care of the property. With a few minor changes, she could make the cottage homey and comfortable. However, that meant unpacking the boxes that remained behind the closed door of the small guest bedroom.

The room she'd avoided opening from the day she'd moved to Oceanside.

Hope didn't need anyone to tell her why she kept those boxes safely tucked away and out of sight. Seeing how much she'd lost, it made perfect sense. Those packing boxes contained the reminders of all the pain and heartache she'd suffered.

Determined to move forward no matter how difficult, she delayed just long enough to put the milk and cottage cheese in the refrigerator and stack the frozen entrées in the freezer.

Walking into her bedroom, she hung up the jacket she'd collected from the dry cleaner. Once in the hallway, she faced the closed guest bedroom door, took in a deep breath, and turned the handle before moving into the room.

The boxes were stacked three and four high against the wall, right where she'd left them. She stood on the other side of the single bed with the rose bedspread that reminded her of her grandmother's small flower garden.

For a long moment, Hope stared at the wall, gathering her resolve.

"This is ridiculous," she said aloud, to convince herself it was time.

Reaching for the top one, she set it down on the shag carpet, and with a burst of energy pried open the top. Peering into the cardboard box, she stared at the contents and swallowed hard.

Talk about leaping into the fire. Inside the very first box was all the pain she'd hoped to forget.

On the very top, carefully covered in bubble wrap, was the photo of her twin brother, Hunter, in his army Ranger uniform. Even before she removed the protective covering, she could see Hunter's serious expression, while his dark eyes, so like her own, sparkled with pride. He'd been proud to be Airborne, proud to serve his country. Hunter had always been fearless and headstrong. It was only natural that he'd think of jumping out of a plane, thousands of feet aboveground, as being a thrill when the very thought terrified Hope. Twins, so different and yet so alike. She sensed it was the same with the twins she had in her class. Callie and Ben, both seniors.

Tears gathered in Hope's eyes as she held the framed photograph against her heart. Hunter, her precious brother, had paid dearly for his commitment to serve his country. More than a year ago, he'd died a hero in some unpronounceable city in an Afghan desert.

Along with the moisture that covered her cheeks, familiar anger settled in her chest, tightening to the point that she found it painful to breathe. With every bit of communication between them while he was on duty, she'd pleaded with Hunter to be careful. She'd begged him not to take any unnecessary risks.

All they had in the world was each other. If she lost Hunter, then she'd be entirely alone in the world. He was all the family she had. All the family she needed. Born as twins, abandoned by their mother, raised by grandparents, Hope and Hunter had always been especially close.

With tears blurring her vision, Hope returned to her bedroom and set the photo of her twin brother on the dresser. Swallowing past the lump in her throat, she turned the frame so she'd see his face first thing every morning, as a reminder that he wouldn't want her to spend her life grieving.

The pain of her loss, that sense of abandonment, of being completely on her own, was too much. Hope needed to escape. Grabbing her purse, she headed out again, needing fresh air. She drove around aimlessly for a while, then parked at the beach. Being by the ocean had always calmed her, and if ever there was a time she needed to find peace and acceptance, it was now.

The tears on her cheeks had dried in the wind that buffeted against her as she left footprints in the wet sand, prints that were washed away by the incoming tide. Gone: just as her twin was forever gone.

Hoping a latte would help her out of the doldrums, she decided to stop off for one of Willa's special lattes. The one friend Hope had made since arriving in town had been Willa O'Malley, the owner of Bean There, the small coffee shop close to the beach. She felt a certain kinship with Willa. Most mornings, she stopped by for a latte, preferring a light breakfast before heading to the high school.

As soon as Hope entered the shop, Willa looked up from the counter and greeted her with an engaging smile of welcome. "I don't usually see you in the afternoons. What can I get you?"

Hope ordered the latte and then took a seat by the window, looking out and looking inward, unable to let go of the sadness that had gripped her heart. It didn't seem possible she'd be able to move on without Hunter in her life. Even now, nearly two years since his death, he was on her mind every day. She felt his loss as keenly as she had when she'd first gotten the news. Against her will, fresh tears filled her eyes. She reached for a napkin and did her best to discreetly wipe away the moisture.

"Hope?" Willa joined her at the small table. "Is everything all right?"

The lump in her throat prevented her from answering. She nodded, wanting to assure her friend all was well, and then just as quickly shook her head. "I lost someone close to me," she finally managed to say, although her words were barely audible. "Some days I wonder if I'll ever get over his loss."

Sitting down across from Hope, Willa stretched her arm over the table and reached for Hope's hand. "You won't, not really, they will always be with you, but I can tell you this, the pain eases with time." Willa's voice trembled as she spoke, as if she, too, had suffered a devastating loss.

Hope looked up. To this point, no one in Oceanside knew about Hunter or the reason she'd moved from California to Washington. "Hunter was my brother, my twin . . . the last of my family."

"Harper was my sister, so full of fun and life with so much to live for. I miss her dreadfully. The world felt empty without her. For a while I was a mess, but time moves on, and that was what she wanted for me, what she asked of me, and so I did."

Their fingers tightened around each other's, as if holding on to the memories of those they'd loved and lost.

A few minutes later another customer stopped in, and Willa left, but not before she leaned down and hugged Hope.

"The pain will always be there, but I promise you that in

time, the love you shared will ease the sting and you'll be able to feel joy again. In the meantime, I'm here whenever you need to talk."

Hope closed her eyes and took hold of Willa's words. Little wonder she'd felt an affinity for the barista.

Hope returned to the cottage, feeling worlds better than she had when she'd left. She wasn't back more than a few minutes when there was a knock on her front door.

She knew only a few people in town and wasn't expecting company. When she answered, she found her landlord, Preston Young, standing on her small porch.

"Hope." He said her name, as if that explained his visit.

She waited, certain there was a reason he'd stopped by.

"I wanted to let you know that as soon as I have a spare minute, I'll get around to repairing the railing on this porch and the faucet. I apologize it's taken me this long."

"It's no problem, Mr. Young."

"Preston, please."

"All right, Preston."

"With the two babies and my work at the shelter, I don't know where the time goes. Mellie's been after me to find the leak under the kitchen sink, and heaven knows I'm no plumber."

Hope felt sorry for the husband, who clearly had his hands full.

"We're desperately in need of volunteers at the shelter," he added, running a hand down his face, as if the weight of it was a burden he didn't need.

As soon as the words left his mouth, he froze and looked directly at her, as if seeing her for the first time.

"You're new in town, right?"

"Yes, a couple months." He should know, since he was the one who first showed her the cottage.

"Other than your students, have you had a chance to get acquainted with anyone outside of the school? In the community?"

Hope wasn't sure where this conversation was headed. "A few." She'd visited a few local churches but hadn't settled on one. The one person she felt she had connected with most strongly was Willa, especially now, knowing what they shared.

"Would you consider doing volunteer work?" he asked, his eyes full of enthusiasm. "The shelter is full, and a lot of the dogs aren't getting the attention they need. If you could walk a few of them, a couple times a week, it would be a tremendous help and very much appreciated."

"I . . ." Hope wasn't sure what to say. When she was a teenager, her grandmother had had the most unfriendly Chihuahua that she'd lavished with attention and love. As far as Hope and Hunter were concerned, Peanut tolerated them.

"Part of your responsibilities would be to present the animals to prospective pet owners."

"I see," she said, drawing out the sentence. "And this will help introduce me to the community?"

"Oh, definitely." Preston smiled, as if this was the opportunity of a lifetime.

"Can I think about it?" she asked, wanting to give the idea some thought. Her evenings were full, keeping up with her classes. If Preston had asked her brother, Hunter would have leaped at the chance. He'd always been good with animals. Even Peanut, who took to growling any time either of them got too close to their grandmother, had eventually been won over by Hunter.

"I suppose it could wait until morning," Preston said, his shoulders sagging, as if accepting defeat.

"I'll let you know then," she said.

"Sure thing," he said, and started to return to the house. "And I promise to get that railing squared away first chance I get."

"Don't worry about it," Hope told him. She was fully capable of pounding a few nails. She'd recognized the problem the first day she'd moved in and knew better than to lean against it or put any weight on it.

Later that evening, after a dinner of an egg salad sandwich and an apple, she graded the pop quiz she'd given to her history class. It didn't surprise her that Spencer aced the test. Both Ben and Scott failed miserably, and Callie missed only two of the ten questions.

Hope did her best to make history come to life so her students would feel they knew the men and women in the pages of their textbooks. History was her first love. The computer skills class, on the other hand, was a challenge. Spencer would likely do a better job of teaching it than she did, although she wouldn't let him know that.

As she readied for the next school day, Hope shuffled

through her closet for what to wear in the morning. As she turned toward her dresser, she caught sight of Hunter's photograph.

"Well, what do you think I should do about working at the animal shelter?" she asked him, wishing he could answer. "The only dog I've ever spent any time with was Peanut, and you remember what he was like."

Hunter continued to stare stoically back at her.

"Some help you are," she said, wanting to groan.

Hunter had always loved animals, forever bringing home injured birds or lost kittens. Their grandparents never allowed him to keep any of his finds as pets. It wasn't until after their grandfather died that Grandma had gotten Peanut, her comfort dog. She'd loved that dog and grieved weeks for him when he died. At the time Hope hadn't appreciated her grandmother's loss. Peanut was only a dog. Only later did she understand the significance of her grandmother's pet. With Peanut gone, a giant hole had developed in her life. With Hunter, the last of Hope's family was gone. The emptiness and loss of connection ate at her. She was alone in the world, so completely alone. Other than her BFF, Tonya, and a few other friends, if she were to disappear no one would know or care. The starkness of that left her feeling vulnerable and lost.

Hope had more than a few questions about what being a volunteer at the shelter would require of her. The one advantage she could think of was what Preston had mentioned: meeting and getting to know members of the community. As an added bonus, it might be exactly what she needed to take her mind off her own losses. Preston had seemed overwhelmed, and it was in her power to help him out. If volunteering at the shelter took up more time than she expected, she would gracefully bow out.

Thinking about Peanut and the comfort he gave their grandmother, Hope decided she could use a bit of comfort herself. No better way than to help these abandoned and lost animals to find their forever home. And that just might help her do the same.

Chapter 2

Hunkering down, Hope stayed a fair distance from the German shepherd inside the containment kennel. Preston had warned her that Shadow, the name given to him at the shelter, was aggressive and hostile toward all who attempted to approach him. Starved and half dead, Shadow had been brought in by Keaton, a friend of Preston's. Keaton had found Shadow lying by the side of the road, too weak to walk, and with a broken chain around his neck and open sores on his coat, especially around his neck. Even in his deplorable and depleted condition, it'd taken some effort to get Shadow into the truck. The sad story of this poor neglected dog tugged at Hope's heart. Somehow the chained dog had managed to escape.

"Hello, boy," Hope said, keeping her voice low and gentle. Stretched out on his mat, Shadow looked back at her with dark, sad eyes. "You're safe now, and there are people here who will take good care of you and love you."

Preston approached, and weak as he was, Shadow lifted his head and growled, baring his teeth. His entire demeanor changed, and he struggled to come to his feet, staggering sideways before catching himself on the side of the kennel.

"Easy, boy," Preston said, in the same calming tone Hope had used earlier. "No one is going to hurt you ever again." Shadow didn't appear to believe or trust him, as he continued to growl.

"I don't know about him," Preston said, his brow creased with concern.

"What do you mean?"

"Anytime he's approached, he becomes aggressive."

"Really? He didn't with me." Hope rose from her knees, and Shadow's gaze followed her before he made a wobbly return to his bed.

"He didn't?" Preston's frown was replaced with surprise. "No one has been able to get near him. The only reason Keaton was able to rescue him was because he was too weak to fight."

"The poor baby. How long has he been here?"

"Since Wednesday."

"Less than four days." She counted the days in her head. This was only Hope's second week of volunteering. Last Saturday she'd planned to spend a couple hours and ended up staying six. She watered and fed the dogs, walked a few, and introduced two dogs to their new families. Seeing these lost and abandoned canines find loving homes had deeply touched her. Both times she'd struggled to hold back tears.

"There's someone I'd like you to meet," Preston said, glancing toward the other end of the shelter.

"Okay." Hope's gaze followed his and spied another one of the volunteers. She'd noticed him earlier; he was hard to miss. He'd briefly looked her way, and when he did, she'd noticed his haunted eyes. He was probably late twenties, early thirties, around her own age. When he walked, she detected a limp. He hadn't said anything when he'd arrived, and she hadn't, either. He seemed preoccupied and she didn't want to intrude.

Preston walked over to the man, who had a dog on a leash. "This is Cade," he said. "Another volunteer. Cade, meet Hope."

Cade wore a camouflage jacket and worn blue jeans. He was a good six inches taller than her, which made him about six feet. He was solid and all muscle. His dark gaze briefly touched hers before lowering.

"Happy to meet you, Cade," she said cheerfully.

Cade nodded, acknowledging her.

"This is only my second week. I've really enjoyed the work so far," she said, trying to be friendly.

"I need to walk Joker."

"Sure," she said, unsettled by his lack of welcome. Cade left, and Hope looked to Preston, eager to know if she'd said something wrong.

Even before she could ask, Preston answered. "Don't be offended. Cade is going through a rough patch. He's been volunteering a few days a week for a month now. Working with the animals seems to be helping him. Give him time, the same way you would Shadow."

"Of course." Cade seemed to want to keep to himself,

which was fine by her. Perhaps eventually he'd feel comfortable around her and she with him. It didn't bother her if he'd rather not be friends. The choice was his. For all she knew their paths might never cross again.

For the rest of the afternoon, Hope worked on the list of tasks Preston had given her when she'd first arrived. Jellybean, a big white Great Pyrenees about the size of a small pony, was collected by Mary Lou Chesterton, a retired teacher. Hope had the privilege of bringing Jellybean out to her.

Ms. Chesterton got down on one knee, so she was eye level with the dog. "We're going to be the best of friends," she told him. She barely seemed to notice Hope, who held on to Jellybean's leash.

"I believe you will," Hope said.

The woman looked up, and when she saw Hope, she smiled. "My husband and I have had three Pyrenees over the years. We really love the breed. Not everyone is suited to caring for these larger dogs. To us, they're a perfect fit."

"I'm sure Jellybean won't disappoint you."

"I'm going to change his name," she said, shaking her head as if finding "Jellybean" over the top.

"I don't blame you. When the animals can't be identified or aren't chipped, the shelter gives them temporary names. Jellybean's name isn't one with any significance." Naming the dogs gave them an identity and a means of helping the shelter know which dog interested a prospective owner.

Running her hand over his thick white fur, Ms. Chesterton stood and took hold of the leash from Hope. "Are you ready to head home, Jasper?"

"Jasper?" Hope repeated, testing the name on her tongue.

"Yes, I decided on the name earlier, after seeing his photo. I took one look at him and knew right away he was a Jasper."

"I like it."

With the paperwork finalized and the fees collected, Jasper was free to go to his new forever home. Even with this short acquaintance, Hope felt confident Ms. Chesterton would be a good dog owner.

As if he knew exactly what to do next, Jasper leaped into the rear of the red SUV and lay down, taking up a good portion of the seat.

Hope watched as the happy couple drove off. Seeing these rescue animals find homes was gratifying on several levels. As she returned to the shelter, she passed the kennel where Shadow continued to lie, weak and sad. The poor boy tugged at her heart.

Once again, she hunched down and placed her palm against the kennel. Shadow's dark eyes met hers. "I see you ate everything out of your bowl. Good boy." In soft tones, she continued talking, letting Shadow know he wasn't alone and that when he was feeling better and regained his strength, he would go to a family who would care for him. He need never worry about anyone mistreating him again.

As she had the week before, Hope stayed for the entire afternoon. When she left, she wasn't able to get Shadow out of her mind. While stopping off for groceries, she wandered through the pet food section and on impulse bought a rope toy for him, thinking he might take out some of his anger on the rope. Shadow had every right not to trust humans. Perhaps with a bit of patience and love he would begin to believe there were good people who would care for him the way he deserved.

Sunday afternoon, Hope returned to the shelter. After signing in, she made her way to where Shadow was confined. Because of his temperament, his food and water were delivered through a small door cut out in the kennel. Again, she noticed that his food dish was empty, which pleased her. With the proper nourishment, he would soon regain his health. Then the real work would begin. When Preston said he wasn't sure about him, Hope was all too aware of what he meant. If Shadow continued to be a threat to others, the shelter would have no choice but to put him down. Hope didn't want to see that happen.

Sitting cross-legged outside his kennel, she spoke in a soft, soothing voice. "Hey, boy," she said, "I brought you a gift." She held up the rope toy, then slipped it through the small door in the kennel. He gave no response and continued to stare blankly at her.

"I'd be careful with him if I was you," Don, the head of the volunteers, said, as he walked past.

"He's okay."

"Just don't go inside his kennel. No telling what he'll do."

"I won't," she assured him, although the idea of gaining Shadow's trust enough to do so started to grow in her mind. If she could visit often enough for Shadow to feel comfortable with her, then perhaps the time would come when he would allow her to get close.

—

That week, every afternoon, as soon as she finished her counseling duties, Hope drove to the shelter and sat outside Shadow's kennel. Each time she scooted a bit closer, inching her way toward gaining his acceptance. It encouraged her to see an improvement in Shadow's physical condition and overall demeanor. Not once did he bark or show aggression toward her, which mystified the staff. Several commented that she was the only one Shadow tolerated.

Three times over the course of that week, Hope saw Cade. They didn't speak, although he always greeted her with a nod. She always smiled back. She noticed how patient and kind he was with the animals, both the cats and the dogs. She found herself watching him, intrigued by his silence and his demeanor. He didn't seem to have struck up a friendship with any of the staff or other volunteers. He came, worked with the animals, and left with barely a word to anyone.

The following Saturday, Hope signed in the way she always did, and Cade stood at the counter in front of her.

After signing in himself, he turned to face Hope. "He waits for you," he said.

His words stumped her until she figured it out. "You mean Shadow?"

He nodded.

"I'm hoping Preston will let me inside the kennel today."

Cade's brow rose in question. "Are you sure that's a good idea?"

"Shadow is learning to trust me."

"He's got a lot of psychological damage."

Coming out of his office, Preston must have overheard their conversation. "Unfortunately, Cade's right. I don't know if the kind of mental damage Shadow's suffered can ever be reversed."

"I agree," Cade said.

Just the way he spoke made Hope think he was referring to more than the issues with Shadow. It came to her that he was speaking about himself. No matter. Hope wasn't willing to give up on Shadow without doing everything possible to give him a chance for a loving home. "I'd like to try going in his kennel. I'm confident after the work I've put in that Shadow won't hurt me." She tried to sound confident, although deep down she didn't know if what she'd said was true. Nevertheless, she was willing to take the chance.

"Sorry, Hope," Preston said. "I can't allow you to take that chance. There's no telling how Shadow will react."

She sighed, certain there had to be a way. "Can we compromise?"

"What do you mean?"

"After everyone has left for the day, can we open his door and see what happens?"

"Not a good idea." Preston sounded adamant.

"I'm willing to take the risk."

"I'm not ready to let you. Let's give Shadow another week. He's getting stronger by the day, which is a good sign. But if he remains territorial and aggressive, then we won't have any other option . . ."

"He doesn't act that way toward me, and as Cade just said, Shadow waits for me to visit."

Preston looked to Cade for confirmation.

"He does. I noticed it for the first time on Thursday when I was here. Shadow looked up every time the door opened. When Hope arrived, his demeanor changed, and he wagged his tail."

"He did?" She hadn't seen any response from Shadow to her visits. It encouraged her that Cade had noticed.

"I saw it myself."

"That's good," Preston said, with an approving nod. "But he's got to be accepting of more than Hope before we can make a decision about the next steps."

"Next steps?" Hope asked, as dread filled her. She knew what Preston meant.

"I'm sure that won't be necessary," she hurried to add, before giving Preston an opportunity to respond.

"Give Hope more time to work with him," Cade encouraged.

"Yes, please," she added, grateful for Cade's support.

"Another week," Preston agreed. "We can assess Shadow then and make a decision after that."

Cade left, and Preston remained. "Don't get your hopes up," he said. "We do the best we can to avoid euthanizing any of the animals. Sometimes we don't have a choice. The fact that Shadow has been this badly mistreated and nearly starved to death isn't a good indication he will ever be able to recover mentally. His spirit has been broken."

"I disagree. He has spirit, I can see it in his eyes. I can feel it here." She pressed her hand over her heart. "He deserves someone who will love him."

"And who do you suppose that would be?" Preston asked. "As you can see, this shelter is full of animals without deep psychological problems. Shadow would never fit into a family with small children. It would be far too dangerous. Few people would risk adopting him."

It was almost as if Preston had drawn a line in the sand. "I'll take him," Hope said, without taking time to consider the ramifications of what she'd said. If she could get Shadow to trust her enough to let her take him home, then she'd willingly adopt him.

Preston's smile blossomed on his face. "That's what I thought you'd say. This isn't a pet, Hope, Shadow is a project. He's going to need a lot of love and a lot of effort if you're going to make this relationship work."

"I know," she said, agreeing with him. She was willing to do whatever was necessary. Shadow needed a home; he needed someone to believe in him. Someone patient who would care enough to overlook his physical and mental flaws.

As she looked past Shadow, her gaze found Cade as he walked a rescue Australian shepherd, his limp more pronounced than usual. Her gaze lingered, and she had the strongest impression that he, too, needed someone to believe in him.

Chapter 3

Cade stood before Judge Walters for his court-ordered ninety-day review. Once again, she'd left his hearing until the last of the day. Ms. Newman, his court-appointed attorney, had heard from the county clerk that the judge had marked her name on his case file. Cade wasn't sure what that meant, other than she seemed to have taken a personal interest in him. Whether that was good or bad remained to be seen.

"I have the documentation before me that you've fulfilled the required physical therapy in addition to the counseling."

"Yes, Your Honor."

She looked up and held his gaze. "Has the physical therapy helped?"

Cade shook his head until he remembered he needed to respond verbally for the court reporter. "It's doubtful." The sessions were pure torture, and his attitude was bad. The only reason he continued was because the judge had made it understood that otherwise he'd be facing jail time.

"Walk for me," she instructed. "Go all the way to the rear of the courtroom and back."

Hesitating for only a moment, Cade did as she requested. Once he returned, she shook her head. "You're wrong, Soldier. Your limp is less pronounced."

"If you say so."

"I do, and I want you to continue, despite the fact that you seem to believe it isn't helping."

"Yes, Your Honor." Cade had hoped she'd be willing to let him discontinue the PT. Far more than the fact that he begrudged every minute of those sessions, he didn't know how he was supposed to earn a living. Counseling, both physical and mental, in addition to all the community service hours he was required to fulfill, made it nearly impossible to find decent employment. He'd gotten a part-time job at a local tire shop and garage, located across from the high school, which hardly paid him enough to cover more than the basics.

"And the counseling?" the judge pressed. "Tell me how that's going."

When he first heard "court-mandated counseling," Cade was convinced it would be a complete waste of time. He hated the very thought and had no intention of revealing his soul to some quack. To his surprise, Cade discovered he quite liked his counselor. Harry Milton was nothing like what he'd expected. He hadn't pressed Cade to discuss anything having to do with his injuries or his combat experience. What Cade found most helpful were the group sessions. As of yet, he hadn't contributed. He needed to get a feel for the others before he'd be willing to share. Listening to their stories, seeing how they had worked their way back from the edge, had helped Cade square his head. It relieved his mind to know he wasn't alone. He'd noticed the nightmares that had plagued him for months didn't happen as often. The group had offered him a lifeline, one he hadn't realized how badly he needed.

"It's going well, Your Honor."

She nodded, looking pleased. "I'm glad to hear it, Soldier. Very glad."

Her continued interest in his case made Cade wonder if his family had something to do with this. He needed to find out if they'd been involved. He hadn't seen or talked to his mother since the day of his sentencing. He had no doubt she'd been quick to tell his father how low their son had sunk. How she'd even known he had a court date remained a mystery.

"You're doing well, Soldier," the judge continued. "I'll schedule another ninety-day review with the clerk. Until then, keep up the good work."

"Yes, Your Honor."

Cade left the courtroom and headed to Harry's for his weekly session. He drove from the courthouse in Montesano to Aberdeen, where Harry Milton had his office. Harry was a vet himself and had served in the first Gulf War. Nearing fifty, he was starting to show his age, with salt-and-pepper hair and a beer gut. His deep blue eyes revealed his own battles with demons who'd followed him from the Middle East. What Cade appreciated most about Harry was the fact that he could read bull faster than anyone Cade knew. He facilitated the group sessions and confronted anyone looking to cover up their feelings with humor, distraction, or other evasion tactics. Harry always cut it off and called it what it was. Cade found the counselor's ability to read into people's psyche nothing short of astonishing. He didn't let anyone, man or woman, lie to themselves or to others.

Harry stepped out of his office after Cade was announced by the receptionist who also served the three other counselors in the VA facility.

"Cade." Harry greeted him with a welcoming smile, leading him into the small office, where a coffee machine rested on the counter. On his first visit, just as he'd predicted, the only two pieces of furniture in the room were a chair and a sofa. If not for the court order, Cade would have turned around and walked out. He didn't look upon it the same way now as he had in the beginning. The overstuffed sofa was comfortable. Harry didn't know much about interior decor, yet somehow the room felt welcoming and soothing, sterile as it was.

"Make yourself a cup of coffee," Harry said.

Cade did, and Harry made another for himself.

They both got settled. Harry sat in a padded chair and Cade sat on the sofa, and without thinking, Cade crossed his legs. He felt the immediate pull of pain at the injured muscle and quickly uncrossed them. It had been an instinctual move, and he realized he hadn't been able to do it ever since his injury. The judge was right; he was making progress. This was the first time he'd done it—not for any real length of time, true, but still, he'd been able to lift one leg over the other for the first time in recent memory.

"So," Harry said, stirring his coffee after adding sugar, "how did your court appointment go?"

"Okay, I guess. Judge Walters wants to see me again in another ninety days."

Harry nodded, as if to say that was what he'd expected.

"My attorney thinks she's put her name on my case file. I have the feeling her interest might have something to do with my father and his law firm." Cade hadn't said a lot about his family situation. Sensing Cade's reluctance, Harry hadn't dug for details. Nevertheless, he seemed to read between the lines.

"As you might have guessed, my father and I are estranged." Before she showed up in court, he would have said the same thing about his mother. He'd expected condemnation and disappointment in her face when their eyes met, and he'd seen neither. He didn't have the ability to read people, not the way Harry did. The only thing he thought he might have detected in her look was regret, and even then, he wasn't completely sure.

Harry uncrossed his legs, set his mug aside, and reached for a pen. "When was the last time you spoke with your family?"

Cade reached for one of the pillows that rested against the back of the sofa and then quickly set it back in place. "Six years . . . not that we talked much before I entered the military. To put it mildly, my father highly disapproved of that decision."

"Any particular reason?"

"Yeah. He had other plans for me."

"And you used the military to escape."

"Probably not the wisest decision I've ever made, but the truth is, given the same options, I'd follow the same path."

Harry nodded without judgment or pressure to continue.

"For your peace of mind, I'll tell you that you're wrong when it comes to Judge Walters's interest in your case."

"What do you mean?"

"Your family, and any influence they might have with the courts, had nothing to do with Judge Walters."

Cade wasn't sure what to make of this. In his mind, he was convinced the judge had been influenced to go light with him. His mother's presence in the courtroom had sealed the conclusion in his mind.

"Judge Walters's son was a marine who served in Afghanistan. He came home a different young man than when he left. He was lost and confused, the way many veterans are. Six months after he was discharged, he ended his life."

Surprise must have showed in Cade, because Harry continued. "Since that time, Judge Walters has made it her goal to help other young men like her son. She read your case file and contacted me long before your court date."

"You're saying my family had nothing to do with my light sentence?"

"I can promise you they did not."

Cade swallowed, seeing the judge with fresh eyes. "Good to know."

"I wouldn't normally share these details, but I wanted to assure you her intentions toward you and others are meant for good and not for harm. They come from her own tragic experience."

"I appreciate knowing this. Thank you." Cade sipped his coffee, needing a moment to clear his head.

Harry leaned back in his chair and looked over the notes Cade had supplied him with regarding his time commitments.

"I see you've spent quite a few hours at the animal shelter this last week."

Cade enjoyed the work. "I'm glad you recommended that as a means of working off my community service. I enjoy my time there."

"I thought you would." He smiled, as if congratulating himself.

"I'd like to adopt a dog myself. Unfortunately, the apartment I'm renting doesn't allow animals." Several times over, Cade had found it difficult to let one of the dogs he'd worked with leave the shelter. It was ridiculous really, because he knew they were going to families and individuals who had much more to offer them than he ever would. Cade's life was chaotic, and he was rarely home as it was.

"How's Shadow doing?" Harry asked.

Cade's head came up. "I mentioned Shadow?" He didn't recall telling Harry about the surly animal.

"Briefly, a couple weeks ago now."

This was the thing about Harry. He had the ability to see beyond the most casual comment and recognize the significance. Cade's mind went back to their earlier conversation. It happened shortly after Hope had started volunteering and he'd taken notice of her. He'd been warned to stay away from Shadow's kennel. They all had, and with good reason. The dog was uncontrollable. Hope hadn't listened. Instead, she'd sat down on the floor outside the kennel and talked to Shadow in that soothing way of hers. It'd intrigued him to watch Shadow's reaction.

"She's got him behaving on the leash." It seemed almost unbelievable. Shadow wasn't exactly licking anyone's hand.

He still growled and showed his teeth with the other volunteers. Yet, when it came to Hope, he was a different animal. Shadow accepted her. To watch the transformation in their relationship had been fascinating.

" 'She'?" Harry asked.

Lost in his musings, Cade frowned. "I'm sorry?"

"You said, she's got him on a leash. Who's 'she'?"

"Another one of the volunteers," he said, downplaying his interest in Hope.

His answer immediately caught Harry's attention. "You'd mentioned Preston felt they were going to have to put the animal down."

"That's what everyone thought."

"Except this other volunteer."

Cade nodded. He'd learned from Preston that Hope taught at the local high school. None of his high school teachers had looked anything like her. She was a knockout, on the petite side, with auburn hair she wore shoulder length. Briefly, he wondered if she was involved with anyone, but quickly dismissed the thought. No way was he ready for a relationship, and no way would someone like Hope be interested in a loser like him.

As if realizing there was more going on than what Cade was telling him, Harry motioned toward him. "Tell me about this volunteer."

The question drew him up short; he was unwilling to walk down this path. "What do you want to know?" he asked, as a delay tactic.

Harry shrugged as if it was of little concern. "I don't know. Clearly she has a lot of heart."

"And patience," Cade added. He'd watched her move closer and closer to the kennel until all that stood between them was the wire. As the malnourished dog regained his strength, his aggression grew less pronounced with Hope's attention and care. Shadow looked for her. As soon as Hope entered the kennel area, Shadow rose to his feet, as if greeting a queen.

"It must have taken a lot of courage for her to go into his kennel."

Cade agreed. He wasn't sure how she'd managed to convince Preston to let her try. He hadn't been around at the time and hadn't heard the details. All he knew was that on his last visit, Hope was in the yard walking Shadow. Granted, it was a short leash, and it was only the two of them. He'd been awestruck, as had the rest of the staff and volunteers. From what he'd learned, Hope had agreed to adopt Shadow.

"Yeah, she's got plenty of that," Cade agreed. As far as he could see, Hope had courage in spades.

"I notice you've increased your hours at the shelter. Is it because of . . . What's this volunteer's name?"

"Hope," Cade answered.

The name seemed to amuse Harry. "Hope," he repeated. "She certainly seems to be giving Shadow hope for the future."

Cade silently agreed.

"And just perhaps, you, too," Harry added.

Chapter 4

Hope sat in her office with Dannie, a junior girl who was weeping over the breakup with her boyfriend, convinced she had lost the love of her life. Hope offered sympathy and a hug. Once Dannie's tears had dried, she rose to leave. Hope walked her out and was surprised to see Spencer Brown standing outside her door.

"Hello, Spencer," she said, surprised and pleased to see him. "What can I do for you?"

As if he regretted being seen, he said, "It's nothing."

Hope arched her brows at his response. "You didn't stop by my office by mistake. Nor did you get lost. Come on in and tell me what's on your mind."

Hope's heart went out to Spencer. He really was her favorite student, mainly because she could identify with him. She'd been supersmart, too, with grades high enough that she could gain a full-ride scholarship and then manage a double major. Spencer's classmates had labeled him an über-geek. She knew he had friends, but, like him, they weren't athletic or particularly popular. They hung out in the lunchroom together and were mostly ignored by the female population.

Spencer's steps were reluctant as he came into the office. He glanced over his shoulder before he closed the door, as though to make sure no one saw him.

"Tell me what's on your mind," she said, encouraging him to speak.

"Not much," he said, shrugging and avoiding eye contact.

"It's clear to me there's something you'd like to discuss. That's what I'm here for, Spencer. What you tell me will remain between the two of us, so feel free to share."

He glanced up, as though he wasn't convinced he believed her.

"You're doing well in all your classes," she said, starting the conversation.

"Yeah."

"Then whatever is bothering you doesn't have to do with your grades."

"No."

Hope could see how difficult this was for him. She suspected she knew what had brought him into her office and broached the subject. "Does this have anything to do with Callie Rhodes?"

Spencer's head shot up, clearly shocked that Hope could somehow read his mind.

"I've noticed the way you look at Callie in class," she said, gentling her voice, wanting him to know she understood.

"We were good friends at one time," Spencer rushed to tell her. "Callie's changed, though, and doesn't have time for me any longer . . ."

"So you two go way back?"

Spencer nodded. "Our families are best friends, or we used to be. Ben and I used to hang out before he got involved in sports."

"When was that?"

"Junior high, mostly. Ben's athletic and that's great. I mean, I'm happy for him, except once he started playing football and ran track, we didn't hang out much, and now we never do. Callie and I were always friends, too, but we grew apart about the same time."

"I understand that Callie and Ben are twins."

"Yeah, they are."

Hope couldn't help wondering if Callie and Ben were close the way she and Hunter had been. They had always relied on each other. For a brief moment, grief over the loss of her twin overwhelmed her as she swallowed down the emotion that clogged her throat.

"Now that we're all in high school, our parents still get together, but us kids aren't included," Spencer continued.

Hope was grateful he didn't notice her reaction.

"Callie speaks to me, and Ben, too, but it isn't like it was when we were young."

People and times change. Hope had come to realize over the years that there were seasons in friendships. Her best friend in college had been Tonya Harrison. Then following graduation from UC Davis, Tonya had married, and she and her husband, Justin, had moved to Texas. Hope and Tonya still kept in touch on Facebook and through text messages every now and again. But it wasn't the same.

"I understand relationships change," Hope told Spencer. "That doesn't mean they need to end."

"I'd like to be more than her friend, Ms. Goodwin. I'd like to be her date for homecoming." He said this squaring his shoulders, as if releasing a long-held secret.

"I see." And she did.

"I know she's one of the most popular girls in school." His eyes lit up, as if another thought had suddenly entered his mind. "Do you think Callie suspects the way I feel about her?" Spencer asked, wide-eyed with both dread and hope.

Hope understood that more than anything, Spencer wanted Callie to know how he felt about her, and at the same time was afraid she did know and chose to ignore him rather than hurt his feelings.

"I don't know." Hope had definitely noticed and wasn't sure if Callie had or not.

"I think about her all the time. I know, I know, it's useless. Callie would never date me. I was thinking if we could go back to being friends that she might be willing to date me eventually. I want to ask her to homecoming in the worst way."

More than he realized, Hope wanted to help Spencer. He had a lot to offer Callie, or any girl, for that matter. Hope didn't approve or disapprove of his choice. She didn't know Callie well enough to say one way or the other. But it discouraged her that all Spencer saw was a pretty face.

"Why don't you start small. Call her."

"I don't have a reason," he insisted.

"Come up with one."

He frowned, as if he'd already considered that. "I'm not good at conversation or making small talk. It would likely be one of the shortest phone calls on record. I thought, you know, if we were together more often . . ."

"So Callie's the reason you took Introduction to Computer Science." Anyone who knew Spencer recognized his computer skills were far and away more advanced than anything the class would teach him.

He didn't deny or confirm her statement.

"You know, Spencer, there are other ways of getting Callie's attention."

He sat forward in his chair. "I'm open to suggestions."

"I don't have any to give you. That is something you need to figure out for yourself. I have every faith that someone as smart as you will be up to the task."

Spencer didn't look convinced. "Smart in getting top grades, but when it comes to girls, I fail every time. I've never attended a school dance. This could well be one of my last chances."

"How many girls have you asked?"

He shrugged, which was answer enough.

"You didn't ask anyone, did you?"

He released a deep, frustrated sigh. "Why bother? I knew they'd all turn me down. I didn't think I could take the rejection."

"Oh Spencer, I can only imagine how many girls would have jumped at the chance to attend any one of the school dances with you."

From his expression, it was clear he didn't believe her.

"Homecoming is in two weeks," she reminded him. "You

should go to that dance, Spencer. If you don't, I think you'll regret it."

"The only girl I'd want to take is Callie," he insisted, even before Hope could suggest a few other names.

"Then ask her."

He hedged, as if giving the idea consideration. Hope could see his mind brewing possibilities before his entire body seemed to slump with defeat. "She's probably already agreed to go with Scott."

Hope had considered that, too, but that didn't keep her from encouraging him. "You'll never know unless you ask."

"If I ask her to homecoming, then Callie will know how I feel about her."

"Isn't that the point?"

"No," he insisted, and then quickly changed his mind. "Well, maybe."

"Whatever happens is up to you."

"I'll think about it," Spencer agreed.

All weekend, Spencer thought about his conversation with Ms. Goodwin. It was terrifying and exhilarating to think that if he were to ask Callie to homecoming, she might agree to go with him. For a time, all too short, he told himself Ms. Goodwin was right, he should ask Callie.

There was one factor he hadn't shared with Ms. Goodwin that kept circling in his mind. He'd heard a rumor that Callie and Scott had broken up after an argument in the school parking lot. A lot of people had witnessed them shouting at each other. But then, a day or two later, they were all chummy again. So much for that.

Even with an effort to be optimistic, he realized it'd be ridiculous to think that Callie would go out with him. By Monday morning, he'd discarded the idea completely. No need to humiliate himself in front of the entire school. If he asked and she turned him down, news of her rejection was sure to be echoed through the halls of Oceanside High.

The last thing Spencer thought would happen was Callie seeking him out.

Monday, after classes were done for the day, Spencer was headed toward the school parking lot. He and his dad had worked on a 1965 Dodge Dart his father bought when he got out of the military. His dad had loved that car, and together they'd worked on getting it running again so Spencer would have a vehicle.

"Spencer."

He knew that voice and turned around as Callie speed-walked toward him, her steps filled with purpose.

Her eyes were bright, and the sun shone down on her until he was convinced a halo had formed over her head.

"I'm glad I caught you." She smiled at him as if they spoke every day and were the best of friends the way they had once been. "How have you been?"

"Good."

His heart was beating like crazy, but he managed to smile back. "I heard you and Scott broke up. I'm sorry."

"We're all right, we'll remain friends," Callie said, frowning.

"Any chance you'll get back together?"

"Not on my part, although I don't think Scott got the message, but that's his problem, not mine."

He managed to appear sympathetic, even if the news made him want to jump up and down.

"Is that the car you and your dad worked on?" she asked, looking at the Dart behind him.

It surprised him she even knew about that. But then, his dad had probably mentioned it to her dad.

It demanded all the fortitude he possessed to answer with an affirmative nod.

"Cool."

"Thanks." He wanted to tell her of all the hours he and his dad had spent rebuilding the engine. In the process, he'd learned a great deal about the inner workings of an internal combustion engine. More important, he'd gained a deepening relationship with his father. While bending over the hood, his dad had talked about his own childhood and teen years. Stories Spencer had never heard before. He'd even spoken at length about his experiences in the military. His dad said the three years he'd been with the army had matured him into the man he was today.

Of course, Spencer told Callie none of this, which meant all he seemed able to do was stare at her.

"Do you have a few minutes?" she asked.

He nodded, rather than risk his voice cracking or embarrassing himself.

"Great. It's been a while, and I thought it was time we caught up."

Callie tucked her hair behind her ear. From his study of her, Spencer knew it was a nervous habit, one that had followed her all through her life. He couldn't imagine why she would be anxious around him.

"Yeah, sure." She wanted to catch up with him? That told him she probably needed a favor.

"I need your help," she told him.

"Okay."

"Okay? You don't even know what I want you to do."

"Whatever you need, Callie. You know you can count on me."

She beamed him a smile. "I know you've got some impressive computer skills."

Spencer and his friends were good. Really good. They pushed one another and had broken through several cybersecurity systems just to prove they could. None of them would ever brag about it, otherwise they could get in serious trouble.

"Who told you that?" He worried that word might have somehow gotten out about his skill and exploits.

She didn't answer for a long moment. "No one, really. I just know how smart you are."

Spencer had to wonder if Ms. Goodwin had put Callie up to this. "Are you asking me to tutor you?" Callie was an honor roll student herself, so that couldn't be right.

"Not exactly . . . It's a bit more than that."

"More what?"

"I . . . I'd rather not say at this point."

This was getting stranger by the second. Whatever it was must be serious.

"I'll admit I'm intrigued," he said, playing it cool—well, as cool as he knew how to be. The thing was, Spencer wasn't a cool guy.

His hesitation seemed to surprise her. "I know I haven't been much of a friend lately," she said, by way of an apology.

"I know how it goes. So what do you need?" he asked, willing to do whatever he could.

"I wouldn't expect you to do this for free. I'll pay you."

"Pay me?"

"Anything you ask within reason. I mean, I have some money saved up. I wouldn't ask if this wasn't important."

Spencer wondered what it was that made her sound so desperate. "I don't want your money, Callie."

"Okay," she said, her face tightening. "We're friends, but I don't expect you to do this for nothing."

"Is there risk involved?"

She bit into her lower lip and glanced down. "Maybe. I can't be sure. That's why I feel I should do something for you in return."

Callie held his gaze, waiting. Anticipating. Eager.

"There is one thing I want."

"Name it."

"I'd like for you to be my date for homecoming."

Her eyes grew shockingly round, as if the request had thrown her off balance. "You want to take me to homecoming? As your date?"

He nodded, his heart pounding so hard it felt as if it was slamming against his rib cage.

"I . . . guess that would be a fair exchange."

Spencer held out his hand. "Then we have a deal."

"Yeah," she said, in a tone that indicated she wasn't happy about this. She'd do it because she was desperate, but she didn't like it.

Even so, for Spencer this was a dream come true. Callie Rhodes was his date for homecoming.

Chapter 5

Hope wasn't at the animal shelter when Cade arrived. Because of his court date, the private and group counseling sessions, plus work, Cade hadn't been to the shelter in several days. That hadn't stopped him from thinking about Hope, though. Unwelcome, she drifted into his mind at the oddest times.

On his way to work on Thursday, he saw her chatting with Willa at Bean There, the local coffee shop. He nearly ran a stop sign when he caught a glimpse of her, stopping partway into the intersection. He was grateful he hadn't gotten a ticket. Judge Walters wouldn't have been pleased.

After arriving at the shelter, Cade kept watch for Hope. It wasn't like her to be late. Shadow remained in his kennel, and, like Cade, looked up expectantly every time the door opened.

Feeling a certain kinship with the canine, Cade walked toward the feral dog and was surprised when Shadow didn't immediately growl or show his teeth.

"She'll be here soon," he commented, and wasn't sure if he said it to reassure Shadow or himself. Most of the time, Hope was at the shelter about the same time as Cade. Although they rarely spoke, he'd started to plan his arrival to match hers, so they often signed in together.

Another hour passed, and Hope remained a no-show. When his curiosity got the better of him, Cade made an excuse to talk to Preston, who stood at the counter outside his office.

"Taffy and Violet were adopted this weekend?" he questioned, although he knew the answer.

"Yep, and we've got five more going to homes today," Preston murmured, while keeping his focus on the paperwork he was currently signing.

"I haven't seen Hope around," Cade commented, wanting to sound casual. "It's going to be a busy day, and we're short one volunteer."

Preston looked up and studied Cade for an uncomfortable moment before a knowing grin showed itself.

"Hope called early this morning to tell me she wouldn't be in. She wasn't feeling well. There's a flu bug going around the high school, and she thinks she might have picked it up. She sounded pretty miserable."

"Yeah, I heard the flu is taking its toll around town." He'd been down with the flu not that long ago himself. It'd been short-lived, a forty-eight-hour bug. But he'd been sicker than he could remember in a long time and was weak as a newborn kitten afterward.

"I didn't know you and Hope were friends," Preston said, looking well pleased with himself.

"We're not, really," he was quick to inform the shelter director. "Like I said, we're down one volunteer, and it's going to be a busy day." The five adoptions were sure to keep them on their proverbial toes.

"Hope's something special," Preston added. "You wouldn't go wrong with her. She's good people."

Cade feared he was digging himself deeper into a rabbit hole but needed to clarify himself. "Listen, I'm not interested in Hope, nor do I plan to be. It's a busy day, and I feel bad for Shadow. He keeps expecting her to show."

Preston continued to study him, and then out of the blue, he added, "You know she rents the cottage from Mellie and me, don't you?"

"No. Don't know why you think it's necessary to mention it."

Preston's slow smile returned. "Thought you might want to stop by and check on her."

"Why would I do that?" No way was he interested in Hope. At least that's what he kept telling himself.

Preston's lips quivered as if holding back a smile. "Why not? You're a healthy young man, and she's a beautiful woman. And from what I can see, you have a lot in common."

Cade bristled at the comment. "We have nothing in common," he insisted, embarrassed now that he'd bothered Preston. The shelter manager was able to see through his questions far too easily.

"Don't be so sure," Preston added, and returned to his paperwork while Cade made a hasty retreat. "From my point of view, the two of you would get along well. You're both new to the town and with no family to speak of . . ."

Cade wasn't listening to anything more as he hurried back into the area where the canines were kept. He was grateful when the door between the office and the kennel closed behind him. For a second, he thought he might have heard Preston laugh.

As he walked the new arrivals, Cade's thoughts wandered, unbidden and unwanted, to Hope. She had no close family? That might mean she didn't have anyone to call to help care for her when she was ill. Well, he definitely wasn't volunteering. Even if he decided to be a Good Samaritan and stop by the cottage, which he had no intention of doing. Besides, stepping in might give Hope the wrong impression. She could read more into his actions than was warranted, and that could have unforeseen consequences. He didn't need to concern himself. Hope had Preston and Mellie. If she needed anything, Cade knew either of the Youngs would be more than happy to help.

By midafternoon, Shadow seemed to accept that Hope wasn't going to show. The dog's entire demeanor changed. Downtrodden, he turned to face the rear of the kennel, so no one could see his face. He remained that way with his head resting on his crossed paws and ignored all the activity taking place around him.

If he felt Shadow would trust him, Cade would be tempted

to enter the kennel and give the dog the attention he needed. Knowing how close Hope was to Shadow, she could be anxious to learn how he was dealing with her absence. Cade wished there was a way for him to comfort Shadow.

Unable to explain it even to himself, Cade felt the same sense of loss and disappointment. He hadn't said more than a few sentences to Hope the entire time he'd been at the shelter. Basically, he'd ignored her. He'd made sure she understood, from the moment they'd first been introduced, that he preferred to keep his own company. Since then, she hadn't said much to him, either. Which was the way he wanted it.

What had captured his attention when it came to Hope was the way she was with Shadow. No one could miss the changes that had come over the dog since she'd started working with him. Her care and dedication to Shadow had left a deep impact on Cade. Rarely had he witnessed anyone with more patience.

From the scuttlebutt going around the shelter, he'd learned Hope planned to adopt Shadow. He knew she'd been working with him every day after school. Her efforts had been rewarded. Shadow had made stunning progress. While he still held back his trust when it came to others, he was far less aggressive.

Before he signed out for the day, Cade approached Shadow's pen. "Don't fret," he told the dog. "Hope will be back when she's feeling better."

Shadow ignored him, which was what Cade expected.

As he headed out the door, Preston stopped him. "Think about what I said," he called, halting Cade.

"You've said a lot of things," he returned, being purposely obtuse.

"About Hope."

Cade waved him off and headed to the rear of the building, where the volunteers were instructed to park.

As he drove into town, he passed the pharmacy, and without making a conscious decision, he turned in. He remembered taking over-the-counter medication that had helped with his symptoms during his own bout with the flu.

For at least five minutes he sat in his vehicle debating the wisdom of what he was about to do. The one thought that prompted him to get Hope medication was that then he'd have the opportunity to tell her about Shadow.

For reasons he didn't want to analyze, he was angry with himself for caring, for what he feared would give Hope the wrong impression. Even at that, he found himself picking up a few items he thought would help, and then driving to the cottage.

He was grateful when he saw that Preston hadn't arrived home yet. That meant Cade could come and go without having to deal with the flak Preston was sure to give him. Walking up the porch steps, he noticed the railing on one side was loose. As Hope's landlord, Preston should fix that. He tested it for sturdiness and briefly thought to mention it until he realized if he did, then Preston would know Cade had stopped by the cottage.

Standing in front of her door, he tapped lightly, thinking she might be in bed. If that was the case, he'd leave the medicine on the porch and drive away.

Only a couple moments passed when the door opened a crack. As soon as she recognized him, Hope opened it all the way. Dressed in a loose shirt and yoga pants, Hope looked dreadful. Her nose was red, her hair hung in strings around her face, and she was pale. Nevertheless, no flu could hide her beauty.

"Cade?" She was as surprised to see him as he was to be there. He should never have come.

"Here." He thrust out the sack. "This helped me when I was sick."

Hope held a tissue to her nose as she accepted the package, looking stunned and not knowing what to say. "Ah . . . thanks."

"No problem." He turned away and made it off the porch before he remembered the other reason for this visit. "Shadow did okay when you didn't show, but I could tell he missed you."

She blinked and looked incredibly sad. "I missed him, too, and I missed being with . . . everyone."

Eager to make his escape, Cade nodded and stuffed his hands into his pockets.

"I'd invite you in, but I don't want to expose you to this bug."

"Wasn't looking for an invitation." He wanted to make that clear up front so there was no questioning his motive.

"I know . . . Thank you, Cade. This was thoughtful."

"Not a big deal." He made a beeline to his truck, wanting to escape before Preston showed. It was far better that the other man knew nothing about this visit. Nor was he mentioning any of this to Harry.

—

Hope had barely closed the door when her phone rang. Checking the screen, she saw the call was from Mellie.

"Hello," Hope said, sitting back down on the sofa, where she'd been camping for the last two days. She had the quilt her grandmother had made when she left for college and the pillow off her bed.

"Was that young man who just left named Cade?" Mellie asked, sounding more than a little irritated.

"Yes. He's another volunteer at the shelter." She paused to blow her nose, which had started to run again.

"I know who he is," she said, sounding less brusque now.

Although Mellie hadn't asked, Hope supplied the answer. "He brought me . . ." She hesitated when she realized she had yet to open the white paper bag. Peeking inside, she withdrew the small box. "Flu medication," she said, "along with juice and canned chicken noodle soup."

Mellie made an indiscernible sound that Hope couldn't decipher.

"Preston must have mentioned I've been under the weather," she said.

"Preston shouldn't have done that." Mellie didn't appear to be the least bit happy with her husband. "I told him not to interfere, and he promised me he wouldn't."

"Interfere?" Hope repeated.

"My husband," Mellie said, with an elongated sigh. "You wouldn't know it to look at him, but he is a romantic at heart. He thinks you and Cade would make a sweet couple."

Hope nearly laughed, and she would have if she didn't have a sneezing fit right at that moment. Her and Cade? It was ludicrous. "Preston's wrong," she said, when she could manage to speak again. "Cade barely says a word to me."

"Yes, so I heard. He doesn't say much to anyone. But according to Preston, Cade watches you."

Busy as she was with her duties and the extra work she put in training Shadow, Hope hadn't noticed.

"I warned Preston to stay out of your business."

"I'm sure he meant no harm."

"I don't care. A promise is a promise."

"I see." Hope didn't know what else to say.

"Furthermore," Mellie added on a sigh, "I don't know if Cade can be trusted."

That piqued Hope's interest. "What makes you say that?"

Mellie paused, as if she'd said more than she should have. "Preston has a connection with Harry Milton, the VA counselor. He recommended Cade complete his community service at the shelter."

"Community service?"

"I don't know what his crime was," Mellie hurried to add. "It couldn't be a felony if his sentence was community service. It isn't my business to be telling you this, and I apologize. I blame Preston for getting involved where he has no right to do so."

"I . . ."

"I apologize on my husband's behalf," Mellie added. "I'll make sure he understands he's stepped over the line. I'm sure Cade isn't dangerous. I'm sorry if I upset you."

"You didn't."

A baby wailed in the background, and Mellie quickly made her excuses and ended the call.

Hope set aside her phone and lay back down on the sofa. She'd been bingeing a Netflix series all afternoon. Following her conversation with Mellie, the series no longer held her attention. Her head spun and refused to return to the storyline that only minutes earlier had intrigued her.

Instead, her thoughts drifted to Cade and his unexpected visit. It'd been a shock to learn his work at the shelter wasn't driven by his desire to help the animals. He was working off court-ordered hours for some unknown offense. That gave Hope pause. It also helped explain his attitude and behavior.

While the hours he spent at the shelter hadn't been his choice, he genuinely seemed to care. More times than she could count, Cade went the extra mile with those dogs who arrived lost or abandoned.

While she didn't know what he had done to get on the bad side of the law, Hope wasn't completely put off by what she'd learned. In her experience, she felt a dog could be a better judge of character than some people.

As far as she was concerned, Cade had proven himself.

Chapter 6

Hope was back at school, following her bout with the flu. Right away she knew something was up with Spencer. Several times during the two classes she had with him, she caught him smiling in her direction. Yet when she looked to Callie, the dance team leader seemed oblivious to him. Nevertheless, something was definitely up.

After her classes, Hope headed for the counseling office and noticed Spencer following behind her.

The instant she was in the door, he said, "I did it!" His eyes were bright with excitement. "I asked Callie to homecoming."

"And Callie accepted?"

"She did." Clearly Spencer was walking on air. "And you know what's crazy?" he asked, much too eager to explain or to wait for Hope's answer. "Callie was the one who approached me."

"Callie did what?" Hope was unable to disguise her surprise.

"She has some computer problem she wants my help with. It was like fate, you know. You'd have been proud of me. After our talk, I kept thinking maybe dating Callie isn't impossible, and then the opportunity practically landed in my lap."

Hope wasn't sure she trusted Callie not to break Spencer's heart.

"We struck a deal. Callie needed my help and offered to pay me. I didn't want her money, so I said I'd be willing to help if she went to homecoming with me."

"And she agreed?" Clearly she had, although Hope had her suspicions.

"I don't think she was especially eager, but a deal is a deal. She broke up with Scott, so this seemed the perfect opportunity."

Oh dear. Hope had a bad feeling that there was more to this than Spencer was willing to admit. She rubbed her palms together, searching for the best way to respond. Callie was using Spencer, and sure as anything, the minute she got what she wanted, she'd dump him like yesterday's garbage, although she could never tell Spencer her thoughts.

"So what do you think?" Spencer asked, waiting, it seemed, for her to congratulate him. He clearly wanted Hope to tell him how proud she was of him for taking the risk.

"That's using the old noodle," she said, doing her best to sound pleased.

And then, because her suspicions were on high alert, she asked, "Exactly what does Callie need help with?"

At the question, Spencer's smile faded. From his body language, Hope knew he was reluctant to tell her.

"Nothing big, just some back-end coding that's a little beyond what she can do . . . It's not a big deal."

Hope wasn't sure she believed him. "You're sure that's all?"

"Yeah." He paused, as if wanting to change the subject. "I'm going to take her in the car my dad and I have rebuilt. It's a classic."

Hope suspected Callie wouldn't have any appreciation for the car, not when Scott drove a newer-model BMW. Again, she resisted the urge to burst his bubble. She feared Spencer wouldn't want to hear it, and she wanted to be careful not to overstep.

"I thought you'd be pleased. You were the one who . . . you know, who encouraged me."

"I am excited for you," she said, forcing enthusiasm into her voice.

"I wanted you to know how much your advice helped."

Hope wanted to be pleased for the young man, but she had doubts. Callie may have agreed to attend the dance with him, but she still completely ignored Spencer in the two classes they shared. She had to wonder if this homecoming date was actually going to happen.

Spencer left the counseling office with a happy bounce to his steps. Hope slumped onto her chair, fearful of the ramifications that were sure to follow. Callie's relationship with Scott was obviously tempestuous, but the last time she saw them together, they were all over each other. Scott likely wouldn't take kindly to this development.

Unsure what she could do, Hope closed her eyes and prayed for wisdom. Before she left the school, she had a bit of paperwork she needed to turn in to the office. As she headed in that direction, she could hear raised voices, followed by a loud banging sound. Afraid someone might be hurt, Hope quickened her pace. To her dismay, she found Spencer slammed up against a row of steel lockers. Scott Pender, the football quarterback and Callie's on-again-maybe-off-again boyfriend, had Spencer pinned there with his forearm securely lodged across Spencer's throat.

Horrified, Hope rushed forward.

"Scott," she shouted. "Release Spencer this minute." The star athlete was a good four inches taller than Spencer and probably had thirty to forty pounds on him.

Angry and red in the face, Scott glared menacingly at Hope before he reluctantly did as she asked. As if turning on a light switch, his demeanor instantly changed. He laughed and looped his arm around Spencer's shoulders like they were the very best of friends.

Spencer immediately gasped. His hands went to his throat, as it took him a moment to recover enough to breathe again.

Hope was furious and had trouble hiding her irritation. She calmed herself. "Scott, I understand you're upset. The girl you thought was your date has chosen someone else. That, however, doesn't give you the right to attack Spencer. You need to come to the office with me to see Dean Wilcox."

"Aw, come on, Teach, we were just horsing around. It didn't

mean anything, did it, Spencer?" Scott glared at the other boy, daring him to contradict.

"He's right," Spencer said, shaking off the other boy's arm and stepping away. "It was nothing."

"See," Scott said, grinning like he'd just won the lottery. "All good here."

"It didn't look like nothing to me," Hope protested, unwilling to ignore Scott's aggressive behavior. She could only guess what might have happened if she hadn't come upon them when she did.

Spencer's eyes connected with hers, silently pleading for her not to make an issue out of this. She returned his look, and while she would have liked to comply, she was unwilling to let this go. Spencer gave his head a small shake as if to say reporting Scott to the dean would only make matters worse for him.

A moment of tense silence followed. Looking from one boy to the next, she noticed the heated look Scott aimed at Spencer. They were like two gunslingers outside of the O.K. Corral. This was exactly what Hope feared would happen. Spencer was out of his depth. Furthermore, she didn't trust Scott.

Hope didn't need a fortune-teller to understand the situation. Scott believed he would be taking Callie to homecoming. It was expected. Scott was a shoo-in as homecoming king. Callie would be giving up the key position as his date if she went with Spencer instead of Scott.

Whatever it was the girl wanted Spencer to help her with had to be something major. Something important. Her mind whirled with possibilities as her suspicions rose. Hope could only wonder what Spencer had gotten himself into and what she could do to help before he got himself into major trouble.

"I've got to get to football practice," Scott said, as if all was forgiven.

"I—" Hope was about to stop him when Spencer cut her off.

"Okay, Scott, see you around."

Scott's eyes darkened. "Sure thing."

Hope read the message in that look and knew this wasn't over. Scott wasn't through with Spencer.

"Are you sure you're all right?" she asked after Scott had left, wanting to issue a warning to Spencer and at the same time knowing it would do no good.

"I said I'm fine."

Hope doubted that was true. "Does Scott know why Callie agreed to go to the dance with you . . . that you're doing her a favor in return?"

He answered with a half-hearted lift of one shoulder. "Maybe. Maybe not. It doesn't matter either way."

"You should ask her to explain before there's another incident."

Spencer adamantly shook his head, and when he spoke his voice was tight with tension. "I don't want Callie to know anything about this. It's bad enough as it is; she'll want to defend me, and that will only make everything worse."

"I'm not sure that's wise, Spencer. Promise me you'll think about it."

Holding her gaze, Spencer didn't respond. "I can take care of myself, Ms. Goodwin."

Hope wasn't convinced Callie would do anything to spare Spencer from Scott's wrath, especially if she felt she'd been coerced into attending the dance with him. Callie was using him, and once she got what she wanted, Spencer would be old news. Former good friend or not.

"I've got to go," Spencer said, and fled as if he couldn't get away fast enough.

The sound of the door closing echoed in the hall. Still processing what had happened, Hope slowly started toward the school's office. Either by luck or by circumstance, Dean Wilcox was sitting at his desk with the door open.

Hope hesitated and then knocked against the door.

Gregory Wilcox glanced up and, seeing Hope, grinned. "Come in," he said, and motioned toward the chair in front of his desk.

At this point, Hope was grateful to sit down. "I just had a run-in with Scott Pender in the hallway," she said. "And I'm not sure what to do about it."

Sitting up straighter, the dean said, "Tell me what happened."

Hope explained what she saw and her speculation about Scott's anger over being cheated out of his date. She didn't go into the details as to why Callie had opted to let Spencer take her to homecoming. Just that she had agreed to go with him. Scott had apparently taken the news personally and was determined to make Spencer pay.

Dean Wilcox listened intently and asked a few clarifying questions. "This isn't the first time Scott has shown aggressive behavior. I think it might be a good idea for me to have a little chat with him. If you hear anything more, let me know. And if there's any further retaliation against Spencer, I want to hear about it."

"I'll make sure you do," Hope said. She hesitated, unsure if she should mention another incident.

"Was there something more?" The Dean asked.

"I don't know if it's worth mentioning," Hope said, feeling reluctant since it was a minor incident and one quickly forgotten. The following day Scott appeared as if nothing had happened and there hadn't been a problem since then.

"Why don't you let me decide that."

"Last week, Scott failed a test. When I gave him the grade he deserved, he blew up at me. He said I had purposely failed him to keep him off the team." His behavior had been aggressive to the point that Hope had been about to call security. A couple of his friends had dragged him out of the classroom before things had progressed further.

The dean listened and reached for his pen. "Thank you. I'll make a note of this incident as well."

Feeling relieved for having unloaded this burden, Hope dropped off the paperwork and left the building. She paused long enough to look out over the football field, where the team was busy with practice drills. She would have lingered a few minutes longer if she hadn't already made plans to stop off at the shelter.

Hope hadn't visited Shadow in four days, and she'd missed him. According to what Cade said, Shadow had missed her, too.

When she arrived, she noticed Cade's truck was in the lot

across from where she'd parked. A small sense of eagerness filled her at the prospect of seeing both Shadow and Cade.

As soon as she entered the kennel, Shadow barked a greeting, his tail wagging. This was a welcome, glad-to-see-you, why-were-you-away-so-long kind of bark.

"I missed you, too, fellow," she said, squatting down at eye level.

"Good thing you're here," Cade said from the other side of the kennel. "Shadow was starting to think you were never coming back."

"I'm so sorry, big boy," she said, and opened the kennel. The door closed behind her, and she got down on one knee as Shadow immediately started licking her face. Rubbing his fur, she whispered, "You did miss me, didn't you?"

Cade walked closer and Shadow tensed.

"Cade's a friend," she reminded the dog, looking at him squarely while petting his neck.

Shadow relaxed, and Hope rewarded him with a treat she had in her pocket. She wondered how many other high school teachers walked around the classroom with dog treats tucked away inside their pockets.

Sitting on the kennel floor, Shadow moved into her lap and laid his chin across her thigh. Content now, he relaxed, and so did she.

Cade moved until he stood outside the kennel. "Glad to see you're feeling better."

"Thanks. I'm glad to be back. Preston thinks I should be able to take Shadow home next week. He's gotten all his shots, been neutered, and has gained the weight he so badly needed."

"Yeah, he's ready," Cade agreed.

"Thanks again for stopping by. That medication helped me over the worst of the bug."

He ignored her gratitude.

"If you're ever sick, let me know," she added. "I make a mean chicken soup. It was my grandmother's recipe and she claimed it cured just about anything."

"Will do," he said, nonchalantly.

He wouldn't call. He didn't need to say it; she could read it in just the casual way he answered.

Because she had a couple errands to run, Hope didn't stay with Shadow long. It would be much more convenient once she was able to take him home. She needed to get the house ready for Shadow to come live with her. To that end, she stopped off at the pet store and got him a big fluffy bed, dog dishes, food, and play toys to entertain him while she was at school. She'd need Preston and Millie's permission to add a doggie door, but she didn't think they'd object. It helped that the yard around the cottage had a fence.

After getting the essentials for Shadow, her next stop was for groceries. Her cupboards were bare and her refrigerator empty. It'd been nearly three weeks since she'd last shopped. An hour later, she checked out with a full cart.

A boy she recognized as a junior helped her carry out her groceries. His name badge told her his name was Pete.

She opened the trunk, and Pete unloaded the bags as they discussed the weather and the homecoming dance.

"Thanks, Pete."

"Glad to help, Ms. Goodwin. I hope I'm in one of your classes next year."

"Me, too," she answered, and opened the driver's-side

door, more than eager to get home and settle in for the evening.

"Ms. Goodwin." Pete stood in front of her vehicle and frowned.

"Is something the matter?" she asked.

He nodded. "It looks like you've got a flat tire."

Chapter 7

Hope groaned as she walked around to the front of her car where Pete stood looking at her flat tire. She was convinced the teenager must be wrong. Those tires were practically new. Less than an hour ago she'd driven without a hint of a problem, running errands from one end of the town to the other.

"Can you call someone?" Pete asked, looking to be helpful.

Hope nodded and dug inside her purse for her phone and her AAA card. Pete returned to the store, and Hope leaned against the side panel of her ten-year-old vehicle to make the call.

The woman who answered was helpful and said it would be up to an hour before a tow truck would be available to respond.

"An hour?" Hope repeated, thinking about the freezer items in her trunk that were sure to thaw before help arrived. The tub of ice cream would be liquid by the time she got home.

"I apologize, there was a four-car pileup on the highway . . . all our drivers are involved in cleaning up that mess."

"I understand." Not that she had a choice.

Ending the call, she tossed her phone into her purse and covered her face with both hands. *Could this day get any worse?* She was concerned about Spencer, fearing her advice would do more harm than good. She didn't trust Scott not to terrorize Spencer in further retaliation. Why hadn't she considered the consequences to Spencer?

Absorbed in her thoughts, she didn't notice the truck that pulled up to the parking spot next to her.

"What's the problem?" The question was barked at her in a voice that was all too familiar.

"Cade?" She whirled around, surprised to see him, and at the same time so grateful she resisted the urge to hug him.

He climbed out of his truck. "I was driving by and noticed you standing here with your hands over your face."

"I've got a flat, AAA can't come for another hour, and my ice cream is melting," she blurted out all in one breath. "These tires are new . . . I don't understand how this happened."

Cade squatted down next to the side of her vehicle to examine her tire. When he looked up, his face was marred by a deep frown. "You piss anyone off recently?" he asked.

Her thoughts instantly shot to Scott Pender. "Why?"

"This tire was deliberately cut."

"What?" she cried, hardly able to believe what he was telling her.

"Take a look for yourself."

Hope crouched down beside him to examine the spot on the tire Cade pointed to. Sure enough, there was a slit in the thick rubber. "Oh dear," she whispered.

"You didn't answer my question. Did you have a run-in with anyone recently?"

She mulled it over, unsure how to answer. The only person she could think of who had reason to cause her trouble was Scott. "He couldn't have done it."

" 'He'?" Cade pressed.

"A student. One of the seniors. Scott failed a test and was upset with me. He's not the only team member on probation, though, so it could be anyone. Only . . ."

"Only?" Cade pressed.

"I broke up a confrontation between Scott and another student earlier and he wasn't happy with me. But he doesn't know that I reported him to the dean . . . Besides, he's at football practice."

"You're positive about that?"

Unsure if she was or not, she answered with a simple shrug.

"Call AAA back and tell them it won't be necessary to send a tow truck."

Although she heard him, he didn't make sense. "But I'm going to need help getting the car to the tire store."

"I'll take care of it," he said, in that no-nonsense way she'd come to expect from him.

"But—" she started to protest, and Cade cut her off.

"Didn't anyone ever tell you not to look a gift horse in the mouth?" He stared her down as if he expected an argument.

That was one of her grandfather's favorite phrases. "Gramps," she said, smiling at the memory of her taciturn grandfather. By contrast, her grandmother was the more nurturing of the two. They'd raised Hope and Hunter from the time Hope could remember. She had few memories of her mother and none of her father.

"Then you know what it means." Even before he finished speaking, Cade went around to the trunk of her car. "Let's get these groceries into my truck. I'll drive you back to the cottage and then come deal with the tire."

"You don't need to do that . . ." Hope didn't know why she was arguing with him, and yet she couldn't help herself.

"Gift horse," he said, reminding her of what he'd said earlier.

"Right." If he was willing to do all that, she shouldn't be looking for reasons to object. She certainly didn't want to stand around in a parking lot for sixty minutes waiting for someone to come rescue her. Not when Cade seemed perfectly willing to help.

It took only a few minutes to load everything and less than five to deliver Hope to the cottage. He helped her cart in the bags of groceries, taking the porch steps two at a time as he made quick work of the task. Hope had called AAA to cancel the tow truck, grateful for Cade coming to the rescue.

As Cade drove off, Hope went to close the front door and noticed her landlady watching from the kitchen window on the other side of the yard. Just as she expected, her phone rang less than a minute later.

"Was that Cade Lincoln?" Mellie asked, and then added, "Again?"

Hope explained the situation.

"Someone purposely knifed your tire?"

"I don't know if it was a knife or not, but it's definitely flat, and clearly it wasn't an accident."

"Someone is apparently unhappy with you," Mellie said, stating the obvious. "Or it could be a simple case of vandalism. Rare, though, in broad daylight." Cade had basically said the same thing, dismissing any thought that it was a random act. He'd convinced her she'd been targeted, and Hope couldn't help thinking otherwise, however uncomfortable.

"Cade stopped to help me," Hope explained.

"So I see," Mellie said, with meaning.

"He's not so bad," Hope felt compelled to tell her. She didn't know many people who would go out of their way to lend this kind of assistance.

"Preston says the same thing, and my husband is a good judge of character. But if Cade gives you any trouble . . ."

"He won't." Hope was convinced Cade meant her no harm and felt the need to defend him. Knowing next to nothing about his background, she had little to go on other than the way he cared for the shelter animals. Yes, he'd been standoffish and uncommunicative, but Hope didn't hold that against him. Learning that he was fulfilling his community service hours didn't discourage her from being his friend. Everyone made mistakes; the key was learning and moving forward, which Cade appeared to be doing.

"I've got to get these groceries put away," Hope said, using that as an excuse to end the call.

"Sure thing. Just know I'm keeping an eye on you."

"No need, Mellie."

"So you say. Fact is, I'm not willing to have you take any chances. If someone has a vendetta against you, then you need to be more aware of your surroundings and keep your eyes open."

"I will, for sure," Hope promised.

Nearly two hours passed before Cade returned. During that time, he'd removed the damaged tire, taken it to the tire shop, and had it examined and replaced. The shop called for her credit card number, which told her there was no saving the tire. Because it was a deliberate act of vandalism and not any flaw having to do with the tire or manufacturer, she was required to pay for the full cost of the replacement.

Cade must have bargained with the salesperson because she was given a discounted price for the tire. When she asked to speak to Cade, the shop owner gave him the phone. When he mentioned the name of the shop, Hope recognized it as the one close to the high school.

"It should have cost more," she said, although she was grateful.

He grunted as if it was no biggie. "I got an employee discount. Remember what I said about a gift horse?" The abrupt way he spoke told her he didn't appreciate her questioning him.

So Cade worked at the tire shop. "Okay, okay, got it. Thank you."

"I won't be long. I'll be by to pick you up in a few minutes."

"Okay."

Sure enough, Cade arrived back at the cottage in short order.

"I can't thank you enough for this," she said, after she climbed into the truck, sitting next to him.

"No problem."

"But it was," she countered. "I mean, this took more than two hours out of your afternoon."

"Didn't have anything going on, so no sweat."

How quick he was to dismiss her appreciation. She wanted to thank him and could think of only one way. While he'd been dealing with her vehicle, she'd cooked dinner. A real dinner, pork chops in mustard sauce, and not something quick that she so often threw together.

Cade pulled into the grocery parking lot and eased his truck next to her car. Even before she could ask him to join her for dinner, he said, "I'll follow you home to be sure there aren't any problems."

Hope decided to wait until they were back at the cottage before she mentioned the meal she'd prepared. "I'd appreciate that."

Her car ran as if there had never been a problem, and Hope was grateful.

And nervous.

She wanted to invite Cade to dinner. Past experience told her he would likely refuse. It came to her how much she hoped he'd agree to join her. She wanted to get to know him better. He'd built a barricade around himself, one as thick as the

Great Wall of China, and she was eager to see the man behind that thick barrier.

After she'd claimed the parking spot next to the cottage, she got out of her car. Cade was already backing out when she stopped him by waving her arm over her head.

Rolling down his driver's-side window, he looked impatient to leave.

"Thanks again," she said, walking over to his truck. As awkward as this felt, she wasn't about to let him go this easily.

Cade kept his hands on the steering wheel. "Like I said, it wasn't a big deal."

"It was to me."

He acknowledged by dipping his head.

"While you were busy dealing with the tire, I cooked dinner . . . I was hoping you'd join me."

"Not necessary."

"It's the least I can do."

"Another time." He started to close the window.

"It's my grandmother's recipe for pork chops in mustard sauce, with fried potatoes and salad."

He hesitated. "Pork chops?"

She nodded, seeing a small crack in his defense. Her grandmother was right when she'd claimed the way to garner a man's interest was to wow him with her cooking. Unfortunately, the handful of recipes she'd gotten from her grandmother was limited. She did make a tasty meatloaf, though.

That crack closed almost as fast as it appeared. "Another time."

It was hard to disguise her disappointment before she accepted his decision. "Okay, I understand you're probably busy. How about I put together a plate for you to take with you?"

He looked away from her and then back. "Thanks anyway, I've got other plans."

Earlier, he'd assured her he had nothing on his agenda. He'd lied in order to get out of spending time with her. Enough said. She got the picture.

"Sure," she said, finding it hard to swallow his rejection. "Another time."

He agreed with a quick nod. Hope knew without him ever saying it that he had no intention of following through.

She stood on her porch steps and watched as Cade drove away. As he pulled out of view, she couldn't help but wonder if she would ever be able to understand what made him tick.

Her phone chirped with a special ring that told her it was her dear friend Tonya.

"Hey," Hope said, happy to hear from her college roommate. "It's been a while."

"You were on my mind. How do you like living in Washington?"

"Love it."

"Meet any interesting men?"

Sometimes Hope wondered if Tonya had psychic powers. "Now that you mention it, I have." For the next ten minutes she relayed her brief history with Cade. "Do you have any words of wisdom?" she asked her friend.

"Patience," Tonya said, without hesitation. "You took the first step. Let him be the next one to reach out."

"And if he doesn't?"

"Then you have your answer. Some men are worth the effort and others aren't. Let Cade tell you into which category he falls."

After briefly catching up, Hope ended the call and mulled over the advice her friend had given her.

The next morning, before her first class, Hope stopped by Dean Wilcox's office. She had to wait a few minutes before he was able to see her.

"More trouble with Pender?" he asked, as soon as she took a seat in his office.

"Unsure. I have a question, though."

"Fire away." He leaned back in his chair and placed his hands behind his head, ready to listen.

"Did you happen to speak to anyone about our conversation after I left the school yesterday?"

Dean Wilcox frowned slightly. "What makes you ask?"

"My car was vandalized yesterday afternoon."

He dropped his hands and straightened. "How so?"

She told him. "Did you mention what I told you about Scott to Coach Simmons?"

"I did, but it wasn't until after practice. Coach said he'd make sure Scott understood if disciplinary action was taken because of his behavior, he'd have to pull him from the team."

If Scott prized anything, it was his standing as the team's quarterback. The reprimand would certainly be taken seriously. That didn't mean that Scott's friends or teammates wouldn't act on his behalf, though. They were just as likely to make Spencer's life miserable as Scott was. Dean Wilcox knew it and so did Hope.

"I'll check into this, and if I find out anything I'll let you know."

"I'd appreciate it," Hope told him.

At this point she would give anything to have not encouraged Spencer to pursue Callie. The price was too high for them both.

Chapter 8

Cade sat directly across from Harry in the group session on Wednesday afternoon. Of the four men and one woman in the group, he probably had the least of the physical injuries. Ricardo, who was close to Cade's age, had lost his left leg and arm. Shelley, a nurse, was without her right hand, Dean was blind, and Silas was badly scarred from burns over a third of his body, including up his neck and over part of one cheek. The extent of their injuries helped Cade appreciate that he'd walked away with a barely noticeable limp. Yes, there was pain. Plenty of that, and not all of it physical.

Dean was speaking. "I'm adjusting to life in the dark. I fought it as long as I could, believing, you know, in some miracle, some new medical discovery that would give me back my sight. With the help of my wife, I'm ready to accept the truth and move forward with my new reality."

Cade could well imagine how difficult it had been for the vibrant young man to be cast into the unfamiliar world of complete darkness. From previous sessions, Cade knew Dean had the encouragement and love of his wife. Still, he knew this hadn't been an easy journey. Dean had struggled hard against the bitterness he felt over his circumstances. This was the turning point for him, and Cade was pleased. He knew the group had been instrumental in helping Dean reach this point.

As was all too often the case, the men and women who were entrusted to love and support those serving in the military couldn't deal with the new normal. When faced with their loved one's life changing injuries, unable to adjust to the pressures, they frequently walked away. Dean was one of the fortunate ones. Silas, not so much. He didn't know about Ricardo or Shelley, as they were relatively new to the group.

Cade had had no one to care if he made the adjustment or not, and that was fine by him. It was his choice. Luke and Jeremy, the two men he'd considered his family, had been killed in battle. Cade had been helpless to stop it. He could do nothing more than watch them die before aid could arrive. He suffered with the guilt of that every single day.

The discussion continued around him. Cade listened but contributed nothing. His mind wasn't with the group as much as it should have been. He couldn't stop thinking about Hope. As much as he'd wanted to accept her dinner invitation, he'd turned her down. He had yet to understand what made him refuse the very thing he wanted most. He was messed up in the head. Troubled. Probably best he stayed away from her. If she knew him, really knew him, she'd be smart to run in the opposite direction.

As though sensing Cade was lost in his own thoughts, Harry asked him a direct question. "Cade, how's Shadow?"

He straightened in his folding metal chair as if he'd been caught speeding and the traffic cop's lights were flashing in his rearview mirror. "Doing well," he answered dismissively.

"Shadow?" Ricardo asked.

"A dog from the shelter where I've been volunteering," Cade answered, and then for reasons he wasn't sure needed to be explained, he added, "Hope is taking him home with her this afternoon."

Preston had made a point of letting Cade know on his way out of the shelter the day before. Hope's good news had been on his mind when he'd happened to catch a glimpse of her with her flat tire.

"Who's Hope?" Ricardo asked.

Harry motioned for Cade to respond. "Shadow's a dog, and Hope's another volunteer at the animal shelter." The words hung in the air as if the others were waiting for more details. Details he wasn't about to supply. The less said the better.

"A woman?" Silas asked. "Hey, man, have you been holding out on us?"

"No," Cade said quickly, probably too quickly, and too adamantly. "The thing is, I'm worried about her."

"Why's that?" Harry asked.

"I'm afraid she's in over her head." Cade briefly explained the circumstances of finding her with the flat tire.

Ricardo shrugged at Cade. "Not your monkey, not your circus, man. We got our own problems. You don't need to make her troubles your concern. You want my advice, stay away from this chick."

"He's right," Silas said. "Look where playing hero got us. I learned my lesson the hard way. As far as I can see, this teacher friend of yours got herself into this mess, then she can get herself out, without any help from you."

In theory, Cade agreed, not that it seemed to do any good. "The thing is, I can't stop thinking about her." Although he spoke to the group, the comment was directed to Harry, seeking his advice, wanting the counselor he'd come to trust to explain this fascination with Hope.

"Let her go before she drags you down," Shelley tossed at him. As the only woman in the group, she usually was the quiet one. The one least likely to speak her mind or offer an opinion.

"I wish it was that easy," Cade admitted. "After I got her a new tire, Hope asked me to dinner. Without even thinking about it, I refused, and then all night I was kicking myself. More than anything, I would have liked to spend that time with her. She'd even cooked my favorite dinner. Pork chops and fried potatoes."

"That was smart, man," Ricardo told him. "You did the right thing."

Cade didn't agree. "Then why did she look at me like I'd kicked a puppy." He glanced up and made eye contact with each member of the group, looking for them to explain what had prompted him to reject the very thing he wanted most. It was an impossible request, seeing he couldn't answer the question himself.

Harry leaned forward. "What frightens you about Hope?" he asked.

The question irritated Cade. "I'm not frightened."

"Oh sorry, I must have misunderstood. She invited you to dinner, and even though she'd cooked your favorite meal and you wanted to spend time with her, you turned her down."

Hearing it put like that, Cade knew he'd been called up short. "I like her," he reluctantly admitted. "Just the way she worked with Shadow. That dog was a mess: feral, mean, and destined to be put down. Hope refused to let that happen. Her patience with him was above and beyond what anyone else was willing to invest."

"That's cool," Silas murmured.

Cade was impressed with her, too, with her patience and determination.

"I think everyone has this wrong," Dean said, addressing the subject for the first time. "Maybe Cade needs Hope in his life."

"Not if she's bringing trouble with her," Ricardo insisted. "We got all we can handle as it is. Taking on anyone else's is a no-win situation."

"Doesn't anyone else see the connection?" Dean gave a small smile. Cade had noticed that his fellow veteran often had insight that escaped the others.

"Tell us what you mean," Harry encouraged.

"It should be obvious," Dean said. "Cade sees himself in this dog. If I've learned anything in these sessions, it's that the psychological injuries require just as much healing, if not more, than whatever else upended our lives."

What Dean said was something Cade should have understood himself, and yet somehow it had escaped him. He had unconsciously seen himself in Shadow. He, too, was angry. And like the feral dog, Cade didn't want anyone befriending him, either. As he watched Hope patiently and gently work with Shadow, he felt inexplicably drawn to her.

"You might be right," Cade was willing to admit. "But that doesn't explain why I would reject the very thing I wanted most."

"The pork chops or Hope?" Shelley asked, and they all laughed.

"Hope," Cade admitted.

"I think it does explain it," Silas said, looking thoughtful, staring down at the floor. "What Cade's shared is something we're all facing in one way or another."

"Say more about that," Harry urged.

"I don't know that I can . . ."

"Give it a try." Harry's voice was encouraging.

Silas continued focusing his eyes on the floor. "When I first arrived home, after several months in the hospital, the family was all over me with sympathy and understanding. My girl was by my side." He hesitated and swallowed hard. "And then she wasn't."

Any number of times Cade had heard the story of how Silas had been engaged to a beautiful, talented woman who owned her own small business. Silas had boasted about her success and how eager he was for them to get married. Only Yvonne had continued to delay making wedding plans. In the end, she admitted she couldn't live with a man so badly scarred.

Soon afterward, Silas had gone on a downward spiral that had resulted in an attempt to take his life. He'd only recently rejoined the group. From what Cade had heard, he'd come a long way since then.

"I had a loving family," Silas continued. "They were with me one hundred percent. The thing is, I couldn't stand to be around them. I wanted nothing to do with my parents or my sisters. That was when the heavy drinking started."

"Why do you think you rejected your family?" Harry asked.

Silas chuckled. "For the same reason Cade turned down a home-cooked meal." He looked up and locked eyes with Cade. "I understand, buddy, I get you."

Cade was glad someone did, because he was lost in his own messed-up head.

"I held on to Yvonne's rejection," Silas admitted, shaking his head as if regretting the fact that he'd spared her a single thought. "I told myself I was glad she called off the wedding. I nursed that pain, held on to it for all I was worth, wallowing in self-pity."

Cade remembered the first session after Silas got the news. He'd sat in the circle and seethed with unmistakable anger until Harry coaxed Yvonne's rejection out of him.

"The pain was comfortable: like my favorite pair of jeans," Silas continued. "And convenient, too, which is why I turned into someone even my mother had trouble loving. I had no desire to move forward, let alone live."

Cade hated to be obtuse. "I don't think I understand what you're saying."

"Let me put it like this," Silas said. "We know you lost your friends in Afghanistan."

"They were my family, my brothers."

"I understand, but you're alive and they're not."

Cade didn't need the reminder. He didn't want to think about Luke and Jeremy, although they all too frequently made appearances in his dreams.

"If you're talking about survivor's guilt, I don't want to hear it," Cade barked. This was an excruciating mental path he'd walked all too often; it had left deep grooves in his brain like ruts in a much-traveled road.

"Not entirely. You're where I was not that long ago." Silas's dark eyes focused on Cade, as if seeking understanding. "You've grown content in savoring your pain."

"That's not true," Cade argued. If it was, he wouldn't be feeling regret about turning down Hope.

"How are things going at the garage?" Harry asked, abruptly changing the subject.

"What does my part-time job have to do with anything?" Cade demanded. Being the focus of this discussion annoyed him to the point that he was ready to walk. As much as he wanted to, he couldn't. These sessions were required as part of a condition for his probation.

"How many friends have you made at the shop?" Harry pressed.

Cade bristled at the question. "I have friends."

"None that you've mentioned," Ricardo said.

"Acquaintances, then."

"Making friends threatens you in the same way Hope does." Shelley made it a statement of fact.

"Hold on," Silas said, raising his hand. "No need to get in Cade's face about this. We're all here for the same reason. If we can't help one another, then we've lost more of our humanity than we realize."

Harry leaned back and smiled, content to let Silas continue.

"By being loners, we feel like we're handling life; we've built this fortress around ourselves. Involving others, inviting them into our pain, is hard. We resist. We don't like it. We feel we can handle it on our own. We're islands unto ourselves, not needing anyone."

Silence filled the circle as they each absorbed his words.

"We hold on to our pain, our loss, our rejections, like a kid with a favorite toy. Why take the risk? Why get involved? It's costly to let go of all the garbage we carry, the pain we've nursed like a colicky baby. That's why we reject the very thing we want most. We're afraid it might lead to something more, something good, and that's what we find downright uncomfortable."

Cade left the session with his head spinning. As hard as it had been to hear, he knew what Silas said was right on. He'd purposely avoided making friends with the other men at the garage.

Without fail, he went to work, did what was asked of him, and left at the end of the day, saying little to nothing to any of the crew. He hadn't included himself in any casual chatter or jokes. He knew next to nothing about the others, and they knew zero about him. That was the way he liked it. Lunchtime was spent by himself, sitting away from the other guys, often eating in his truck.

It was the same at the animal shelter. Hope was the only volunteer he'd spoken to other than to answer questions. He had infrequent short conversations with Preston. The longest conversation he'd had with the other man was when Hope hadn't been around for a couple days. And look what that had led to: bringing her provisions when she was sick, helping her with her slashed tire, turning down her dinner invitation and now regretting it.

Hope.

His mind all too readily flew to her and the sadness he saw in her eyes when he'd rejected her dinner invite. If he could turn back time, he'd gladly do it. He could picture himself sitting across the dinner table from her and laughing at something she'd said. A warm sensation filled his chest akin to happiness. Happiness he'd refused to allow back into his life. Feeling any sense of joy had died with his friends on a foreign battlefield. If what Silas said was true, it was all because he was afraid to let go of his loss, of his pain, for fear of what the unknown future might hold.

Cade needed to think. Needed to sort through his feelings. It wasn't going to be easy to change the way he viewed relationships. As if his troubled mind had a will of its own, his thoughts zoomed to his mother. She'd come to the courthouse, and according to Harry, it wasn't because of any connection with his father. It made him wonder if she had regrets over what had taken place between Cade and his father. If she had been looking to build a bridge back to his family, he wasn't convinced it was a road he could travel.

The fight was technically between him and his father. But his mother had remained silent when he'd felt confident she'd stand by his side instead of turning a deaf ear to what he was saying. He'd been angry with her, furious that she hadn't stood up for him when he needed someone to believe and understand that he wasn't a clone of his father.

In retrospect, Cade could see that his mother had been trapped between the two most important men in her life. Maybe she'd had no choice but to remain silent. Now it was too late. Too much time had passed. Even if she had come looking to make peace, her efforts were wasted.

Arriving at the beach, Cade parked his truck, climbed out, and started walking. Time spent at the ocean had the power to calm him. It always had, which is one of the reasons he'd chosen to live in Oceanside.

The constant pounding of the surf, the pattern of it, the assurance that when one wave left, another would replace it, comforted him. That and the strong wind that buffeted against him, along with the cry of the seagulls as they drifted along, seemingly without effort, letting the wind take them where it would. To be so carefree, to have a life this simple, was beyond his imagination.

As his steps carried him to the water's edge, he noticed children flying colorful kites and a woman sitting in the sand with a large dog at her side.

Only it wasn't any woman.

It was Hope with Shadow.

Chapter 9

Shadow, on his first day away from the kennel, was tucked close against Hope's side as they sat on the sandy beach. She'd grown close to this stray. A bit of the pain of being alone in the world dissipated as she ran her fingers through his dense fur. Shadow needed her and she needed Shadow. It was one of those incidents when she could ask who had rescued whom.

With the wind in their faces, completely content to sit side by side, they stared out at the rolling waves as the water splashed against the shore, leaving a thin zigzag line of foam.

For the first time since getting the heartbreaking news about Hunter, Hope was at peace. With patience, love, and persistent training, it was as if Shadow was a completely different dog. While he remained guarded and leery of people, he no longer snarled or acted aggressively whenever someone approached. Hope was proud of the work she'd done and the changes she'd made in his life. And he in hers.

She hadn't mentioned Hunter to anyone, the pain debilitating even now, a year following his death. Working with Shadow had helped her deal with the loss of her twin. In some unexplainable way, this feral dog had eased the tight hold grief had wrapped around her heart. She was alone now, starting over, building her life from scratch. Only she wasn't so much alone as when she'd first arrived in Oceanside. She had Shadow and he had her.

Willa was the first person Hope introduced her canine companion to once the adoption papers had been completed. He was now officially hers. Willa surprised Shadow with a special concoction she'd called a puppuccino. He'd loved it, slurping it down in quick fashion, to both Willa and Hope's delight.

"I'm hearing good things about you," Willa said, as she handed Hope her drink.

"Oh?" She brightened. After the incident with the flat tire, Hope had to wonder.

"A lot of the high-schoolers stop by after class, and I hear them chatter about what a good teacher you are. One recently mentioned she went to you after class to talk about troubles at home and how much she appreciated the advice you gave her."

Hope figured that was probably Morgan, a junior girl. She hadn't felt she'd given her advice that was anything special. What Morgan really needed was a listening ear, and Hope had provided that.

"Good to know," Hope said, grateful for the positive feedback. "And thanks."

"Any time," Willa said, and turned her attention to the next customer.

Hope left and wandered down to the beach. Shadow walked steadily at her side, keeping close and alert.

As it often was at the beachfront, the wind was strong. Kids raced up and down the shoreline with their kites, the long tails flapping in the breeze. Couples strolled along the wet sand, savoring the sunshine.

For early October, the afternoon was glorious. Hope had been assured days like this would be rare, as the rains were sure to hit the Pacific Northwest soon. It seemed as if God had smiled down on her, making this day even more special as she had Shadow with her.

Because her gaze was focused on the activity along the beach and the water, Hope didn't notice Cade until he stood almost directly in front of her. He had his hands in his pockets and looked ill at ease. Her heart raced as she recalled Tonya's words about letting him make the next move, if there was to be one. She'd trusted that advice, although that hadn't kept thoughts of him from drifting into her mind.

"Hey," he said, his greeting carried with the wind.

"Cade?" Despite her effort to appear casual, she couldn't keep the surprise out of her voice. She stopped herself from starting a conversation, letting him take the lead.

He didn't quite meet her eyes as he asked, "Do you mind if I join you?"

"Ah . . . sure." She found it difficult to hide how pleased she was that he was there to share this special moment with her.

Lowering himself down beside her, Cade seemed uncertain and eyed her dog. "Do you think Shadow will mind?"

"Guess we'll find out." After all her work socializing the canine, this would be a valid test. Tightening her hand around Shadow's leash, she was prepared for however her dog responded.

Cade carefully sat down on the sand, maintaining a fair distance between him and Shadow. He was close, but far enough away to show that he posed no threat. As expected, Shadow focused his gaze on Cade and regarded him warily.

Hope waited impatiently for him to speak. In their brief history, he had avoided speaking to her, although she didn't know why.

"It's a beautiful afternoon," Cade said, as if he didn't know where to start.

"Sure is." She raised her face to the sun and briefly closed her eyes, soaking in the warmth.

Shadow was alert, his head up, watching every small move Cade made. With his knees up, Cade placed his hands between them, as if to show her dog he was a friend.

"The other night when you invited me to dinner . . ." He hesitated, as if unsure what to say next.

"What about it?"

He heaved a huge sigh. "I wanted to spend time with you, I really did."

"You could have fooled me." She hadn't meant to be so blunt, but his rejection had felt exactly that way. His refusal had left her confused and unsure, as if he regretted stopping to help her.

"I know . . . I wish I could explain what was going on inside my head." As though frustrated with himself, Cade rubbed a hand over his chin. "I would if I'd understood it myself. I have a group of . . . friends I meet with, and they sort of set me straight."

"How so?"

He grimaced before he answered. "They basically told me I was an idiot, and I should've leaped at the chance to know you better, and to be honest, they couldn't understand me turning down a home-cooked meal."

Looking down, Hope did her best to hide her smile. "I like your friends."

"I want to make it up to you," he said. "Would you be willing to go out to dinner with me tonight?" Then he added in a rush, "I know it's last-minute and that you probably already have plans, so if tonight doesn't work, I'll understand. Or if you'd rather not see me at all, I'll understand that, too."

Hope wanted to go to dinner with him, badly. "I can't."

Cade's face fell.

"I'd love to have dinner with you, but I can't leave Shadow locked up in the house on his first day with me."

"Of course, I should have realized that." His shoulders slumped forward for a moment before he straightened. "I could always get us take-out. Would that work?" Cade asked. "I could meet you back at the cottage or you could bring Shadow with you to my place, although it's small."

Hope loved how eager he sounded. "It's so peaceful here, do you mind if we stay right here?"

He relaxed. "I think that's a perfect idea." He glanced over his shoulder, looking toward the parking area where the food trucks assembled. Most had left after Labor Day, although a few remained, eking sales from the last days of the season.

"How do you feel about hot dogs?" Cade asked.

That sounded exactly right. "Hot dogs are the best part of a picnic."

"Do you think Shadow would like one?"

She cracked a smile. "You're joking, right?"

Cade grinned before he leaped to his feet and brushed the sand off his backside. "Don't go anywhere. I'll be back before you know it."

She watched Cade walk away, and there seemed to be a bounce in his step. "Well, well," she said to Shadow. Her pet placed his chin on her thigh as he relaxed. Gently petting his head, she couldn't keep the smile from her face. "Will wonders never cease," she whispered.

Within fifteen minutes Cade returned with a large container holding two large drinks and a paper bag.

"That didn't take long," she said.

"I didn't go far. I didn't want to risk you changing your mind."

"No chance," she said, smiling up at him.

Cade's returning smile was huge as he sank down into the sand next to Shadow, closer this time. He handed her the soda and then set his own aside before he opened the brown paper bag.

"Are these from Wee Willie's Wiener Wagon? I didn't realize he was still at the beach." The wiener wagon was her favorite of the food trucks, although several sold hot dogs. She thought Wee Willie had left for the season, as she hadn't seen him in his usual parking spot up from the beach.

"It's his last day. He took over one of the more popular spots since it was vacant," Cade explained.

He handed Hope the hot dog wrapped in shiny foil. "I should have asked what you like on your bun. I guessed and added mustard and relish."

"That's perfect."

He removed a second hot dog, unwrapped it, and then tore it into small bites to feed Shadow a little at a time. Given to him whole, Shadow would have immediately inhaled the entire hot dog in one giant gulp.

As she expected, Shadow was in doggie heaven. Wieners weren't the best diet for him, however, today would be the exception. After everything he'd endured, he deserved to be a little spoiled now and again.

Hope had eaten half her dog before Cade had a chance to dig into his own meal. As the sun started to set and sink below the horizon, they ate in companionable silence, content to simply sit side by side.

When they'd finished, Cade gathered all their trash and delivered it to the proper container before rejoining her. When he sat back down, she noticed Shadow seemed to have completely accepted him. Her faithful friend rested his chin on Cade's thigh the way he'd done with her earlier.

"My hope is that this will be the first of several dinners." He looked her way as if this was a question rather than a statement.

"I'd like that."

He stretched his arm across Shadow's back and reached for her hand. They linked their fingers together. "Tell me what brought you to Oceanside."

She inhaled and held her breath. Certain details of her life were private, Hunter's death being one of those. The pain of his loss was her own and she held it close, not wanting sympathy or welcoming it. Talking about Hunter made her realize how alone she was and often brought tears to her eyes. This was a path she wasn't ready to walk with Cade, since they were just getting to know each other.

Unsure where to begin, she started with her childhood. "My mother abandoned my brother and me when we were toddlers. We grew up in southern California and were raised by my grandparents."

"That's rough," he said.

"Our grandparents loved us to the best of their ability. I'm sure raising two rambunctious children wasn't how they'd expected to spend their retirement years." More than once, Hope had felt their resentment that they couldn't travel and do all the things they had planned, because they were saddled with her and Hunter.

"Hunter, that's my twin brother, joined the army as soon as he graduated from high school. I was smart enough to get a scholarship for college, and moved out as soon as I could, to give my grandparents the freedom from responsibility of looking after us." Hope had worked two part-time jobs, plus concentrating on her studies. Hunter helped her out financially when he could.

"Why did you decide to become a teacher?"

He didn't know she had a double degree, and this wasn't

the time to point that out. "California had a shortage of teachers at the time, and I knew I'd be able to get a job."

He nodded, as if urging her to continue.

"Then I lost both my grandparents within a short amount of time, which was really sad. Grandpa went first and then Grandma with breast cancer. I had no idea that older women are more prone to that form of cancer.

"She was lost without Grandpa and died about a year later. Her death certificate said it was cancer, but I knew the real reason. I had moved back in with her to help. She was lost and lonely without him and didn't have the will to live."

Cade gave her hand a gentle squeeze. "That partially answers my question. With Hunter serving in the military and both your grandparents gone, you had no reason to remain in California."

"Exactly. I'd lived in the Los Angeles area nearly all my life, and I wanted to experience life in a small town. Once I'd completed the paperwork, I applied for teaching jobs in a number of small towns in Washington." Oceanside hadn't been her first choice. It'd turned out to be the best, though. "Now, what about you?" she asked, eager to turn the conversation away from herself.

Leaning back, Cade stretched out his legs and crossed his ankles. "Raised in Tacoma, graduated from Pacific Lutheran University," he stated the bare facts. "After that, I had some problems with my parents, my father in particular." He hesitated, as if unsure he should continue. "My dad demanded that I follow in his footsteps, career-wise. I rebelled. That didn't sit well with my mom and dad. We've basically been estranged ever since."

How unfortunate to have a family and to walk away. "I'm sorry, Cade," she said, genuinely sad for him.

"You have nothing to be sorry for. You didn't do anything."

"I know that. I'm sorry that you don't have a good relationship with your family." Because she was completely alone in the world, Hope would give anything to have known her birth parents. As it was, she had only fleeting memories of her mother. As far as she knew, her father had never been part of her life. From tidbits she'd overheard from her grandparents, their mother was a lost cause. Hope wasn't exactly sure what that meant, although she suspected it had something to do with drug addiction. From the time Hope and Hunter arrived at their grandparents' home, they had never, not one time, received any communication from their mother. Hope had no idea if the woman who gave birth to her was alive or dead, and had to assume she was the latter. According to their grandmother, it was likely Hope's mother didn't know who had fathered her and Hunter.

"I wish it was different, too," Cade confessed. "The problem is we're both too stubborn to admit we were wrong."

"You can't go back?" Surely there was a way to move forward.

"If I reach out to my father, he'll assume I'm admitting I was wrong and will bend to his plans for my life. That's not going to happen. I'm not cut out to be an attorney."

"What about your mother? Can she help?"

Cade straightened. "It took a long time for me to forgive her for not backing me when I needed it most. I was desperate for her to stand at my side. It's only been recently that I've come to understand what a difficult position she was in, trapped between me and my dad." He hesitated, bending his head down. "I saw her not long ago." His voice was low, uncertain. "I should probably tell you . . ."

"That you're on probation?"

His head shot up. "You know?"

"Mellie, Preston's wife, told me."

His face revealed his shock. "And you're still willing to spend time with me?"

She nodded. "I've seen how you are with the animals at the shelter. As far as I'm concerned, you've proven yourself. You went out of your way to help me when it would have been easy to drive off. I don't believe you're a dangerous person, Cade. I trust you."

"Do you know even what crimes I committed?"

"No, and I don't need to unless you feel it's something you want to tell me."

He sighed and closed his eyes before he spoke. "I was drunk and got into a bar fight. It wasn't my finest moment. I didn't deserve any leniency; the judge took pity on me and gave me time served and probation with certain stipulations."

"Community service?"

He nodded. "Harry . . . a friend, suggested the animal shelter."

They'd gotten sidetracked a bit. "You mentioned you'd recently seen your mother. That's encouraging, don't you think?"

"It would be, if it hadn't been inside a courtroom." He expelled his breath. "I hated that the first time I'd had any contact with her in over six years was when I stood before a judge. It humiliated me for her to see how low I'd gone."

"Oh Cade." She tightened her hold on his hand.

"The worst of it is she was sure to tell my father, and knowing my dad, he probably ate it up."

"You can't be sure of that."

"You don't know my father," Cade argued. "The minute he learned I'd joined the army, he went ballistic. He was convinced I did it to spite him and that it was the biggest mistake of my life."

Cade's voice had grown tight with pain and frustration. He'd revealed a vulnerable part of himself that she was certain he didn't discuss often, or at all. Darkness had settled over the landscape and over them. The moon slowly started to rise over the horizon.

Cade pulled his hand from hers and settled it on Shadow's back. "Now that you know the worst, I'll understand if you'd rather not have anything to do with me."

Hope thought over his comment, and while she probably should have some reservations when it came to Cade, she went with her gut. She'd liked Cade from the beginning and trusted him.

"I have a question for you," she said.

"Okay." He'd tensed right along with his voice.

"Do you have plans Saturday night?"

She felt, more than saw, his head swivel toward her.

"No. Why?"

"I'm chaperoning the homecoming dance at the high school, and I'd like to know if you'll be my date."

Chapter 10

Cade sat across from Harry, his head down, his thoughts whirling at tornado speed. Harry waited for Cade to speak. Five tense minutes into the session, Cade was finally able to look up.

Ever patient, Harry appeared content to wait him out.

"I spoke to Hope," Cade mumbled.

Nodding, Harry encouraged him to continue.

Cade had been shocked when Hope mentioned chaperoning the homecoming dance. He'd been unsure what to say. "She asked me to attend a dance with her at the high school," he blurted out, like it was a request for him to leap off the Narrows bridge or swim to Hawaii. "You and I both know that's impossible. I can't dance. Even standing for an extended length of time can be problematic."

"What kind of dance is this?" Harry asked.

"Homecoming. She's one of the chaperones and she wants me to join her: like I won't stick out like a scarecrow in the middle of a cornfield."

"Being a chaperone doesn't necessarily mean you have to be on the dance floor."

Cade expected Harry's questions. He had plenty of his own.

"I understand we won't be crowned the king and queen." His voice betrayed his sarcasm. "But Hope's going to expect at some point that I'll want to dance with her."

"Seems to me you're making assumptions."

"I can't dance," Cade insisted, growing irritated with himself more than with Harry. "We both know that kind of physical activity would be difficult for me with my . . . limitations." Cade had come to hate his leg and all the problems it caused him. The pain was a constant reminder of that fateful day and the helplessness he experienced as he watched his friends die. He should count his blessings: the very fact he was alive. When he couldn't, he felt guilty, sinking into a black hole that wanted to suck him up.

"Do you know exactly what your role would be?" Harry always seemed to ask the right questions. He'd relentlessly zoom in to a problem the way a hawk goes after its prey.

Thinking back over their brief conversation, once Hope mentioned the dance, Cade hesitated before answering, realizing his error. "No."

"Then it seems to me you're making another assumption."

Cade felt like he'd backed himself into a corner. He wanted to dance with Hope. Not dance, especially, but hold her tight against him. All night, he'd tossed and struggled with the sheets, tugging them one way and then another, as his mind filled with thoughts of the pleasure of holding Hope in his arms. Half-asleep, he could smell the scent of her perfume and feel the comfort of her pressing against him. He wanted that more than he wanted anything. Then his mind would shoot to his disability and the embarrassment he'd feel if his leg gave out from under him. It'd happened before and it would again. No way would he put himself in that position. Eager as he was to hold Hope, he couldn't let himself do it.

And yet . . .

Their conversation from the day before had been a turning point for him. It'd felt monumental to sit at her side, share Wee Willie's hot dogs, and enjoy the late afternoon as if he hadn't a care in the world. It'd been years since he'd experienced any moment as freeing until . . . until she'd mentioned the dance.

With this new understanding between them, Cade had shared a sensitive part of himself that only Luke and Jeremy had heard. Harry hadn't dug much into his family background, and Cade hadn't mentioned his parents in the group sessions, either. For some unexplained reason, he'd felt compelled to tell Hope.

"Did you agree to chaperone with her?" Harry asked.

This was the problem. "I . . . I didn't say anything one way or the other. It was as if she assumed I'd agreed because she went on talking, giving me details about the night. At some point, she must have realized I hadn't said I'd go and went silent. Harry, I don't know what I'm going to do." He wanted to bury his face in his hands. He was right back where he started when he'd refused her dinner invitation. Even though he was strongly attracted to her, he had declined the very thing he wanted most. And here he was doing it again.

His time on the beach with Hope had been perfect until she'd mentioned the dance. He'd planned on kissing her, but as soon as she brought up him chaperoning with her, he'd frozen. No question, he needed counseling. He needed help to figure out why he kept turning his back on Hope when he hungered to have her in his life.

"She was willing to let you get away with not answering?"

"She said she'd accept whatever decision I made."

"And have you decided?"

Cade had mulled it over from the moment they parted. "I've thought about it every minute. I was grateful our session was today so you could help me sort all this out; tell me what would be best."

Harry chuckled. "You don't honestly think I'm going to advise you one way or the other, do you? This is on you, Cade."

On him. Harry was right. He was the one who had to find peace about this. Part of him was eager to be with Hope, no matter when or what the occasion. From the moment he'd met her, the reality of his physical limitations had caused him to keep his distance.

His leg, at times, had a mind of its own. One wrong move and he would writhe with pain so severe it took every ounce of strength he possessed not to cry out. Although he had to admit the physical therapy was working, he wasn't to the point where he could twirl Hope around a dance floor.

"How long are you going to wait before you give her an answer?"

Time was quickly evaporating. Every tick of the clock was a reminder that he had to decide one way or the other. They'd parted with the understanding that he'd let her know sometime before Saturday evening when the dance was scheduled.

Although Cade was a relative newcomer to Oceanside himself, he'd been around long enough to know the high school football games were huge events. The stands were crammed during each home game with students, parents, and local supporters from the community. Friday-night football was big entertainment in a small town, and Oceanside was no exception. The players were treated like royalty. Businesses waved flags bearing the Oceanside Eagle logo, hyping up each game.

As a compromise, Cade decided to attend the game with Hope, even if it meant he would need to climb the bleachers. Stairs could be a painful challenge. Putting all his weight on his injured leg often caused debilitating pain. To alleviate that, he often took one step at a time, attracting unwanted attention. To face those pitying looks while half the town's population stared at him sent a chill up his spine.

Silence filled the room as Cade was lost in his thoughts.

Harry interrupted Cade's musings. "Didn't you recently mention that Hope had some kind of run-in with the team's quarterback?"

At the memory, Cade's entire body stiffened. In that instant he had his answer. Hope alone at the dance, unescorted, could possibly make her a target. Cade hadn't gotten all the details of what had happened or exactly why, but he knew enough. He'd even done a bit of homework himself. He'd asked to view the security camera of the grocery's parking lot. The equipment was old and outdated, and the picture too fuzzy for him to make any clear identification, although it clearly showed that the tire had been vandalized.

Cade had his suspicions. Whoever was responsible looked young, likely a teenager.

"I have to go to that dance," he said, with newfound determination.

"You aren't obligated, Cade. This isn't your concern."

"Hope is my concern."

Harry crossed his legs. "What if, at the end of the evening, she wants to dance with you?"

Leave it to Harry to force him to face the most uncomfortable aspect of this. All he could do was be honest. "I don't know. I guess I'll figure it out when the time comes."

Harry was all smiles.

"That pleases you?"

"It does," Harry said. "You aren't focusing your attention on yourself or your limitations. Your concern for Hope has overridden your fears, and that's a step in the right direction."

"If you say so," Cade grumbled.

Fifteen minutes later Cade left Harry's office, and he noticed his step was lighter. Now that he knew what he was doing, he felt good inside. At their first meeting Cade hadn't wanted anything to do with counseling. These days, he was grateful for Harry, who would be the first one to tell him to pull his head out of his butt and make it sound like Cade's suggestion. The guy had a gift.

This dance with Hope wasn't about him and his limitations. His focus was on the woman who had caught his attention. Being by her side, protecting her from any potential problem, was what was important. Whatever embarrassment he suffered would be worth keeping her safe.

Instead of meeting Hope at the game an hour before the starting time, Cade showed up at her cottage.

Her eyes revealed her surprise when she opened her door. Shadow was at her side and didn't so much as bark when he saw it was Cade. It seemed Shadow accepted him and all it'd taken was a single hot dog.

"Come in," Hope said. Her eyes filled with expectation as she waited for him to explain the visit.

Moving into the house, for a moment, Cade couldn't take his eyes off her. She was already dressed for the game in skinny jeans and a school sweatshirt with the Eagles logo. She was beautiful. Her silence reminded him she had no idea why he'd stopped by.

"I decided to be your plus-one for the dance," he said.

Her face dissolved into a huge smile. "I'd love that, and thank you. I wasn't looking forward to attending the dance alone."

"But you should know I have certain limitations, and if that embarrasses you—"

"Stop," she said abruptly, and reached out to grab hold of his forearm. "You're being ridiculous. I know you have an injured leg. It doesn't bother me, and it shouldn't bother you, either. Now, enough said."

Cade couldn't resist. Even before she finished speaking, he drew her into his arms and kissed her. It was impulsive and out of sheer relief that she understood and accepted him with his many flaws and shortcomings. He took her by surprise because her mouth was closed, but she quickly adjusted, opening to him. Her arms went around his neck, and she leaned in to him, sucking on his bottom lip, giving herself to him. He wasn't sure how long they kissed. Not long enough. One taste of Hope and it left him craving more.

When she opened her eyes, Hope looked up at Cade with the sweetest smile. "That was nice."

It was all he could do to acknowledge her with a nod. He swallowed. "Very nice."

"Tonight will be fun," she assured him. "We're going to attend the game and cheer on our team with half the town, and then Saturday night we'll meet up for the dance."

The tension between his shoulder blades dissipated and Cade relaxed. He could do this. Hope needed him, and he wouldn't disappoint her.

By the time they arrived at the football field, it was hard to find a vacant parking spot. This game was a big deal. Oceanside was playing against their strongest rival, the Montesano Bulldogs. The Oceanside Eagles remained undefeated. Although it was early in the season, the Eagles were expected to go all the way to the state finals. The previous year, both the football and baseball teams had been awarded the championship for Washington State's A classification. With the school's population around three hundred, they played against other schools with a larger student count from which to pull talent.

Much of the credit went to the coach, Wade Simmons. As far as Oceanside was concerned, the man walked on water. Cade didn't blame them. Coach inspired and encouraged his team with a strong work ethic. Nearly every afternoon if Cade passed the high school, he noticed the team running drills and scrimmages on the field. Coach was strict but fair, and Oceanside loved him for the way he'd shaped the young men on and off the field.

Hope wrapped her arm around Cade's elbow as they approached the field, her eyes filled with excitement. "Willa's here," she announced. "She's with her husband and Dr. Annie, too."

Cade knew Willa but hadn't met Sean O'Malley, her husband. He was some hot shot photographer whose photos were often featured in *National Geographic*. Seemed funny a successful professional like Sean would choose to live in a little town like Oceanside. To each his own.

Cade hadn't needed any medical attention outside of what he got from the VA hospital and the physical therapist he worked with in Aberdeen, so he wasn't familiar with Dr. Annie. He knew her husband, Keaton, from the animal shelter. As he recalled, it was Keaton who'd delivered Shadow to the facility. Since Cade had been volunteering at the shelter, Keaton had stopped by several times. The man was large and intimidating at first glance, until Cade had been around him awhile. He was big-chested, close to seven feet, he'd guess, with hands nearly twice the size of a normal person's, and it seemed his heart for helping others matched his size.

Hope waved to Willa, who immediately invited them to

join her and Sean. Naturally, they sat more than halfway up the bleachers. Cade tensed right away, knowing the climb would be awkward.

Instead of rushing forward, Hope remained patiently at his side, taking one step at a time with him, as if he were the one helping her up the stairs.

She paused halfway up when she spied one of her students. "Hi, Spencer," she said.

The kid looked up and then glanced away. As crowded as the stands were, there was plenty of space left on both sides of Spencer. It was as if he were being given the cold shoulder by his schoolmates. Clearly no one wanted to sit next to him.

"Where's Callie?" Hope asked. "Shouldn't she be with you?"

Several other students stared in his direction. "She's on the dance team," Spencer explained.

"Right," Hope said, as if she should have remembered that bit of information.

Once they were seated and friendly introductions were made with Willa and her husband, Cade asked about Spencer.

"He's the young man I mentioned. Scott Pender's girlfriend is the one Spencer is escorting to homecoming."

"Not his former girlfriend?" Cade asked.

Hope hesitated. "I'm not sure. They seem off and on, so I have to assume this is an off time."

If not, that could mean trouble at the dance, Cade mused.

Although he didn't know Spencer personally, Cade was sympathetic. "You mentioned him before, but not by name. He's the one who finagled the deal with Callie, right?"

"Right. She had some computer problem she wanted him to resolve."

Cade wanted the facts straight in his mind. "Which Spencer agreed to do if she became his date for homecoming?"

"Exactly."

He could only imagine what the girl had wanted, and suspected Hope did, too. "Do you know what it was she asked of him?"

Hope's arm that remained wrapped around his tightened. "That's the problem, he hasn't told me. Spencer always manages to change the subject. I'm afraid he's gotten himself tangled up in something over his head."

Cade let that settle in, wondering what the poor kid had agreed to do for this girl all because he'd lost his head over a pretty face. From what Hope said, it sounded as if Callie couldn't care less about Spencer or the consequences from her former boyfriend.

"I'm concerned," Hope added. "At this point, though, there's nothing I can do."

"You can't blame yourself."

"But I do. I should never have advised Spencer the way I did. He told me that their families are good friends and at one point they had been, too. All Spencer really wanted was for things to go back the way they once were: to be friends with the hope of something more. He wanted a chance to let Callie know how much he liked her. Spencer is such a great kid." Lowering her voice, she added, "I know I shouldn't have favorites, but I can't help it with Spencer. Yes, he's smart, but he works hard. Not everything comes easy for him. He isn't like the others; he's mature for his age, works part-time with his dad, and has manners and respect for others. You wouldn't believe how rare that is in this day and age."

"You're afraid Callie is using him."

"I have no doubt. She's pretty and popular and seems completely self-absorbed. I'm convinced she made sure everyone in school knows that she'd been manipulated into this date with Spencer."

"I'm surprised he's going through with it."

"Actually, I am, too."

Cade could imagine Spencer had paid the price for the audacity of even asking Callie to homecoming.

"Has the harassment continued?"

She expelled a heavy sigh. "If it has, Spencer isn't saying."

"But you have your suspicions."

Hope nodded. "I heard that Spencer had his head shoved into the toilet, and it was posted on social media. I asked him about it, and he refused to answer. Then there was talk over some social media post that was an unflattering caricature of Spencer. He's been the brunt of jokes ever since. I have to admire the way he ignores the taunts."

"And Callie has stood by and said nothing?" Cade hadn't met the girl and he already disliked her.

"Apparently so. There's been other stuff happening, too, whispers and laughs in the hallway whenever Spencer is there. He hasn't complained or reported anything. I don't think the staff know the half of it."

"Poor kid." Spencer had Cade's sympathy.

The band started to play the school song, and spontaneous applause arose from the crowd as the Oceanside Eagles charged out of the locker room and ran onto the field.

Everyone in the stands leaped to their feet and cheered for what was sure to be a good game against a worthy opponent. Despite their undefeated record, Oceanside wasn't a favored win against the rival Montesano Bulldogs.

Cade had the feeling Spencer wasn't favored to win, either.

Chapter 11

Spencer parked in front of Callie's house. While she'd agreed to be his date for the homecoming dance, she'd gone out of her way to make him regret ever agreeing to help her. It was hard to believe that at one time they'd been friends. Whatever it was they'd shared when they were younger was over, only he'd been too infatuated with her to accept the truth of it.

Ever since word had gotten out that she was his date, he'd been the brunt of every joke. In the days leading up to the dance, he felt like an outcast. He would forever be grateful to Joel and Brian, his true friends, who had stuck by his side. But neither of them was attending the dance, so Spencer was on his own.

Before his foolish mistake of asking Callie to homecoming, he had been so smitten he wasn't able to see past her beauty and charm. Since then, his eyes had been opened, and he had a clear view of Callie's personality. She was nothing close to what she'd once been. Because he took great pride in being a person to keep his word, he'd followed through with his end of the bargain.

The big ask had to do with her twin brother, Ben. For the last couple months since school had started, she'd noticed an alarming change in his behavior. Determined to discover the source, Callie made it her mission to find out what she could about it.

Which was when she had found a bag of pills in his backpack. Ben had caught her in his room, going through his stuff, and had been furious. He'd refused to tell her who gave him the drugs and insisted she mind her own business. That hadn't stopped Callie, however. She'd been determined to expose whoever was responsible, and she had her suspicions. All she needed was confirmation. For that she required Spencer's help.

Callie needed Spencer to hack into Ben's computer for evidence, convinced he would find a trail, either there or on Ben's phone. She'd determined this by the protective way Ben hid both from her and from everyone else. Spencer had given it his best effort and come up blank. Because of that, Callie felt that he'd failed her.

Strengthening his resolve, Spencer climbed out of the car and headed to Callie's front door. The dance was sure to be her most opportune moment to complete his humiliation.

Spencer was determined not to let that happen.

He stepped back after he rang the doorbell and waited. Her father answered the door and looked at Spencer before a huge grin spread across his face. "Spencer!" He slapped him hard against his back. "Callie didn't mention you were her homecoming date."

That didn't come as any big surprise.

"It's been a while since we've seen your mom and dad. How are they doing?"

"They're good." He didn't elaborate.

"The last time I talked to your dad he was telling me about the two of you working on his old car. How's that going?"

"We're finished."

Bill Rhodes's eyes went from Spencer to the car parked on the street. His eyes widened in appreciation.

"That's the 1965 Dodge Dart?" he asked. "Wow, I can hardly believe it. You two put a lot of work into it."

"We did." The car was Spencer's prized possession, especially after all the time he and his dad had spent on it.

"That Dart was your dad's first car."

"It's mine now. We rebuilt the engine." He didn't mention it'd taken months to get everything they needed to make it purr as it once had.

"Would you mind if I took a look at it?" Even as Callie's father asked the question, he was halfway down the front steps.

"Not at all." Some of the tension tightening Spencer's shoulders dissipated. He followed Mr. Rhodes to the curb, pleased that he appreciated how special this car was.

Walking around the vehicle, Bill Rhodes nodded several times, showing his admiration. "What a sweet ride. Be sure and let your dad know how impressed I am."

"I will for sure," Spencer said, unable to hide the pride in his voice.

He turned to Spencer and beamed at him. "It's about time my daughter showed some sense. Makes me proud that she's dating you."

"We aren't dating." Spencer wanted to clear away any misconception before matters escalated and their parents got involved.

"I hope that changes after tonight," Bill said. "Between you, me, and the goalpost—no pun intended—I've never been enthusiastic about Callie dating that football player she seems so fond of. The kid has more brawn than brains."

Bill had always been a good judge of character.

"Come on back to the house, and I'll see if Callie's ready."

Spencer followed him into the entryway. It'd been a few years since his last visit and there were some changes. The sofa was new, and the carpet, too. Callie was nowhere in sight, and he wondered if she'd linger until the last minute to avoid any extra time spent in his presence.

After a few minutes, when Callie remained absent, Claire, her mother, went upstairs to collect her. Another five minutes passed before Callie descended the stairs like royalty, her head held high. She avoided making eye contact with Spencer, which was fine by him.

The sooner this night was over, the better all around.

When he did chance a look at her, he was again struck by her beauty and had to remind himself, after everything she'd put him through, that it was only skin deep. Long gone was the girl he once knew. When she reached the bottom of the stairs, Spencer handed her the obligatory small wrist corsage.

"White roses," Claire said, with a meaningful sigh. "For my first big high school dance, my boyfriend gave me a corsage with white roses."

Callie rolled her eyes.

Spencer noticed she didn't produce a boutonniere for him. That was par for the course.

"Pictures," her mother insisted with girlish excitement. "I want pictures." Before either Spencer or Callie could object, she held up her phone and snapped several.

"Get one of them by the car," Bill added, following them out of the house.

They were delayed another five minutes while Claire Rhodes took one photo after another of the couple alongside the Dodge Dart.

Callie's parents stood on the lawn, their arms around each other as Spencer started the engine and drove off.

The silence in the car was as thick as a rubber tire. Neither said a word until Spencer parked outside the school gymnasium. It was time to break the silence and get this over with as quickly as he could.

"I know you aren't happy that I'm your homecoming date, Callie. You've made your feelings clear from the beginning. When I suggested dinner, you flatly refused reminding me you had only agreed to the dance. Fine. I did my part and now you will do yours."

She sat like a stone statue beside him. "You manipulated me into going with you," she reminded him.

"No, I didn't, we made a deal. Trust me when I say it's been one of the biggest regrets of my life. And you went out of your way to make sure of it."

She turned to glare at him. "It doesn't help that you weren't able to do what you said you could."

"I said," he reminded her, trying to control the irritation in his voice, "I'd do my best and I did. At the risk of who knows what, I hacked into Ben's phone and email accounts and found nothing. You were the one who seemed to think I'd find some hidden information there."

"He guards his phone and his laptop like it's the Holy Grail. What else was I to believe?"

"If you remember, I said straight up that no drug dealer would be stupid enough to leave an Internet trail."

She didn't answer him. Her arms were crossed and her nose so far up she'd drown in a rainstorm.

Spencer drew in a breath before he spoke. "I do want to thank you, though."

"Oh?"

"You taught me a lesson I'm not likely to forget."

"Not to manipulate people," she said, with a smug twist.

He hesitated. "That's where you're wrong. You agreed. You could have turned me down, you know. Trust me, I won't make a mistake like this again, but what I really learned has to do with you."

"Really?" She glanced at him and then away again.

"I thought you were beautiful. I couldn't keep my eyes off you."

A small smile cracked her tight lips.

"And it wasn't just your looks. In my eyes, you could do no wrong. But you're definitely not the girl I remember. I hardly recognize who you've become. You're a fake."

"What do you mean by that?" she challenged, turning to look at him once again, her eyes narrowed into thin slits.

"You're selfish, mean, and spoiled."

Her mouth sagged open. "I'm not going to sit here and let you insult me."

Spencer was done with Callie. The last thing he wanted was to attend this dance with her. It would have been easier to call the whole thing off. However, pride wouldn't let him. "As far as I'm concerned, you and Scott Pender deserve each other."

Callie climbed out of the car and slammed the door with unnecessary force. "If you think I'm going to enjoy being your date, then you're sadly mistaken."

Spencer was out of the car by this time and stopped her. "Oh no you don't. I held up my part of the bargain and it cost me. So you better do yours."

"Or what?" she challenged, as if he had no recourse.

"As you already know, I have good hacking skills, and so do my friends." He almost hoped she'd defy him, giving him the perfect excuse to make her life as miserable as she'd made his.

Her arms were tucked around her middle. "Not that those skills did me any good."

"Because there wasn't anything there to find."

"Ben isn't talking," she insisted. "You don't think I've tried? When it comes to my brother, I might as well be talking to a brick wall. It might have helped if you'd made the effort."

"Me?"

"Yes, you. Ben trusts you. Or he did at one time. The least you could have done was ask him."

Spencer shook his head. "Are you serious? Do you honestly think Ben would confide in me when he refuses to talk to his own sister? His twin?"

"I thought you could help. Boy, was I wrong."

"I don't understand why you didn't take this to your parents." Bill and Claire were good people and would do whatever it took to help their son.

"I can't. Ben would never forgive me. He'd be pulled from the football team and lose any chance of getting a college scholarship."

"If he's on drugs, he's headed for a downward spiral as it is. Come on, Callie, if you're serious about helping Ben, you need to involve your family."

"Not yet. Honestly, Spence, this is eating at me like nothing else. I can't sleep for fear of what Ben's gotten himself into. I haven't got a clue how he's paying for the drugs. He doesn't have a job, and I'm afraid he's stealing to supply his habit."

Spencer heard the worry in her voice. "You're sure it's a habit?"

She nodded miserably. "I hardly recognize him anymore, and my parents are clueless. Ben is up early and arrives home late after practice, and then heads up to his room. I'm the only one who seems to notice the difference. Then I found those drugs, and I had my answer."

"What about asking his friends?"

"I tried with Scott, but he isn't talking to me at the moment."

"Because you agreed to go to homecoming with me?"

Callie lowered her head. "I don't know. Don't care, either. I don't mind dancing with you, Spence, but really . . . every dance?"

No chance on him backing down. "Yup. After what I've been through, I'm claiming every single dance."

"Even though you hate me." Her eyes flickered with regret.

"I didn't say I hated you." He almost wished he could.

"Yes, you did."

"No," he clarified. "All I said was that you aren't the girl I remember, the one who used to laugh and tease me. We used to be friends, Callie. Good friends, and I thought . . . well, it doesn't matter what I thought. You've changed, and honestly I found those changes weren't for the better."

"I care about my brother, and I hoped you'd be able to help."

"You used me, Callie, and to be fair I guess I used you, too."

"We used each other," she agreed.

"I apologize for my part. Like I said, lesson learned."

"It hasn't been a bed of roses for me, either, you know," she returned.

This was too much. "Please, Callie, tell me how you've suffered. I'm all ears."

Embarrassed, she hung her head.

She had the good grace to say nothing.

"I can't imagine what story you made up as to why you agreed to be my date."

"I know you did your best to help me, Spence. You're right, I used you. I probably should have gone to my parents about

Ben instead of coming to you for help. Then when you wanted to take me to homecoming, I felt people would think . . . I don't know what they'd think."

"You didn't want any of our classmates to believe you were attracted to me. The über-geek. Trust me, the message was received."

"I'm sorry," she whispered.

"Well, that's progress. We understand each other. Now let's go into the dance and do our best to have a good time."

He waited, hoping she'd understand why this was important.

Callie looked up at him again, her doe eyes pleading with him. "Even after everything that's happened, would you be willing to help me find out who's supplying my brother with drugs?"

He hesitated, even now finding it difficult to refuse her.

"Ben was your friend once, and if ever he needed a friend, it's now," she said, her eyes wide and pleading.

Spencer found it hard to find his voice. It went without saying Ben wouldn't listen to him and likely would resent any effort he made to reach out. "I'll think about it."

She swallowed and impulsively hugged him. "I knew I could count on you."

"Callie, listen. Even if I agree, you need to understand there's only so much I can do. Are you sure you don't want to bring your parents in on what's happening?"

"I can't. Not yet. I will if I have to, but not yet."

Spencer could understand her hesitation because of all the ramifications that would come down on Ben.

"I need to find who's giving him the drugs," Callie said, looking thoughtful, as if her mind was reviewing who it might possibly be.

"Come on, Callie, you have to know nothing is going to deter Ben if he's addicted. He'll simply find another dealer, and trust me, there are plenty of them out there."

"He won't," she insisted. "I won't let him."

"And you're going to stop him how?"

"I haven't figured that part out yet. I'm hoping that once whoever is doing this is exposed, the school will step in."

"What about Ms. Goodwin?"

"What about her?"

"Talk to her. Explain the situation."

Automatically Callie shook her head. "I can't. She'll be obligated to take it to the authorities, and that would be even worse than telling my parents. Mom and Dad would never forgive me for not going to them first."

She was right. Still, if Ben was truly addicted, he'd take his business elsewhere. The one hope Callie had was to involve her parents so they would get Ben the help he needed. "You're convinced it's another student?"

"It has to be. I mean, Ben's entire life is at school. He doesn't have a job, all his friends attend here, and he's serious about getting a football scholarship. All the scouts are looking at him this year. I only want to help my brother."

Spencer understood her dilemma.

"I'm sorry about everything, Spence. I really am. I'll be your date tonight. Your real date."

"I'm sorry, too," he said, and he was.

They started walking toward the gym, her arm tucked in

his. He heard the loud music even before they entered the building. After checking in, they stepped inside. It seemed everyone close to the door turned to look at the two of them. To his delight, Callie was all smiles.

"Hey, LeAnn and Steve," she called and waved. "Good to see you."

Others in the group around them raised their hands in greeting, all the while keeping close watch on Callie and him.

"Come on, Spencer, let's dance." She took his hand and led him onto the polished dance floor. The song was a ballad, and she looped her arms around his neck and smiled up at him.

"You know what?" she said. "After the rough way this night started out, I didn't expect to enjoy myself."

"You mean you are?"

She smiled. "Surprisingly so, yes. I hope you are, too."

Callie was in his arms just the way he'd dreamed about. "I don't have any complaints," he said, grinning at her.

"Me, neither," she whispered.

Chapter 12

Hope could feel the tension rise in Cade as soon as they entered the school for the homecoming dance. She knew he'd had reservations when he agreed to chaperone with her. His willingness made her appreciate him all the more, knowing this dance was completely out of his comfort zone. She also knew he was doing this for her, for the simple reason that she'd asked.

Seeing Cade come out of his shell, a little at a time, had delighted and encouraged her. Like Cade, Hope had a protective guard around her own heart, for fear of being abandoned again, as her mother had done, and Hunter, who had left her, too, although not by his own choice. She struggled in facing life alone without any family connection.

The gymnasium was filling up. Lois Greenly had been assigned to check the QR code for those who had paid for the dance. The DJ had started the playlist, and a few brave souls had already taken to the dance floor. Even from the far side of the room the music was loud enough to hurt her ears. It'd been a long time since Hope had attended a high school dance, and she'd forgotten how deafening the music could be.

Cade paused as if he, too, was taken aback by the sound blast. With the volume high, it was nearly impossible to decipher the words to any of the songs. From what Hope knew of the more recent chart-topping hits, it was probably better that the lyrics remained obscure. As soon as more couples entered the dance floor, the worst of the noise was muffled somewhat.

"You best tell me what the responsibilities of a chaperone are?" Cade leaned close to ask.

Hope had needed clarification herself. While working in California, she'd taught fifth grade. Most of the extracurricular activities she did were field trips, so this experience was new to her, too. It helped that she'd been given a list and would be trading off with the other chaperones. Lois Greenly and Hope were both on the faculty. Two other chaperones were on the PTA board.

"Our first job is to man the beverage table," Hope told him.

"All night?"

"No, just the first hour. We're trading off assignments with the other chaperones."

"What else?"

"We'll need to monitor the doorway to make sure no one leaves and then wants back inside. No good will come from letting anyone return to the dance from the parking lot."

"They can't bring any food or drinks in, either, right?"

"Right. Lois is doing the initial check-in. She's got a good eye and won't let any contraband through. We'll man the table later, but by then the majority of the kids will have already arrived. A few stragglers are bound to make a showing, though." Hope had asked for the assignment later in the evening so Cade would have a chance to sit down.

"Anything else?"

"Before the end of the evening, we'll have our turn as floaters."

"What's that?" He sounded skeptical.

"We drift around the room, and make sure everyone is having a good time. And we'll have to check the bathrooms. I'll check the girls' room and you can check the boys'."

"Okay. Do we have any other responsibilities? Like me having to dance?"

"Nope, you're free and clear. The dance is for the teens, not us."

"So that's it, then?"

"That's it," she said with a smile, sensing his relief. "Told you it wasn't a big deal."

"Big enough," he muttered.

"Come on, soldier boy, it's our turn to man the refreshment table."

Weaving their way to the back of the room, Hope noticed everything was set up and ready for them to take over. Seeing that it was early, they didn't have many takers.

At one point, she glanced up to see Spencer dancing with Callie, unsure what to make of the scene.

"Is something wrong?" Cade asked.

Hope slowly expelled her breath, unsure and suspicious. "That's Spencer. He's the boy I was telling you about, remember?"

"What I remember is that you got a flat tire because of him." Cade was looking toward the dance floor and frowning.

Hope felt the need to defend the teenager. "That wasn't Spencer's fault."

Cade continued to watch the couple dancing. To Hope's eyes, it seemed as if the two were having the time of their lives. Callie had her arms linked around Spencer's neck and she seemed to only have eyes for him. Every once in a while, she would press her head on his shoulder, and he would tighten his arms around her waist. If Hope didn't know better, she'd think the two were a real couple.

This sudden change in behavior went against everything she knew about Callie and her treatment of Spencer. From the moment Spencer had asked Callie to the dance, she'd gone out of her way to avoid him. It was as though he was invisible. And not just Callie, but nearly everyone in the entire school. His friends had stuck by his side, she knew, but that was only a few students.

"This is unexpected," Hope whispered, more to herself than to Cade.

"What do you mean?" he said. "It looks like they're enjoying themselves."

"Callie made sure he regretted asking her to the dance, going out of her way to ignore him with a lot of other students following suit. Something's changed, and I'm not sure what."

"From where I'm standing, Spencer doesn't seem to mind."

Hope agreed. Spencer seemed to be eating up Callie's attention, and that worried her. The kid was so infatuated with his childhood friend, he might actually believe Callie was sincere. The sudden change was suspicious, to say the least, and it worried Hope.

"If Spencer is as smart as you say he is, then he'll figure it out soon enough."

Hope's thoughts were spinning, and she barely heard Cade. "Callie's after something. I need to find out what her angle is."

"Hope," Cade said, gently squeezing her hand. "Let the kid enjoy the evening."

Cade was right, she should let matters be. If Spencer reached out to her, she could discuss it with him then. For now, the best she could do was keep her eyes on the couple and hope nothing would disrupt the evening. Looking around the dance floor, she spied Scott Pender as he walked over to the edge of the dance floor, abandoning his date, and stared at Callie and Spencer. A dark scowl came over him.

"Oh dear," she whispered, immediately concerned.

"What's wrong?" Cade was instantly alert.

Before she could explain, Scott approached Callie and Spencer. Hope eased closer to the edge of the dance floor to step in if warranted.

Scott shoved Spencer aside and grabbed hold of Callie by the waist. Spencer stood back as if unsure what to do. By this time, several of the couples dancing close by had stopped to watch the exchange.

Callie wrestled away from Scott and grabbed Spencer by the hand. "I'm not interested in dancing with you," she said, glaring at Scott. "Spencer is my date for the night."

"You don't care about him," Scott challenged. "Who do you think you're fooling?"

"You don't know who I care about, so keep your opinions to yourself."

Scott turned to face Spencer. "You're more of an idiot than I thought."

Spencer remained silent.

Just when matters looked to get heated, Coach Simmons stepped onto the dance floor, and that was all it took to defuse the situation. Scott glanced at the coach and then laughed, as if it was all a big joke, slapping Spencer hard across the back. Without another word, he walked to the other side of the dance floor, where his date waited, looking none too pleased.

Hope breathed a sigh of relief. She wasn't sure what she would have done if Scott had pushed Spencer into an altercation.

It was a relief when Scott went back to his date. Coach Simmons must have noticed her interest, because a few minutes later he approached Hope and Cade.

"Good to see you, Ms. Goodwin."

"You, too, Coach."

He looked to Cade, and Hope made the introduction. The two men exchanged handshakes.

"I'm grateful you stepped in when you did," Hope told him.

"Scott's a good kid, talented and destined for great things on and off the football field, if he can learn to keep his cool."

Cade eased closer to Hope, placing his arm around her middle. "Are you aware Hope had a run-in with him recently?"

Coach was immediately concerned. "I know she found him

harassing the Brown boy. Is there something else I don't know about?"

"Her car was vandalized."

Coach's eyes narrowed. "What happened?"

Hope felt the need to step in. "Cade, please. It isn't fair to accuse Scott when we have no proof it was him."

"Please," Coach insisted. "I want to know."

As Cade told him the details, it was clear Coach took the incident seriously. For sure he didn't look happy. When Cade finished explaining about the tire and the security feed he'd watched, Coach's face was hard and determined.

"If anything, and I do mean anything, like this happens again by any one of my boys, I need to know about it."

"Of course."

"I'll handle it personally," he added.

"All right," Hope reluctantly agreed. She understood Coach wanted to protect his team by taking matters into his own hands. Losing a key player due to discipline problems could well mean losing the chance of winning the state championship for the second year running.

They stood together for a few minutes longer before Coach nodded toward Cade and then walked over to join one of the parent chaperones.

The rest of the dance proceeded without incident. At the end of the evening, Hope was exhausted. She hadn't done any real physical work, so it seemed silly to find herself yawning.

With the other chaperones, they stayed for cleanup. Cade was a big help. They remained with Lois as she locked up the gym after the DJ had packed up his equipment and left.

"All in all, it wasn't such a bad night, now, was it?" she asked Cade, as they walked out into the dark to the nearly empty parking lot.

"I confess I actually enjoyed myself." His arm was around her, and she could hear the smile in his voice.

"I'm glad."

"What was there not to like? I got to spend the evening with you, didn't I?" he said.

"And I wasn't at the dance alone." Hope had spent so much of the last two years by herself, it felt good to feel a connection with another person, even if that thread remained fragile and was still relatively new.

Cade drove Hope back to the cottage. Although it was after midnight and she was tired, she didn't want the evening to end.

"Come in for a few minutes," she said, when they arrived at her place.

Cade hesitated. "Are you sure?"

"I'm not asking you to spend the night, Cade. Neither of us is ready for that just yet. I need to let Shadow out, and I thought I'd put on a pot of chamomile tea and relax for a minute."

"All right." He didn't hesitate, and that encouraged her. Before, he always needed time to think through each invitation, as if to sort through the implications of being with her, and what that might mean.

Once she unlocked the door, Shadow was there to greet her and then immediately went outside to do his business.

"I hate keeping him locked up all day," Hope said. It was her one regret with owning Shadow. "Mellie's been kind enough to come and let him out once or twice a day while I'm at school."

"Didn't you mention getting a doggie door?"

"I did, but I need to find someone to install it."

"I'll do it," Cade said, with an eagerness that surprised her.

"I didn't mention it so that you'd offer, Cade." She didn't want him to feel obligated.

"I know. I'd be happy to do it, really. That's just the sort of thing I enjoy."

His enthusiasm was unexpected and welcome, as it helped solve a problem for her. "I'd appreciate it, but I can't let you do it for free."

"Why not? If I needed a favor, would you turn me down?"

She laughed softly. "It depends on the favor."

He dismissed the question. "I'll stop by tomorrow afternoon, and while I'm here I'll secure the railing on your porch."

That railing was in bad shape. Hope didn't dare put any weight on it for fear that it would become completely dislodged. "Preston's been meaning to look at it for some time now, but he's busy at the shelter and with his family. I haven't wanted to pester him about it."

The kettle on the stove whistled, and Hope filled the teapot that had once belonged to her grandmother. She'd kept a few mementos from her grandparents and treasured each one. They were her one link to the past.

"Preston's got enough on his mind without worrying about this, especially when I can fix it without a problem."

They sat at her small kitchen table and Hope poured the tea. It was too hot to drink right away. Cade stretched his arm across the tabletop and took hold of her hand.

"Thank you," he whispered.

She smiled. "You're thanking me for dragging you to a high school dance?"

"I'm thanking you for everything. When we first met . . . I wasn't in a good place."

"Are you now?" she asked.

He didn't answer right away. "Not completely, but I'm getting there."

Hope felt she was getting there, too. Like Cade, she had a way to go, but she was making progress.

Chapter 13

Hope wasn't home when Cade arrived late Sunday morning. He knocked several times before he realized she wasn't there. He could hear Shadow barking on the other side of the door. He checked to see if she'd locked the door, and sure enough Hope had left it unsecured. She was far too trusting.

Speaking calmly, letting Shadow know it was him, Cade eased open the door. As soon as it was wide enough, the dog shot outside. It was a relief to know Shadow had seen Cade enough times to know he wasn't a threat, with or without Hope's presence.

Shadow immediately went into the yard to do his business and then lay down in the grass to watch as Cade went to work testing the railing. As he suspected, the wood had rotted and needed to be replaced.

As he was dismantling it from the porch, Preston came out of the house. "I've been meaning to get to that for weeks," he called out as he approached. "Hope isn't one to complain, so it was easy enough to let it slide."

"No worries, I enjoy this kind of stuff. But it looks like it's going to take more than a few nails to set this in place, there's wood rot here."

"I thought as much. I bought the wood to replace it a while back. I've got it stored in the garage."

"Great, that will save me a trip to the hardware store."

Together they walked over to Preston's garage, and Preston moved a few items aside to reach the stacked pieces of lumber that rested against the garage wall. Together they carted what was needed back to the cottage.

"The entire porch could do with a paint job," Preston said, "but that will need to wait for better weather."

Intent as he was on the task, Cade hadn't noticed the darkening skies.

"Listen, I know you're doing this as a favor to Hope, but this is my responsibility," Preston said. "I'd like to pay you."

"No need." Cade was quick to brush aside the offer. He wasn't doing this for the money. He'd been looking forward to the project. From the time he could remember, he'd loved taking things apart and learning how they worked and then reassembling them. He was good with his hands and figuring out problems. His father had never understood that part of Cade. In fact, Cade felt his father had never understood him at all.

Preston wasn't hearing it. "I'll give you what I feel your time is worth and I won't accept an argument. Fair is fair."

"Okay, fine," Cade reluctantly agreed, "but you aren't paying me for putting in the door for the dog."

"Agreed." Preston nodded, accepting the deal.

They chatted for a few minutes longer before Preston returned to the house.

Cade had removed the rotted railing when he noticed Shadow quickly coming to his feet. "What is it, boy?" Cade asked.

The words had barely left his mouth when Hope's car turned the corner and parked in her spot beside the cottage. He wondered where she'd gone and been disappointed when he arrived to find she wasn't home. She knew he was coming, and he was a bit annoyed that she'd left.

Hope was all smiles as she climbed out of the vehicle. Cade noticed a Bible in her hand, which gave him the answer. She'd been to church. It'd been a good many years since his figure had darkened a church door. As a kid, his mother had faithfully attended and dragged him along to Sunday school class. He remembered he'd been awarded a Bible for memorizing the names of all sixty-six books that made up the Bible. He had no idea where that was now and guessed it was stored somewhere in his old bedroom closet. His father had never been interested in faith or religion, so it came as no surprise that his mother attended alone.

"Cade," Hope said, "I wanted to be back before you returned. I didn't keep you waiting long, did I?"

"Not long at all." His slight irritation immediately evaporated. "Preston got me started and I have everything I need."

She lingered outside for a few minutes, petting Shadow's head as he came to stand at her side. "Do you need me to do anything?" she asked.

"Nope," he said with an easy smile. "Got it under control."

"Okay. I'll change clothes and put something on for lunch." She bounded up the few stairs and ever-faithful Shadow followed behind her. It came to him that the shelter had aptly named him. Hope's pet had become her shadow, following her wherever she went.

Now that he had everything gathered, Cade went to work. Just as he finished measuring and cutting the two-by-four to nail into place, he felt the first drops of rain. He didn't let that deter him, as he continued pounding the new railing into place.

A couple minutes later, Hope appeared in the doorway in jeans and a plaid shirt with a red sweater vest. She'd changed out of black slacks and a wool blazer. The easy transformation from a fashionable sophisticated woman to a down-home country girl got his attention. He liked both versions.

"Get out of the rain, soldier boy, lunch is ready."

Cade grinned and joined Hope and Shadow inside the cottage. The table was already set. She had toasted cheese sandwiches on a plate and was dishing up steaming bowls of tomato soup.

Cade washed his hands and sat down. Already his mouth was watering. He was hungrier than he realized. All too often he subsisted on take-out or something prepackaged. He had to admit his diet wasn't the best.

"I could hear you whistling," she said, as she carried the first bowl to the table.

Hearing that was news to him. "I was whistling?"

She paused before placing the bowl down. "It sounded familiar, but I couldn't place the tune."

Cade didn't remember doing that. He hadn't whistled since he was a teenager. Talk about childhood regression. Then he remembered he was always happy when he whistled, and there was a song he'd always loved.

"It might have been an old Roger Whittaker tune. I used to whistle 'The Last Farewell,' but that was ages ago."

"That's the song! I've always loved that one. It's so romantic, the sailor going off to war."

"Trust me, there's nothing romantic about war," he felt obliged to remind her.

She sat down across from him. "I realize that more than you know."

He wasn't sure what she meant, and while momentarily tempted, he didn't question her. It seemed they each had their secrets. She didn't pry into his, and he refused to pry into hers. With a brother who was currently serving in the military, she was of course well aware of the ugliness of war.

His phone rang just as they were finishing lunch. Checking, he saw that it was Silas from his therapy group.

"Cade here," he answered.

"Hey," Silas said, sounding upbeat and cheerful. "You get things squared away with that woman you mentioned?"

"Yeah, I guess."

Silas didn't stop to question his response. "I met someone myself."

"Good going, man."

"We're going to meet later at The Logger around five. I wanted to know if you and your lady friend would like to join us."

Cade didn't correct him by explaining that Hope wasn't officially his girl. But he realized he quite liked the idea of being linked with her. At this point they'd been together only a few times, yet he was more at ease with her than he had been with anyone in a long time.

Cade knew this was a big step forward for Silas, especially after he'd been dumped by his fiancée. Hearing the excitement and knowing his friend was anxious, Cade understood what Silas really wanted. Backup. If this date went south, he needed someone who knew his situation close at hand.

Before he agreed, Cade needed to clear the invite with Hope. "Give me five minutes and I'll get back to you."

"Sure thing."

Cade disconnected and looked at Hope. "That was a friend of mine," he said. "He invited us to join him later this afternoon for a beer. Is it something that would interest you?" Being out of practice, he felt a bit awkward asking.

"Sure, that sounds like fun."

"Okay, I'll text him back." Before he finished typing, he felt he needed to tell Hope about Silas. Looking up, he made eye contact with her, unsure how much to say, although now was as good a time as any, he decided.

"What's wrong?"

"There's something you should know before you meet Silas."

"Okay." She held his gaze, waiting.

Cade inhaled a deep breath. "Silas and I are in a therapy group together."

"That's nice." She made it sound like a small thing, and

maybe to her it was. He hadn't mentioned his counseling or his need for it, or that it had been court-mandated. Telling her was harder than it should have been.

"Silas has been through hell and back. He was badly burned in an IED explosion. His face is partially scarred and it's off-putting to some people. I thought you should know so when you first meet him, you won't be taken back by his appearance."

"Cade, honestly," she said, with a small huff. "I'm not the kind of person to be bothered by something like that. You like and trust Silas?"

"I do."

"Then that's good enough for me."

Relieved, Cade sent a text to let Silas know they'd meet him at five as planned.

Even though it was raining, Cade finished the railing and got the dog door installed before he left. He returned to his tiny apartment to shower and change clothes before picking up Hope.

Thinking he needed a few more details before he introduced Silas, Cade connected with his friend.

"You aren't changing your mind, are you?" Silas asked first thing.

Cade could hear the tension in his friend's voice.

"Not at all; we're looking forward to it. I wanted to know a bit more about this woman you've met."

"Like what?"

"How'd you meet?"

Silas didn't answer right away. "Technically, we haven't. We connected online."

This didn't sound good. Little wonder Silas wanted a side-kick.

"Jada suggested we meet for coffee, but I hate the stuff. I don't think she's fond of beer, but she likes wine. The way I figure, if she's looped, she might be able to ignore my ugly face."

Cade carefully broached the subject, afraid of the answer. He'd seen the before photo of Silas and he'd been a good-looking guy. "Did you send Jada your photo?"

"Of course."

"Before or after?"

"After. She knows she's not getting any shining knight with me," he said with a short, tense laugh. "I did assure her I'm a prince of a guy, though."

"That you are, my friend, that you are."

"I appreciate you doing this, Cade. I have to tell you this is the first woman I've connected with since Yvonne dumped my sorry ass. I'm nervous."

Cade was nervous for him, too. From their therapy sessions, he was all too aware of the emotional damage Yvonne had inflicted on his friend when she'd called off their wedding. Silas had made great strides since his suicide attempt, but he remained vulnerable. They all were.

At five, Cade picked up Hope, who had changed back into her black slacks and blazer, which was probably a little over-dressed for The Logger. The plan was, if everything went well, the four would go from sharing a beer, or in Jada's case, wine, to having dinner. Cade and Silas decided to see how matters went first before suggesting that.

Cade was silent as they drove into town.

"You aren't whistling now," Hope commented, as he found a parking place on the street outside The Logger. The tavern was a longtime establishment that served as a meeting place in town. It did a thriving business and had been part of the community since the 1960s, when lumber was king. Back then, much of the local economy was built around the lush forests of the Pacific Northwest. These days, Oceanside was a tourist town, having had to reinvent itself when several of the lumberyards and mills went out of business.

"I'm on edge for Silas," he said, to explain his silence. "All I can do is hope that Jada is prepared for Silas's reality. He claims she knows about his scars, but a picture is one thing. Seeing him face-to-face is another."

"It'll be fine," Hope said. She was an optimist. Cade, not so much.

Silas was sitting at a table and looked up when Cade and Hope arrived. Cade made the introductions, and Hope didn't so much as blink when they shook hands. Silas had lost two of his fingers from burns and his hands were also badly scarred. Reassured by her reaction, Cade wanted to hug her.

Cade ordered them each a Budweiser. "You okay?" he asked his buddy.

"I don't think she's coming," Silas said, glancing at his watch for the third time in the last minute.

"Is she late?" Hope asked.

Silas nodded.

"By how much?"

"A minute," Silas confessed.

Both Cade and Hope laughed. Silas, however, didn't find anything comical in their response.

Silas seemed to have trouble holding still. He crossed and uncrossed his legs, shredded the paper napkin, and nibbled on the corner of his mouth. "I should have known this was a bad idea."

The door opened and the three looked up as a stunning, tall woman made her way into The Logger. She glanced around before she spied them, paused, and then smiled. Cade glanced at Silas and saw his friend visibly relax.

Without hesitating, Jada walked directly over to their table. She smiled when she looked at Silas. "Like you said, I wouldn't have a problem finding you in a crowd."

"Told you I stood out like a sore thumb." He stood and pulled out a chair for her. "These are my friends."

As Jada extended her hand, Cade saw the burn scars that ran up her arm. Hope caught his gaze as she saw them, too. In that moment, Cade knew everything was going to be just fine with Silas.

And just maybe for him, too.

Chapter 14

When Spencer pulled into the school parking lot, he noticed Callie lingering outside, sheltered from the rain by the overhang. With dreary weather, most everyone had headed inside the building. Callie stood with her arms wrapped around her books, holding them tightly against her front. She appeared to be waiting for someone.

He hoped it wasn't Scott. She seemed pretty adamant that she wanted nothing to do with the football player at the dance. Things change, though. Scott wanted Callie. His ego wouldn't let her walk away, especially after the way she'd publicly rejected him.

Another thing. Spencer didn't think Scott would let him walk away unscathed. The way the football star glared at Spencer at the dance had let him know Scott wasn't done with him.

Climbing out of his car, Spencer made a beeline for the school, his feet splashing through the rain puddles as he rushed toward the door. Callie opened the door for him, and to his surprise followed him inside.

He didn't have a clue what this was about. While he'd agreed to help her with Ben, he'd been having second thoughts. She'd ignored his best advice about going to her parents. Bottom line, Spencer couldn't do anything more than what he'd already done. He planned to tell her that as much as he wanted to help, he couldn't.

"Spencer, wait up," Callie called, trotting behind him.

He stopped at his locker.

Callie looked unsure of herself, which wasn't like her. While it'd been nice to hold her in his arms, he was all too aware that had all been a façade.

"Listen, I know what you want."

Her face immediately relaxed.

"The thing is, I already did everything I could for you."

"You could talk to Ben. He might listen to you."

"Callie, you don't understand. No way will Ben listen to me. He'd resent me even trying. If I thought it would do any good, I'd try." It didn't help that Ben and Scott were constantly together. Besides being best friends, they were teammates.

"I don't know what to do," Callie said, her shoulders sagging in defeat.

"Involve your parents." Spencer didn't understand her reluctance. They would find out soon enough, and when they did, they'd be upset that Callie had known and said nothing.

"I can't do that, Spence, not until I've done everything I can on my own."

"Then there's nothing more to say." They may have been friends at one time, but that was long ago. The only reason she'd paid him attention now was because she wanted something.

"I had a good time Saturday night," she said, all sweetness, as if that would be enough to sway him to do what she wanted.

He took what he needed out of his locker, intent on getting to his class.

"Didn't you?" she demanded.

"It was nice," he said, as he closed his locker and started down the hall. "I'll admit you did an admirable job of pretending to like me."

"I do like you."

Evidence said otherwise. Before homecoming, she'd barely spoken to him, and then only when she wanted something. Like now. He didn't know what she expected him to do. It wasn't like he had a magic wand that would make Ben realize he was putting everything at risk. Nor could he speak to Ben one on one. Not when her twin was part of the crowd that had tormented him.

"But you said . . . ?" She followed behind him.

"I didn't make any promises," he reminded her.

Just then the bell rang, indicating the first class of the morning was about to begin. This was Spencer's means of escape. He knew Callie's English class was on the other side of the building, and if she didn't hurry, she'd get a tardy slip. Earlier in the year he'd made a point of learning where each of her classes were so he could be nearby with the hope she might notice him. It embarrassed him to think of what a fool he'd been to think things would ever go back to the way they had once been.

"We'll talk later," she told him, as she raced down the crowded hallway, weaving her way among students also rushing to class.

No need, he wanted to shout after her, but resisted.

Spencer and Callie both had first lunch. The cafeteria could accommodate less than two hundred, so lunch times were divided between fourth and fifth period. Spencer collected his tray and joined Joel and Brian, his two best friends, as usual. The three of them generally sat at the table alone. The popular girls congregated at a table on the other side of the cafeteria as far from "the nerds" as possible. The jocks sat close to the girls, which made sense. In between was everyone else, those not cool enough to be especially popular.

When Callie carried her tray over to their table, Spencer's friends stared at him as if they didn't know what to think.

"What's she doing coming over here?" Joel asked, in a stage whisper.

"Beats me," Spencer said, although he knew. She wanted to continue the conversation from that morning.

Callie placed her tray on the table and beamed a smile at Spencer and his friends.

"Hi, guys," she said, as if she sat with them for lunch every day.

Before Spencer could suggest her joining them might not be such a great idea, Callie sat down. She leaned forward as though she'd been waiting all morning for this minute, which no doubt she had been.

"Seems to me you're a little lost," he said, hoping Callie would take the hint.

"Not at all," she said, as though slightly offended by the comment. "Like I said earlier, I had such a good time at homecoming."

"We both did," Spencer said. That was the impression he'd wanted to leave, and the sole reason he'd followed through by attending homecoming. Although in retrospect, he wondered if anyone had really believed her act.

One thing about Callie. She knew how to get attention. First at the dance and then now. It seemed everyone in the cafeteria was watching the exchange. Spencer glanced toward the jock table and noticed Scott frowning in their direction. That wasn't a good sign. The sooner Callie left, the better it would be for him and his friends.

"My dad hasn't stopped talking about your car," she said, as she picked up her ham-and-cheese sandwich. "He called your dad and the two were on the phone for a good thirty minutes."

Spencer had heard about the call. It seemed their parents decided to do some outing together later in the month.

"Dad thinks it's great that the two of us are dating. He never was overly fond of Scott."

Spencer let the dating comment slide. They weren't dating, and he had no intention of them dating. It had been his dream at one time, but no longer.

Joel leaned closer to Spencer and asked, "What does she want?"

Really, could Callie be any more obvious?

"Who says I want anything?" Callie asked, as though wounded by the suggestion.

"Experience," Brian answered, before Spencer could.

Callie smiled encouragingly at his two friends before she took delight in announcing, "Spencer and I have an agreement."

"No, we don't," he corrected. He refrained from reminding her he hadn't agreed to anything.

"Yes, Spencer, we do," she said, with emphasis as she lowered her sandwich back to the plate. "You know, the one I mentioned before the dance."

He slowly shook his head. "I already told you what you need to do."

She pouted ever-so-sweetly. "You know I can't do that, and you know the reasons why."

"Sorry, Callie, but either way, I'm out." Spencer realized he'd need to be blunt if she was going to get the message.

Callie frowned. "This is important. You can't just brush me off like this. I made a stand at the dance, and now Scott and all his friends are giving me grief. I did it so you'd help me find whoever is involved in . . . you know what." She lowered her voice, as if afraid of being overheard.

"Told you she wanted something," Joel said, with more than a hint of righteousness.

"We didn't find anything before, and we would have if it'd been there," Brian said.

"You told your friends?" Callie's gaze shot to Spencer.

"Well, yeah. You didn't think I did that search alone, did you?"

Her gaze shot to Brian and Joel. "So you two know about Ben?"

Both nodded, as if marionettes.

Brian returned his attention to Spencer. "You aren't going to agree to help her, are you?" he asked, as if Spencer would be crazy to agree.

No question in his mind. "She has my answer."

"Spencer, please." Callie's eyes misted with what he assumed were fake tears. He hated to be so skeptical; Callie was someone accustomed to getting what she wanted.

"I'm not likely going to be the class valedictorian because I'm stupid," Spencer reminded her.

His response seemed to shock her, as if she hadn't considered any ramifications that would fall on his head if he were to get involved in this. If someone from the school was dealing drugs and he started snooping around, who did Callie think they would go after? He might as well paint a bull's-eye on his chest.

"Spencer won't be taken in by you batting your eyelashes at him," Brian told her.

Both his friends glared at her from across the table.

"You have your answer," Joel, the more levelheaded of his friends, said. "Spencer's not interested."

Callie looked stunned, as if she found it hard to fathom that anyone, especially Spencer or his friends, would ever refuse her.

A commotion on the other side of the cafeteria broke out as Scott and Ben leaped from their chairs, sending them crashing to the floor. The two stood nose-to-nose, glaring at each other. Everyone in the room diverted their attention away from Callie to the other side of the room.

The lunch monitor, Mr. Sullivan, hurried over to separate the two, coming to stand between them as they continued to glare at each other. After a few minutes, they righted their chairs and sat back down.

"That was my fault," Callie whispered, and lowered her head. This time it looked like the tears that flooded her eyes were genuine.

"What do you mean?" Spencer asked. Despite his determination not to care, he couldn't help himself.

"Ben's defending me."

"To Scott?"

"I already told you," she blurted out. "Scott's upset, and when Scott gets angry like this, it's not good. He's always had something of a temper, and ever since Coach chose him to be the quarterback, it's gotten worse. It's like he feels it's his right to be king and everyone should bow to whatever it is he wants."

"Kind of like you?" Joel asked.

"Exactly," she said, and released a deep sigh. "I embarrassed Scott at the dance and now he won't stop bad-mouthing me in front of my brother."

Both his friends swiveled their heads to Spencer, looking for him to explain.

Personally, he'd like to forget about the dance, put it out of his head, because if he didn't, he'd find himself considering helping Callie and he knew better.

"Scott wanted to dance with Callie," he told his friends, "and she basically said she'd rather be with me."

Callie seemed to think this was the golden opportunity to prove herself. "I promised Spencer every dance and I stuck to my end of the bargain."

Spencer wasn't hearing it. "The only deal I agreed to was to hack into your brother's accounts, which I did. It isn't my fault nothing was there."

"Yeah, nothing," Brian said, and then added with a small display of pride. "Trust me, if there was anything to be found, Joel and I would have caught it."

Spencer wanted to be sure she understood. "It was a mistake to ask you to homecoming with me. We were friends once, and I hoped to recapture that." He'd wanted more but realized how impossible that was. They were different people now.

"We both made mistakes," Callie agreed. "The thing is, you're the only one I can trust. I need your help."

It demanded all the resolve he could muster to refuse her. "I'm sorry, Callie. I did my part and that's as far as I'm willing to go."

Callie let that settle in for a moment before she turned her attention to Joel and Brian. "What about you two? Would you be willing to help me save my brother?" She made it sound like she was Joan of Arc, desperate for someone to fight alongside her.

The question hung in the air like one of those barrage balloons that hung protectively over the city of London during World War II. Spencer had read about it in Ms. Goodwin's history class and been fascinated by them.

"I don't know," Brian said, looking to Joel as if to see if he was tempted.

Spencer knew Brian also had a soft spot for Callie.

"No way," Joel said, adamantly shaking his head. "I saw what happened to Spencer once he got tangled up with you. I'm not interested."

She turned her attention to Brian. "What about you?"

"Joel's right," he said, shaking his head. "No way."

"But . . ." Callie looked from one to the other, as if she expected them to change their minds.

"I'm sure this is a temporary setback with Scott," Spencer told her when he noticed her gaze drift across to the other side of the cafeteria. "Give it a day or two of you being all sorry and humble, and he'll take you back."

Callie swallowed hard. "Who said I wanted to get back together with Scott?"

"Makes sense, you two have been dating for over a year."

Callie shook her head as if the idea was repugnant. "I don't care about him anymore. He hasn't been the same in a long time. We're through and he knows it."

Taking her untouched lunch with her, Callie left the table and headed over to where her friends sat. They scooted aside to let her in.

"It's for the best," Joel said.

"Yeah," Brian agreed, and then, leaning forward, braced his elbows against the side of the table. "Did she really dance every dance with you?"

Spencer nodded.

"What did she want you to do this time?" Brian asked, as if he wasn't completely convinced Spencer had made the right decision.

"She wants me to find out who's dealing, like I have some magical powers or something."

"Could be more than one person. Everyone knows anyone who wants drugs can get them." None of them ever had, and they didn't know anyone who attended Oceanside High who was into that. The price was too high. The school was a drug-free zone and possession would mean immediate expulsion.

"Her finding out isn't going to stop Ben if he's hooked," Joel said. "Callie's barking up the wrong tree. I mean, what would she do once she discovers who it is?"

"Exactly," Spencer said. She was asking them to go on a wild-goose chase. She should have gone to her parents the way he advised. They would know how to help Ben.

To some degree, Spencer understood why she hadn't. College scouts were looking at Ben for a possible scholarship. If word got out that he was doing drugs, then any hope of that happening would be over. An academic scholarship was out of the question, since, unfortunately, Ben wouldn't qualify for one.

"You tempted?" Joel directed the question to Spencer.

He remembered having his face shoved into a toilet bowl and held there by three of the biggest members of the football team. He wasn't looking forward to a repeat.

"Not even close." Only that was an exaggeration. He couldn't help being sucked in by Callie's tears, even though he realized he'd be setting himself up for even more trouble if he gave in.

—

That afternoon, Ms. Goodwin stepped outside the counselor's office when she saw Spencer. He was headed toward the main office when she waylaid him.

"Is everything okay?" she asked.

"How do you mean?"

She crossed her arms. "I saw Callie sitting with you at lunch today."

"Everything is fine," he assured her.

She hesitated, as if she expected him to elaborate about his conversation with Callie. Although he would like to have gotten her advice about Callie finding the drugs on Ben, he couldn't. That would betray her trust and have huge negative consequences for Ben.

"Are you sure about that?" she pressed.

Spencer nodded, eager to be on his way, and then hesitated. Ms. Goodwin had her suspicions, and that wasn't a good thing.

"It was no big deal, really. If you must know, Callie needed a bit of help understanding some of the technical aspects of the computer. I was able to advise her."

Spencer could tell by the way she regarded him that she didn't believe him.

"I heard about Ben Rhodes and Scott getting into it this afternoon at lunch. Did that have anything to do with you and Callie?"

"You'll need to ask them," Spencer said, unwilling to divulge anything more.

"Coach wasn't happy."

Spencer snickered. "I bet not."

"Apparently both Ben and Scott have trigger tempers."

Spencer was all too well aware of that.

"You don't need to worry, Ms. Goodwin, it's all good."

She appeared relieved.

As he left the school, Spencer noticed Scott and Ben out on the track field running laps. Coach Simmons stood on the outskirts with his arms crossed. Both boys looked exhausted.

Spencer couldn't have kept the smile from his face, even if he'd tried.

Chapter 15

Something changed between Hope and Cade following Sunday evening when they'd met up with Silas and Jada. After a fun evening together and dinner out, Cade had driven Hope home. It was late, and they both had to be up early for work the next morning.

Even though it was well past Hope's usual bedtime, she hadn't wanted the evening to end. It seemed Cade didn't, either. For the longest time they continued to sit in his pickup and talk. She found it easy to be with him. The changes in him the last few weeks were almost night and day. It was like watching the wall he'd built around himself come crumbling down one stone at a time.

As they sat in his truck, with only the dim moonlight, Cade talked about the friends he'd made in his therapy group.

"I didn't want to go and was determined to hate every minute. I had no intention of talking, and for the first few sessions I barely said a word."

"What changed?"

"Me, I guess. As I listened to the others, I realized they'd all gone through hell, the same as I had. The thing was, they were learning to accept the past and move forward. For some reason, I can't even explain why, I thought if I didn't hold on to that day . . . those memories, that I was somehow betraying my friends. I realize now that I had to let go of Jeremy and Luke. Knowing them as well as I do . . . I did, that was what they'd want. I was the one holding on to something nothing I could ever do would change."

"That doesn't mean you'll forget your friends."

"No, never. I can't. I'll carry them with me for whatever remains of my life."

He snickered softly, causing Hope to wonder what he was thinking.

"What?" she asked.

"I was just remembering something Harry said. He's the counselor who leads the group. He has a way of knowing exactly the right questions to ask. I swear he's a mind reader. Have you ever met anyone like that?"

For a long moment, Hope said nothing. It had always been like that between her and Hunter. It was as if they knew each other's thoughts. Living with grandparents who loved them, and at the same time resented them, they knew they would always be there for each other. Then Hunter was gone.

After an embarrassing silence, she whispered, "I know

what you mean." She didn't elaborate and was grateful Cade didn't pry. She had things in her life she wasn't comfortable enough to share. He probably did, too.

A short comfortable silence followed before Cade spoke again. "I'm a disappointment to a lot of people," Cade said suddenly. "Harry and the others have helped me realize how far I have yet to go."

Hope guessed Cade was talking about his relationship with his family and knew it weighed heavily on his mind. "You aren't a disappointment to me," she said, giving his hand a reassuring squeeze. "The fact is, I think you're wonderful. I want you to know how much your friendship has helped me."

Her words appeared to shake him. It seemed he didn't know how to respond. After a few moments, he said pensively, "I didn't ever think . . ."

"Think what?" she pressed.

"That I would meet someone like you."

Unsure what he meant, she asked. "Like me?"

"Someone so good."

Unable to stop herself, Hope laughed. "I'm not that good, Cade. Please, whatever you do, don't put me on a pedestal. I'm as flawed as anyone."

His face shone with doubt in the moonlight. "I guess what I'm trying to say is, I didn't expect to meet someone this accepting of me and my . . . problems."

"If you're talking about your leg . . ."

"It's more than my leg. It's my head. I'm struggling, looking to find where I belong. To fit back into life, to escape the nightmares that haunt me from my time in Afghanistan." He paused, as if carefully measuring his words. "I'd gotten comfortable in the black hole I'd dug myself into."

"I know what it's like to be in a dark place myself," she whispered. Seeing that Cade had shared this painful part of himself, Hope knew she needed to tell him about her twin brother.

A couple times since they'd started seeing each other, Cade had brought up Hunter. Hope had cleverly managed to sidestep his questions, and he seemed comfortable with that. Hope assumed it was because he feared she might ask him questions about his own service. She felt it would be better to leave any such discussion at his discretion.

"When I moved here, I was looking for a geographical cure," she admitted. "I thought a fresh start would help."

"From a broken heart?" he asked, and seemed to think the pain she carried was over the loss of a man she'd once loved.

"No . . . this has to do with my brother."

"Hunter? What's going on with him? Is he okay?"

Her throat clogged with emotion. "No, he's not okay."

Although it was awkward in his truck and a bit uncomfortable, Cade wrapped his arm around her shoulders.

"Hunter . . ." She stopped and bit her lower lip, hardly able to mention her twin's name without the instant rush of loss and grief.

"Tell me," he whispered, as if he was willing to help her carry any burden, any weight too much for her to bear.

A sob broke loose.

"Hope, what happened to Hunter?"

"He's gone, Cade. He's the reason I left California. He died in Afghanistan nearly two years ago. I thought if I moved away, if I wasn't constantly bombarded with memories, that I'd be able to move forward. That hasn't happened. Every day is a struggle. I can't let go of him for fear if I do, I'll be left completely alone, floundering. I have no family. No one."

His arms tightened, and he buried his face on the top of her head. "Oh baby, I'm so sorry. You aren't alone any longer. I'm here and I'm not going anywhere."

His words washed over her, giving her a reason to look forward instead of back to all she'd lost. She wept, comforted in the warmth of his embrace, absorbing his tenderness and his gentle care.

"We've both suffered losses," Cade whispered, calming her by stroking his hand across her back in a soothing caress.

How long they sat there, in silence, holding on to each other, Hope couldn't say. When she yawned, Cade said, "It's time for me to leave."

Although she didn't want him to go, she knew it was for the best. For him and for her. Ever the gentleman, Cade walked her to the door. Shadow had been sitting on the porch, patiently waiting for her. Cade paused long enough to give him an affectionate pet.

Before she went inside, Cade gathered her in his arms and kissed her. This wasn't the first time they'd exchanged kisses. But it felt different. Somehow sharing the pain of the losses in their lives had broken down unseen barriers between them. They clung to each other as Cade kissed the tears from her cheeks. Hope found it difficult to let him go.

"I hate to leave you," he whispered, seeming as resistant for their evening to end as she was.

"I know."

She went into the house with Shadow at her side, and then stood in the doorway with her arms around her waist, as she watched Cade return to his truck and drive away.

The next morning, Hope woke to a text message from Cade that left her smiling.

No nightmares for me. I dreamed of you instead. I've got a counseling session this afternoon. What time will you be free from school?

Hope sent a quick text back. *I'm glad you know about Hunter. I should be home around five. I've got a couple errands to run after classes.*

Hope's head was buzzing with a warm feeling from Cade's text as she stopped off at Bean There for her morning latte.

Willa greeted her with a knowing smile. "Something tells me you're in an especially good mood."

"I am," Hope said, on a cheerful note, as she paid with her debit card.

"I don't suppose this has to do with that handsome young man I saw you with at the football game?"

"And I would say that it most likely does." Hope had dated a bit while in college. However, between school and her part-time jobs, there'd been precious little time for relationships. Then, after getting the news about her twin, it felt as if her whole world had imploded. She'd been too depressed and melancholy to even think about dating. Eventually she realized she needed a fresh start and had found one in Oceanside.

And with Cade.

"I remember what it was like when Sean and I first started seeing each other," Willa said. "It seemed every day was full of sunshine even when it was cloudy and raining."

"That's how I feel," Hope said. Happiness seemed to bubble up inside her as she waited while Willa brewed her drink.

"It was dark for a long time after my sister died," Willa added. "I'll be forever grateful for how patient Sean was with me."

"You were right, you know, the pain never leaves, but it gets to the point that it's tolerable."

"I glad you're coming to that place," Willa said.

Only someone who had experienced devastating loss would understand the importance of finding a home, a place where they belonged and were appreciated.

"You should know," Willa continued. "When Dr. Annie first arrived in Oceanside, she'd recently lost her entire family in a horrible mudslide. She found love and a home here, and you will, too. In fact," she added, "it sounds like you've got a good start. I don't know Cade very well, but I like what I see."

"I do, too," Hope said.

How confident Willa sounded about Hope's future. That reassurance was exactly what she needed to hear. "Thank you," she whispered, and gave Willa's hand a quick squeeze before collecting her latte and heading to school.

Hope loved her job. This was her first year teaching teenagers, and she found she enjoyed her classes. In the computer science class, she noticed Callie broke away from her traditional seat and sat down in the chair across from Spencer.

She wasn't sure what exactly was going on between them, but it seemed as if their dynamic had changed.

In her U.S. History class, the last one of the day, Callie once more made a point of sitting across from Spencer. Hope watched as she slipped Spencer a note. He returned it without opening or reading it.

At the sound of the bell, her class raced out the door. She watched as Callie gathered up her things and charged after Spencer.

While she was grateful that Spencer was showing some backbone where Callie was concerned, Hope couldn't help wondering what was so important for her to chase after Spencer. Although she'd subtly tried to get Spencer to talk to her, he'd brushed her off.

Since this wasn't one of her assigned counseling days, Hope gathered up her own things. She paused long enough to check her phone to see if she'd gotten another text from Cade. Her thoughts were full of him.

Sure enough, she found one waiting for her.

I'll stop by after therapy

Sounds good

Hope was smiling to herself when she started out of the building. The football field was in view, and she noticed the team running practice drills. They had narrowly won the last game and Coach wasn't letting the players get overconfident. She admired the relationship he had with the team and how closely he kept tabs on each player, making sure their studies were up to par and their behavior, too.

She was almost to her car when Lois Greenly called out to her. "Hope, there's someone in the office asking for you."

"For me? Man or woman?" She didn't think Cade would come by the school; he might, though, if his session had gotten canceled.

"Woman."

Doing an about-face, Hope headed back into the school and to the receptionist desk.

Just as Lois had told her, an elegantly dressed, middle-aged woman stood as Hope arrived. The first thing Hope noticed was the thousand-dollar Louis Vuitton handbag. The only reason she recognized it was because she'd recently seen one like it advertised in a woman's magazine and looked it up on the Internet. The price tag was far and above anything she could afford.

"I understand you're looking for me," she said. She didn't recognize the woman and was sure if they'd met previously, she'd remember. The woman was cultured and attractive.

"You're Ms. Goodwin?"

"Yes." She guessed this must have to do with one of her students. Perhaps a parent. The other woman seemed far too young to be a grandparent.

The woman blinked and seemed ill at ease.

"Would it be possible for us to speak privately?" she asked.

"All right." Hope led the other woman into the room she used as a counselor.

"What can I do for you?" Hope asked, turning back to face the woman.

She continued to study Hope as though unsure where to start. For a long moment, she didn't say anything.

"I suppose I should start by introducing myself," she said, and raised her chin slightly in a proud gesture. "I'm Sara Lincoln."

It didn't take Hope long to make the connection. "You're Cade's mother."

Chapter 16

Hope sat across from Cade's mother at Bean There. When the assigned counselor came to reclaim the room, Hope had suggested they continue the conversation at the coffee shop. She ordered tea for them both. Willa was gone for the afternoon, home with her toddler and her husband, Sean, who Hope had learned that morning was about to head off on another photographic journey.

"Thank you for agreeing to talk to me," Sara Lincoln said, as soon as they'd collected their tea and found an empty table.

"Of course." She'd decided to let Cade's mother do the talking. Hope didn't feel it was her place to mention what she already knew about the situation. Trust was a huge issue with Cade, and Hope refused to say or do anything that would break that fragile bond.

Sara glanced up from staring at the tea as if the leaves

would part and foretell her future. "How's my son?" she asked, in a pleading tone, as if desperate for information.

"He's doing well." Hope almost added that he was getting better, but quickly changed her mind. If his mother wished to speak to Cade, all she needed to do was reach out to him herself. Hope didn't know what she could do to facilitate that and preferred not to get involved.

His mother kept her gaze lowered.

"How did you know about Cade and me?" Hope asked. From what he'd told her, he'd had no connection with his family for the last six years. Hope couldn't help wondering if they'd kept tabs on him by some other means.

"It was a lucky break," Sara said, warming to the subject. "I suspected Cade was living in Oceanside because this was where he'd gotten into trouble." She paused, and then, stricken, glanced up. "Oh dear, you do know about his . . . arrest, don't you?"

"I do." She didn't elaborate.

Sighing with relief, Sara continued. "Every now and again, I drive into Oceanside, on the off chance I might catch a glimpse of him."

"You saw him with me," Hope guessed.

"I did. He was at one of those food trucks near the beach. It was such a lovely afternoon, I sat in my car and watched him walk to where you were sitting with a dog."

Hope remembered well what she considered her first date with Cade. Wee Willie's Wiener Wagon would always have a special place in her heart because of it. Every time she thought about the name of that truck, she found herself smiling.

"He looked . . ." His mother struggled to find the right word. "Better," she said, after a moment.

Hope smiled. She'd like to think she might have had something to do with the improvement in Cade. And perhaps she did, but only a little. The biggest help Cade had received was from therapy and the work he was doing on himself because of that.

"I'd caught a glimpse of him a few times before. He always looked so sad and dour. That day he was smiling, and I felt sure it was because of you. I got out of my car and approached a man who was painting a mural. I was intimidated at first because he was so big. I asked if he was familiar with the community, and he told me he'd lived here nearly his entire life."

"That sounds like Keaton."

"Yes, I believe that was his name. He's very talented."

"He is," Hope agreed.

"Anyway, Keaton told me he thought you were the new high school teacher in town. He couldn't remember your name, so I did a bit of investigative work on my own and found you on the school webpage."

Now that she knew how Sara had discovered her, she felt obligated to ask: "You went through a lot of effort, but shouldn't you be talking to Cade and not me?"

She blushed with embarrassment. "The truth is, I'm not sure my son wants anything to do with me. I tried to talk to him a while back and he refused to even acknowledge me."

"In the courtroom?" Cade had mentioned the encounter.

"Yes, I wasn't there to embarrass him or make him feel

guilty. I went because I wanted him to understand I was there to support him . . . I was there for him."

From their conversation, Hope knew Cade had been mortified to find his mother witnessing one of his darkest moments.

"When was the last time you saw him before that day in the courtroom?" Hope asked.

Sara looked as if she was about to break into tears. She drew a tissue from her purse and wadded it up in her hand. "Six years ago."

"You didn't go to see him after he returned from Afghanistan?" His injury had been extensive. Surely his family had been informed. The fact that they hadn't shown their support then said a great deal.

"We knew nothing about his injuries," Sara said quickly, defending herself. "I would have moved heaven and earth to get to my son had I known."

From the vehement way she spoke, Hope tended to believe her.

"You must think me a terrible mother," Sara said, and dabbed at her eyes with the tissue. "I have failed Cade in so many ways. It isn't any wonder he wants nothing to do with us."

"I don't believe that's the case." As much as she wanted to comfort and reassure Sara, she had to believe Cade would be willing to mend fences with his family under the right circumstances. Cade had said so little about his parents. What she did know had been painful for him to discuss. From what she'd learned, the real disagreement was between him and his father.

"His father and I realize we were wrong. We want our son back in our lives. He's our only child . . . perhaps if I'd been able to have more children, things might not have gone so wrong. You see, my husband pinned all his hopes on Cade. He never once considered that our son wouldn't want to follow in his footsteps. When he learned Cade had no intention of becoming an attorney, it nearly destroyed John."

"I'm so sorry," Hope said, in a comforting tone.

Sara sipped her tea and took that time to gather her composure.

"Does your husband know you're here?"

Sara shook her head. "His pride is standing in the way. He wants Cade to make the first move toward reconciliation. I disagree and hoped there was some way I could bring our son back into our lives."

"Are you telling me your husband would disapprove of you being here?"

She hesitated, studying her tea, and for a moment Hope wasn't sure she intended to answer the question. "I can't rightly say," she whispered tightly, as if she found it difficult to speak the words aloud. "I believe he'd be disappointed in me, but frankly I don't care what I have to do to reach Cade."

The picture Cade had given her of his father took shape in Hope's mind. He appeared to be a stubborn, unyielding man, too full of pride for his own good.

"John isn't a bad person," Sara was quick to add. "He loves our son; I know he does. Cade's decision not to follow in his footsteps has been hard on him. All the Lincoln men, as far back as his great-great-grandfather, have chosen the law. It's tradition. It was expected. I knew it, and so did Cade."

"But Cade doesn't want that." Hope felt the need to defend him.

"I guessed as much early on and tried to prepare John. When Cade finally made it clear he had no intention of attending law school, John took it as a personal rejection of him, Cade's heritage, and our family. He was convinced Cade did it out of spite."

"Do you believe that?"

"No. Never. Cade was not cut out to practice law."

Her voice wobbled with this last bit as she struggled to hold back the tears.

Seeing how difficult this was for Sara, Hope gave the other woman's hand a gentle squeeze.

"The sad part is that Cade and John are alike in so many ways. They're both stubborn and full of pride."

"And reserved in their feelings," Hope added, seeing how hard it was for Cade to open to her.

"Yes, oh yes," Sara agreed. "They both tend to keep everything bottled up inside and refuse to show any weakness."

They sat in silence for a moment. Hope knew Cade's mother hadn't come to pour her heart out. She'd made the drive because she wanted something from Hope. Something she was nervous to ask.

"You want my help," Hope said, broaching the subject before Sara had a chance.

"Yes . . . please. I know I have no right to put this on you. I wouldn't ask if I felt there was any other way. I'd like, if possible, for you to speak to Cade on my behalf."

Hope swallowed hard, unable to respond.

Sara's eyes were wide with appeal. They were so like Cade's that Hope found it difficult to look away.

"Would you tell him how much his father and I love and miss him? Would you ask him if he'd be willing to forgive us?"

Oh dear, that was something Hope didn't feel she could do. Automatically she shook her head while she struggled to find a way to explain. She had been seeing Cade only briefly. Their relationship was in its infancy. "I can't get in the middle of this, Sara. That would sabotage every bit of trust between us. Cade would view it as a breach in our relationship, and I can't and won't do that."

"But he likes you and . . ."

"Why don't you talk to him yourself," she advised.

"I tried that, remember?"

"Sara, think about it. You were in that courtroom. You were the last person Cade wanted to see at that moment. He was at a low point, and it humiliated him that you were there to witness it." Then, because she had to know, she asked, "Did your husband know about his arrest?"

Sara nodded. "An attorney friend, a rival really, was doing pro bono work for the county when he saw Cade's name on the list of recent arrests. He took delight in letting us know."

Hope could well imagine Cade's father's reaction. His son's arrest must have cut him to the quick. Perhaps Cade's trouble with the law was the very thing that had opened his eyes.

"I'm sorry, Sara, I really am, but I can't get involved in this situation. If there's going to be healing, then the three of you will need to work it out yourselves without any interference from me."

"I understand," she said, sadness weighing down her words. "It was too much to hope for, I suppose."

"I'm sorry, I truly am."

"It was presumptuous of me to ask. I thought . . . I hoped, you know, that you might have some insight into how best to bring Cade back into our family."

"I wish I did." She was sincere in that. Hope would do anything to have known her mother, to have had a father in her life. That was never in the cards for her. At some point, she prayed Cade would be able to find a way to bridge the differences he had with his family. That would need to come from him, though, and not from anything she said or did.

"Would it be all right if I called you now and again?" Sara asked, her eyes bright with hope. "It would mean the world to me if we could talk every so often."

As much as she hated to disappoint Cade's mother, Hope didn't want to do anything behind his back. "I don't think that's a good idea."

Sara's face fell.

"I would be willing," she revised, "but only if Cade knows, in which case, I believe he would probably prefer to talk to you himself."

Sara didn't appear convinced. "He's as stubborn as his father, so I wouldn't count on that."

"I'm sorry, I wish I could do more."

"I do, too," Sara said.

They finished their tea and left at the same time.

—

An hour after she was home, Hope had expected to hear from Cade. When she didn't, she sent him a text.

How'd your session go?

Good.

Before this point, his text messages hadn't been this abrupt.

Can you stop by later?

No.

Is everything okay?

Just dandy.

Hope's heart rate accelerated.

Cade, what's going on?

You tell me.

What do you mean?

A full minute passed before he responded.

Did you have a good afternoon?

He knew. He must have seen Hope and his mother at Bean There. She'd assumed he was at his therapy session and wouldn't be in town.

Hope didn't want to have this discussion via text, so she tried to phone him. He didn't answer.

It isn't what you think! Let me explain.

Hope waited for a response and saw that the text wasn't delivered. She tried several more times and then realized why they weren't going through.

Cade had blocked her.

Chapter 17

Hope remained stunned. Without listening to a word of explanation, Cade had blocked her. His action infuriated and frustrated her. He was being judgmental and completely unfair. She wanted to stomp her foot and retaliate. The best way she could think to do that was to block his number, too. If, at some point, Cade wanted to apologize, he would feel the same annoyance she had.

Her little temper tantrum lasted for all of five minutes before she changed her mind and unblocked him. She wanted to talk to Cade, to explain that she hadn't broken his trust. Maybe, she told herself, he'd realize he'd overreacted and would reach out.

But he didn't. She waited, trusting and believing he'd realize his mistake, only to face disappointment.

"If that's what he wants, then fine," Hope told Shadow, as she slammed around the kitchen.

By now it was well past dinnertime, so she threw a few leftovers into a salad. Then she found she couldn't eat it, and slapped her fork down on the kitchen table, startling Shadow. Her stomach was in knots, and she blamed Cade for the loss of appetite. Tossing the remains into the garbage, she determined if Mohammad wouldn't come to her, then she'd go to Mohammad.

Although she had never been to Cade's studio apartment, she knew the general vicinity of where it was. If she drove around long enough, she was bound to see his truck parked out front.

She brought Shadow with her and took off, doing her best to contain her irritation. It distressed her that he thought so little of her that he would cut her from his life, as if everything they'd shared meant nothing.

While she was driving around, her mind whirled with all the things she planned to say to him. She'd explain the situation, reassure him that he'd been wrong in whatever he had assumed. Being the forgiving person she was, she would accept his apology and they would move forward.

Cade's truck was nowhere in sight. After an hour of driving around, she realized she was wasting her time. Cade had likely guessed she'd be unable to leave matters as they were and went out of his way to thwart her efforts.

With no way to connect with him, Hope decided to sleep on it and pray that by morning Cade would have a change of heart. If she didn't hear from him, then she'd decide what to do next, if anything. Her one hope was that in time, Cade would realize he should at least listen to what she had to say.

While the different scenarios played out in her mind, sleep eluded her. She tossed one way and then another for what seemed like hours. Her thoughts drifted from Cade to her classes, to Spencer and Callie, bouncing from one thing to another and then back again.

"Come on," she muttered, as she pounded her pillow into submission. "Go to sleep." Her alarm was set early, and every time she glanced at the clock, she calculated how many hours she had left before it rang.

Not enough. Not nearly enough.

Sensing her mood, Shadow decided to sleep curled up in the living room rather than on the fluffy bed she'd purchased for him and kept in the bedroom. It seemed even her most faithful companion knew it was best to avoid her when she was in this mood.

Sometime well after midnight, when she was half asleep, her phone rang. She had it charging on her nightstand and blindly reached for it.

Glancing at the ID, she saw that it was Cade. She had half a mind to let it go to voice mail. It was what he deserved for the way he'd ruined her night. It was his fault she hadn't been able to sleep.

She answered, though. As much as she wanted to frustrate him the way he had her, she couldn't make herself do it.

Picking up on the fourth ring, she said, "Hello?"

"Did I wake you?" The voice didn't belong to Cade. Ear-splitting discordant music played in the background, making it difficult to hear.

"Who is this?" she asked, thinking it might be a prank. Only the number was Cade's, and the voice was vaguely familiar.

"It's Silas."

"Silas?" she repeated. Her mind screamed to a halt. Her concern was instant, and she needed to know why Cade's friend would have his phone.

Before she could ask, he said, "We met last Sunday, remember."

"Of course I remember. Where's Cade? Is he all right?"

He hesitated. "Ah . . . not really."

"What's wrong with him?" She sat up in bed now, fully awake, worried. Silas wouldn't reach out unless it was serious.

Cade's friend hesitated. "Did you two have a falling-out, a disagreement or something?"

She noticed he didn't answer her question.

"Not exactly." Cade hadn't given her a chance to argue her point. He'd abruptly ended their text conversation long before she had a chance to talk to him.

"Well, something's happened," Silas told her, "and my guess is it involves you."

"What's going on?" she asked, more insistent this time. She pressed the phone closer to her ear, the background noise making it nearly impossible to hear him clearly.

"Cade called me a couple hours ago from this bar. He wanted me to join him, said he was having the time of his life."

That wasn't what Hope needed to hear. While she'd been fretting and stewing, Cade was out on the town. The perfect ending to a miserable day.

"Where is he?" she asked. None too pleased.

"Aberdeen," Silas told her, and mentioned the name of the bar. Hope wasn't familiar with the area. However, from the background noise it appeared to be a hopping establishment.

Aberdeen was a good thirty- to forty-minute drive from Oceanside, depending on the traffic, which she had to assume would be light at this time of night.

"He's been drinking," Silas told her.

She'd already guessed as much. "I suppose he's drunk." Her irritation grew with every bit of information Silas gave her.

"He might have had a couple beers, but I don't think he's completely soused."

"Why call me?"

Silas didn't hesitate. "Because he needs you, and the sooner you arrive, the better."

"You mean right now?"

"Yes. I'll do my best to keep him from making an idiot of himself until you get here."

"I need to know what I'm walking into, Silas."

Silas must have gone outside, because the noise level dropped significantly. "I don't know what happened between you two," Silas said, with an edge to his voice. "All I can tell you is that when Cade first joined the group, he was in bad shape mentally. Everything changed for the better when he started seeing you."

While hearing that was gratifying, it didn't answer her question.

"Tonight, when he called, he might have claimed he was having a good time, but I knew he wasn't. I could hear it in his voice. When I asked him if something had happened, he refused to answer. When I pressed, he hung up on me."

Hope placed her hand over her heart, which had started to beat erratically.

"I don't have the insight Harry does," Silas continued. "But I'm smart enough to know something is off."

"Harry?" she asked.

"He's our counselor. Like I said, I might not be a professional, but I know a cry for help when I hear it."

"What did you find when you got there?" she asked, needing to know.

"Cade in a corner with a . . ."

"A woman," she finished for him.

"Yeah. A woman. I asked about you and got a look that would curdle milk."

She felt obliged to explain. "Cade has issues with his family, deep-rooted ones that go all the way back into his childhood. His mother sought me out, and Cade saw the two of us together."

"That explains it."

Hope wasn't sure that it did. Several other factors seemed to be in play.

"Will you come and talk some sense into him?" Silas pleaded. "You need to resolve whatever is between you before he self-destructs."

Hope bit into her bottom lip, and her throat clogged as she debated the best course for her to follow. "I don't think my showing up will help," she said, speaking through the tightness in her throat. "Especially when Cade has apparently already found comfort from someone else."

"Hope, have a heart. The guy's in a bad state."

"I'm sorry, Silas. I really am. I can't rescue Cade; he has to find what he needs within himself. I'm not his savior. First off, he leaped to conclusions and refused to give me a chance to explain. He blocked my number and shoved me out of his life."

"Will you at least talk to him?" Silas begged.

"When he's ready, I will."

"I mean now."

"Tonight?"

"Yeah, on the phone. Just a sentence or two. Something that will bring him to his senses."

"Like what?"

"I don't know. Women always seem to know the right thing to say. I can only do so much. I'm here. I won't let him do anything stupid like get in a fight or take this woman home with him."

She swallowed hard at the image of Cade with another woman. "I don't have a clue what you expect me to say."

"Think, Hope."

Silas was asking the impossible. "He'll probably hang up on me."

"Then that's on him."

"All right, all right. Give him the phone and I'll think of something."

"Thank you." The relief in his voice was evident.

Silas must have returned to the inside of the bar, because the noise was back as loud as ever. She knew Silas was talking to Cade. Although she strained to hear the exchange, she couldn't make it out.

"Who's this?" This time the voice was Cade's. Clearly Silas hadn't told him she was on the line.

"It's Hope."

"Hope," he snapped, "I have nothing more to say to you."

"That's fine with me, but I have one thing to say to you, like it or not."

He didn't immediately disconnect, which told her he was willing to listen.

She prayed he'd hear her and understand. "When the two officers came to deliver the news that Hunter had been killed, I quietly listened, and accepted their condolences. Then as soon as they left, I trashed my apartment and destroyed the very things I loved most, punishing myself. It made no sense. I deeply regretted it the next day, and I continue to live with the regret of what I'd done in my anger and grief."

"Is that all?" he asked sarcastically.

"Yes," she whispered. "That's all I have to say."

"If you believe I'm on a path of destruction because of you, then you're wrong. You fooled me, Hope, and I fell for you only to learn you're like everyone else: full of duplicity. I trusted you."

"What you're forgetting, Cade, is that I trusted you, too. It didn't take much for you to look elsewhere, did it?"

"This conversation is over."

"Yes, it is. Good-bye, Cade," she said, her heart breaking as she disconnected. If he said anything more, she didn't hear it.

Chapter 18

Cade sat in Harry's office with his head down, avoiding eye contact. Neither man spoke. It'd been five minutes of silence, and Cade knew Harry would wait patiently for Cade to begin the conversation, even if it took the entire hour.

He kept his gaze focused on the gray carpet. Funny, he'd been in this office multiple times and had never paid much attention to the carpet pattern of white swirls on a gray background. It was easier to concentrate on the intricacies of the rug than on what was happening in his own life.

"It hasn't been a good week," Cade finally said, when the silence grew too heavy for him to ignore.

"What made it such a miserable week?" Harry asked. He leaned back in his chair and crossed his legs.

"Hope." He didn't elaborate.

Harry waited, apparently wanting Cade to fill in the details. It came to him that perhaps the counselor had already heard everything he needed to know about the situation from Silas.

"Silas told you, didn't he?" Cade remained angry at him. Silas had no business contacting Hope. They'd had words that night, and Cade said things he'd regretted almost as soon as they left his mouth. In the space of twelve hours, he'd lost his girl and his best friend. It was a tragedy worthy of a Shakespearean play.

"I haven't spoken to Silas," Harry stated calmly. He made a notation on the pad in his lap, as if this information were of some significance.

"He butted in where he didn't belong," Cade snapped, looking up from the carpet and meeting Harry's gaze. He wanted the counselor to understand that not only had Hope betrayed him, but so had the man he'd called his friend.

"What exactly did Silas do?"

Cade refused to answer; anger simmered just below the surface as he silently reviewed the events of that evening.

"You should know the only reason I'm here today is because it's court-mandated."

To his shock, Harry laughed.

"You find that funny?" Harry was full of surprises. Cade couldn't figure the other man out, no matter how hard he tried. He had a gift of extracting information that Cade never intended to reveal. Cade supposed that was what made Harry a good therapist, even if Cade found him irritating.

"No, actually, I find your honesty refreshing. All along I assumed you came because you found my company scintillating."

Cade snickered but was unable to hold back a smile. Harry was doing it again, and Cade didn't like it. He wanted to stay angry. Anger was comfortable.

"It's either my sparkling personality or maybe, just maybe, the deep-seated need you have for peace. Peace of mind, peace from your past, and peace to move forward."

Cade let his words soak in. As much as he was loath to admit it, Harry was right. He thought he might have found the path to it when he'd first started seeing Hope. For weeks he'd watched her with Shadow. He identified with the mistreated dog. He didn't want anyone close to him, either. He was angry, inimical, hostile to anyone who tried to befriend him. Then Hope came into his life.

He'd admired her determination, her grit and courage in taking a savage canine that was destined to be destroyed and transforming him with patience and love. Only he'd been misled by her, misled and betrayed. She was nothing like what he'd assumed. Once again, he'd been fooled.

It'd been devastating to inadvertently find her speaking to his mother. Her betrayal had felt like a knife thrust into his chest.

"I saw her with my mother," Cade blurted out, unable to hide his anger and indignation.

"I assume you're talking about Hope?"

He nodded. "I'd told her things I hadn't told anyone, and then she turned and betrayed me with what she learned."

"You mean to say you've been holding out on me?" He gave a pout, but Cade knew it was all for show.

Once again, the silence stretched between them while Harry patiently waited for Cade to continue.

After several awkward moments, Cade spoke. "I left home six years ago, and I haven't been back. The last time I saw my mother was in a courtroom, just before I was sentenced."

"In other words, you decided six years ago that you wanted nothing more to do with your family."

"It was a mutual decision."

Harry cocked his head to one side. "It appears your mother doesn't share those feelings."

Cade knotted his fists. "She was there to gloat."

"Did she say so? Did she use the opportunity to tell you what a disappointment you were? Or anything that would give you that impression?"

Briefly reviewing the scene, he murmured, his voice so low he could barely hear himself. "We didn't speak . . . She tried, but I wasn't listening." He'd been too embarrassed. Humiliated.

"I see," Harry said.

Anger sparked in Cade. "I hate it when you say that. You see what? You have no clue, making judgments like you've been gifted with psychic powers that enable you to read minds. Well, I've got news for you. You're as much a fraud as Hope and Silas."

His words fell like boulders off a hillside, bouncing on their way down, destroying the landscape. Cade knew Harry wouldn't respond to anger. Cade had tried before and had been unable to get a rise out of him.

Harry continued as if Cade hadn't spoken. "I can see your family is a sensitive issue. I believe, from what you've said, that while you remain estranged, your mother seems to have had second thoughts."

"You don't know that," Cade challenged. At one point, he'd been sympathetic toward his mother. No longer. If she'd been genuinely interested in healing the breach between them, she would have made the effort to connect with him instead of with Hope.

"True," Harry agreed. "But I wonder if you should look at what you saw in a different light. Do you sincerely think Hope sought out your mother? Or is it possible that your mother found Hope?"

"How would my mother even know about Hope? No one in my family knows anything about me." Cade had made sure of it. When he cut those ties, he never intended to return.

"Your mother knew you were in the courtroom," Harry reminded him. "I assume you weren't the one to tell her."

"Hardly," he said with a snicker, "but that doesn't mean Hope is innocent in this. She knows how I feel about my parents. That she would even talk to my mother is in itself a betrayal."

Harry seemed to measure his words. "You're telling me you sincerely believe Hope would go behind your back, do an extensive search to find your family, and arrange a meeting. Not only would she do all this, but then take the risk of meeting your mother in Oceanside with the possibility of being seen by you."

Cade quickly dismissed the idea. "Hope knew I would be at group therapy that afternoon."

"Only a water pipe burst, and the session was canceled at the last minute."

"Yes," he confirmed. Harry had tried to cast doubt on the scenario, and while Cade would like to believe Hope was innocent, he was convinced otherwise. This anger, this darkness he'd been living with the last three days, was familiar, almost welcome. He'd started to trust the light only to learn the light couldn't be trusted. It was an illusion like a desert mirage.

"When you confronted her, what was Hope's explanation?"

This was the question Cade had dreaded. "I didn't give her a chance to lie."

"Really?" Harry gave him a look of disappointment, which Cade chose to ignore.

"You mean you went with your gut," the counselor said, "and are finished with her."

"Exactly." He didn't care to hear anything Hope had to say. He knew what he saw. As far as he was concerned, that was the end. He wanted nothing more to do with her.

"And this is where Silas stepped in." It was more statement than question.

"He contacted Hope." It tightened his jaw just thinking about what his friend had done. The last person Cade wanted to see or speak to ever again was Hope, and Silas had forced him into it.

"Why would he do that?" Harry asked, and seemed genuinely curious.

Cade huffed out a long breath. "That was my mistake. I called Silas and asked him to join me at Hooters."

"Hooters," Harry repeated slowly. "This was soon after you saw Hope with your mother, I take it?"

"Yeah, I needed to think, you know." A lot of military men frequented the bar there. Being around other veterans was comforting. Well aware of the consequences, Cade knew enough not to get drunk. He wasn't looking for a fight. Wasn't looking for anything other than a sympathetic ear. He'd called Silas, thinking his friend would empathize with him. He never got the chance. Before Silas arrived, a woman, Cade couldn't remember her name, had made it her mission to fulfill his every need. It didn't take him long to realize her ulterior motive. She wanted Cade to pay for her drinks. When Silas arrived, Cade had been embarrassed at his inability to get rid of her. The woman had more arms than an octopus and was crawling all over him.

At some point, he wasn't even sure when, Silas had taken his phone and called Hope.

"I don't know what Silas was thinking," Cade said, regretting nearly everything about that night. It'd been a big mistake to contact Silas and an even bigger one heading to Hooters.

"I'll admit it seems out of character for him," Harry said, thoughtfully, "unless there were extenuating circumstances."

"Like what? I wasn't drunk."

"Then what do you think prompted him to reach out to Hope?"

Cade knew and hadn't wanted to bring it up. "There was this woman I met."

"Ah," Harry said, in that knowing way of his.

He wanted to groan with frustration. "It's not what you think."

"Now who's reading minds?" Harry asked.

Cade ignored the question. "I couldn't get rid of her. She planted herself in my lap, her hands in my hair, and then she

was kissing my neck like it was the world's finest chocolate."
He had the bite marks to prove it.

"I know the type," Harry said, sounding sympathetic.

"Yes, well, the next thing I knew, Silas arrived. We tried to
talk, but this woman was all over me."

"Do you think Silas guessed the problem with your sudden
change of affection?"

Rather than answer, he shrugged.

"It seems to me Silas was looking more for information
than to interfere," Harry said, and then added, "Of course, I
could be wrong."

"Maybe so," Cade was willing to admit. "But that isn't the
worst of it. He handed me the phone and said it was for me.
He'd called Hope. I didn't want to talk to her; Silas had to
know that."

"It's possible," Harry agreed. "In my experience, we all, at
one time or another, try to fix things that would be better off
left alone."

No doubt about it. "This was definitely one of those times."

Harry uncrossed his legs and was silent for a moment, as
though mulling over everything Cade had told him.

"If you don't mind my asking, I'd be curious to hear what
it was Hope had to say."

Cade snickered. "She was ridiculous."

Harry's brows arched. "In what way?"

"She lost a brother in Afghanistan. He was her twin . . .
the last of her family. I had this woman hanging around my
neck and Hope told me she trashed her apartment when she
learned Hunter had been killed."

Harry mulled that over for several moments. "Interesting. How did you respond?"

Cade wasn't proud of what he'd said. "I told her if she assumed I was trashing my life because of her, she was off base. She means nothing to me. Not anymore."

"Am I correct to assume you haven't spoken to her since?"

"You're damn straight."

Harry nodded. "And she hasn't made an effort to contact you?"

"I blocked her number."

"So you don't know if she has or hasn't reached out?"

Time for truth. "She hasn't. I unblocked it the next day."

This, too, appeared to interest Harry, but he didn't comment, and Cade was just as glad. "I thought I might, you know, inadvertently see her at the animal shelter," he admitted.

"You haven't, though?"

A dozen times in the last few days, Cade wanted to ask Preston about her. He hadn't, although it took tremendous willpower on his part. He believed she'd purposely stayed away because of him. It didn't help that the tire store was across the street from the high school parking lot. He'd watched as she'd pulled in that very morning. There seemed to be no escaping her. Anger simmered below the surface. Anger at Hope, yes, but with himself. He looked for her and couldn't seem to make himself stop.

"Are you sure you want to end this relationship?" Harry asked.

"Yeah, I'm sure." Cade knew it was his pride speaking. Despite his determination to put Hope out of his mind, he'd epically failed. Disenchanted as he was, he couldn't stop thinking about her. One minute he wanted nothing more to do with her and the next he missed her like a severed appendage. She had quickly become part of the fabric of his life. He longed for Hope. The fact that he'd been weak enough to feel like he needed her infuriated him even more. It was best that they both move on. She had become a crutch. The time had come to walk alone.

When the session ended, Cade's mood hadn't improved, but then he'd arrived with a bad attitude. He had several more community service hours to fulfill, and that was the reason he gave himself when he drove from Harry's office to the shelter.

Preston sought him out after Cade had signed in, giving him a short list of what tasks needed doing. While Preston was speaking, Cade's gaze wandered around the area, seeking out Hope.

To avoid her, of course, and for no other reason.

"Are you looking for Hope?" Preston asked, seeming to sense he didn't have Cade's full attention.

Before he could stop himself, Cade responded, making the inquiry as casual as possible. "I haven't seen her around for a while."

"Yeah, I know. She's dealing with midterms."

"That explains it."

"Come to think of it, I haven't seen you at the cottage, either."

"Yeah, I've been busy."

The look Preston gave him said he hadn't been fooled. Something was wrong and he knew it. Unlike Silas, Preston chose not to push or step in where he wasn't wanted. For that, Cade was grateful.

After Cade had finished working an hour at the shelter, he headed to his apartment. Driving past the cottage, he noticed Hope's car parked in her usual spot. All was well with her, it seemed. He found that reassuring and then was furious with himself for caring.

The last thing she'd said to him was good-bye, and it seemed she'd meant it, which was fine, because he did, too.

Chapter 19

The football team remained undefeated, which made Scott, Ben, and all their friends even more insufferable. Spencer hadn't attended any of the games since homecoming, where he'd been treated like he had a communicable disease. One good thing was that Callie had stopped pestering him. It'd taken her long enough to get the message.

"You going to the game?" Joel asked, as he slid his lunch tray onto the table across from Spencer. The cafeteria was buzzing with talk about the upcoming game taking place that night.

Spencer gave him the look.

"Hey, just asking."

"Are you?" Spencer said to his friend. This would be a first for Joel.

"Maybe. Oceanside is first in the league. No one expected us to beat Montesano, and now the entire state is paying attention. I heard one of the Seattle television stations is planning on being there."

Spencer wasn't interested.

"Come on, dude, that's huge."

No doubt Scott and his friends were eating it up, too. If what Callie said about college scouts looking at her brother for possible scholarships was true, then this was big news. Spencer wished Ben well. He didn't have anything against him, other than the trouble Callie had brought into Spencer's life because of Ben's reported drug use.

Brian had joined them in the middle of the discussion.

"I'm thinking of going; Brian is, too," Joel announced. "You should come with us, Spence."

"I'll think about it." His decision was already made. He couldn't care less how well the team did or their state ranking. In a few months, he'd be graduating and moving on to college.

U.S. History with Ms. Goodwin was his last class of the day. He'd noticed a subtle difference in her this past week. She wasn't as quick-witted as she usually was. Nor did she laugh as easily. He was certain she'd gotten some kind of bad news and wished he knew how best to cheer her up. Although it concerned him, he wasn't good with that sort of thing.

His mood didn't lighten when Callie followed him out of the classroom. Instead of heading to his locker, he tried to ward her off by going straight to the parking lot. To his dismay, Callie raced out the door after him.

"Hey, wait up," she called. School buses belted fumes as they pulled into place, preparing to load up students.

Seeing he wasn't likely to escape Callie, Spencer turned around to face her.

She held her handbag tight against her side. Gone was the smile, the happy look she usually wore. A dark frown marred her face.

Something was definitely wrong. "What's going on?" he asked.

"I found out who's giving Ben drugs."

Spencer inhaled deeply. "Who?"

"Scott," she whispered, almost as if she feared being overheard, which was highly unlikely with all the activity taking place around them.

Scott. That came as something of a surprise, but Spencer had his doubts. Scott's father was a prominent attorney in town, and he came from money.

"And you know this how?" Spencer asked.

She nervously glanced around and lowered her voice. "I saw him hand a bag of pills to my brother."

"Are you sure that's what you saw?"

She nodded. "Positive. I was right there. I'm not stupid, I know what was in that plastic bag."

"Did you tell anyone?"

"Not yet . . . I confronted Scott."

"And he denied it, of course." Spencer wouldn't expect Scott to own up to the truth.

Callie nodded as if she'd expected more.

"What did you say?" he asked.

"First of all, I threatened to tell Coach and Scott just laughed at me. He said I should go right ahead. Coach isn't stupid. His team is first in state, and he wouldn't do anything to ruin the school's chances of collecting the title."

Spencer knew Scott was right. Coach would whitewash anything that could destroy their chances of winning. Especially with the rumors floating around that Coach Simmons was being considered as an assistant coach for the University of Washington. It wasn't only Coach, either. All of Oceanside was excited about the team. Spirit ran high. Everyone in town was behind them. With only a few tourists around at this time of year, the team's success gave the community something fun to focus on and cheer for. No way was Coach going to destroy that.

Tears welled in Callie's eyes. "Did you hear me, Spencer? Scott laughed at me."

"What did you expect?" he asked, not unkindly. "You called him out, and he thinks—the entire team thinks—they're invincible. Nothing can touch them."

"I . . . did something you're not going to like," she confessed, refusing to look at him.

Spencer's shoulders deflated with an exasperated sigh. "What now?"

Callie looked down at the pavement as though she had lost her courage. "You have to understand I was angry and frustrated. Scott acted like this was all one big joke. He didn't take me seriously. He treated me like I was an idiot and didn't think I had the guts to tell anyone."

That she expected anything less was telling. Because Callie was pretty and popular, she believed she could say what she wanted to without consequences.

"What did you do?" Spencer asked. She hadn't chased after him wanting to let him know she'd been made to look like a fool.

"It was my last resort. I had to do something; otherwise, they would continue to go on as before."

"Callie."

She bit into her lower lip. "I did consider telling my parents."

"Why didn't you?"

"If I told Mom and Dad that Ben is using, and his supplier is Scott, then they'd go to Scott's parents. I mean, they're friends and all, so that's a natural conclusion, right?"

Unsure, Spencer remained silent.

"And when they did, Scott would say I was making it up because . . ." She hesitated and glanced at him.

"Because Scott wouldn't take you back after you went to homecoming with me," he guessed.

"I didn't want to go back to Scott," she insisted. "I was finished with him when he got all aggressive with me when I refused to dance with him. I was through even before the dance. He's not like he used to be. He's mean and vindictive."

"Because of the drugs?"

"I think so."

"Did you or did you not tell your parents?" He could only hope she had.

"No. My parents might trust me, but not Scott's. It's too easy to avoid the truth when it would mean they'd need to take action that would hurt their son's chances on the football field. They love the attention."

Callie was right.

"You did something that involves me, didn't you?" This was what this entire conversation was leading up to.

She swallowed. "I told Scott that I wasn't the only one who knew."

"You gave him my name?" Even though he asked, he already knew the answer. Memories of the humiliating Instagram post returned to his mind. That had been even worse than his face in the toilet. The entire school had seen it.

"I'm sorry, Spence."

"Great. Just great."

To her credit, Callie seemed genuinely regretful. Her actions told him there was more she wasn't telling him.

"What else?"

"I tried talking sense into Scott. If he hadn't been so cocky, I would have walked away. But he was so awful, mocking me and calling me ugly names. I couldn't let him get away with that." The blowback must have been a harsh lesson.

"Ben wasn't there?" Callie's brother had defended her in the past, and Spencer knew Ben would do it again, no matter the circumstances.

"No. I hoped, you know, that Scott would listen to reason."

Callie's foot found a pebble, and she kicked it around with the toe of her shoe. "I told him you were onto him and that you were determined to get all the evidence needed to take to Sheriff Terrance."

Spencer closed his eyes and groaned.

"I know I shouldn't have said that, but I couldn't think of any other way to show Scott I was serious."

"You mean throwing me under the bus was your only option." Briefly he wondered if he could finish out the school year with virtual learning. He had enough credits to graduate. It would mean only a few months of hiding.

"I know it was a stupid thing to do. I wasn't going to tell you."

"Spare me, please." He was angry now. Furious. Biting his tongue from saying something he'd regret, he whirled around and left her standing in the middle of the parking lot with tears streaming down her face.

Needless to say, Spencer stayed away from the football game that Friday night. He pretended to be sick on Monday morning and was dead bored by noon. As much as it appealed to him, he couldn't hide for the remainder of the school year. His parents would want to know why, and he'd never been a great liar.

A dozen ideas floated in and out of his mind. The best one was also the most direct. He'd find Scott, tell him Callie was dead wrong. He knew nothing, and even if he did, it wasn't his business.

The more he thought about it, the stronger the urge grew. He considered sending Scott an email. He had the quarterback's email address from when he'd hacked into Ben's computer. While the idea had seemed good, Spencer decided it was best to talk to Scott face-to-face. He'd make sure there were plenty of people around, too, which would lessen his chances of getting beaten to a pulp. Not so close that anyone would listen in on their conversation, though, which left him with few options.

Tuesday morning, Spencer returned to school. He hadn't told Joel or Brian what Callie had done. While he could use their support, he didn't want to drag his friends into this mess. He half-heartedly looked for Scott and was almost grateful when he didn't see him.

He was sitting in his last class of the day, determined to approach Scott before he left, when he heard a noise that sounded something like a firecracker outside in the school parking lot.

Looking out the window, he gasped, horrified at the sight in front of him. His car was on fire.

Not thinking about anything else, Spencer raced out of the classroom.

Ms. Goodwin shouted for him to stop, and when he didn't, she hurried after him.

Taking off his jacket, he started beating against the flames that had engulfed his 1965 Dodge Dart, while Ms. Goodwin tried pulling him back.

Chapter 20

Cade heard what sounded like a gunshot coming from the high school. He was working on aligning the front end of a Chevy truck and whirled around at the unexpectedness of it. What he saw made the oxygen freeze in his lungs.

Flames leaped from one of the vehicles in the school parking lot.

To his horror, he saw Hope racing after a teenage boy as the kid barreled straight toward the burning car. Hope was mere inches behind him, placing herself in imminent danger. He couldn't let that happen. With a force stronger than his will or any fear for himself, Cade tossed aside the wrench in his hand as he took off after her. His heart pumped like a race car piston with the terror of what could happen if the car exploded.

As he hurled himself across the street, his legs moving

faster than he thought possible, he saw another teenager, a girl this time, following both Hope and the guy. The boy quickly removed his jacket and started beating at the flames. His efforts were futile and put him and Hope at even greater risk.

Anyone could see it was useless, but that didn't stop him. Nor did it deter Hope, who was desperately trying to drag the teenager away from the burning vehicle.

Terrified the fire would reach the gas tank and explode, killing Hope and the two students, Cade rushed as fast as he could, despite the pain in his leg. No matter the potential cost to him, he refused to let harm come to Hope. Images of his friends burning on the ground flashed through his mind. Not again. Never again. He'd rather die himself than watch someone else he loved suffer a horrible death.

Fire engines screamed in the distance as he reached Hope. Frantic now, he grabbed her around the waist and hauled her back. She stumbled and nearly fell in her struggle to escape him before she realized it was him.

"Get Spencer," she screamed. "Get him away from the fire."

Even before she finished speaking, Cade grabbed hold of the boy, dragging him away from the burning vehicle.

By that time, two of the other mechanics from the garage had joined him, and several of the high school staff had stepped outside of the building. They stood back, helpless to do anything but watch the scene unfold before them.

Safely away from his car, Spencer sank onto the pavement and buried his face in his hands. Callie stood over him with tears glistening in her eyes.

Looking to Hope, Cade was frantic to make sure she hadn't been hurt. He ran his hands over her face and down her arms as if to check for any injuries, needing the assurance that she was okay. "Were you burned?" he demanded to know.

"I . . . I don't think so."

"You should never have gotten that close to the fire."

"But Spencer . . . I needed to get to him."

"I know . . . I know." Cade stepped back and braced his hands on his knees and paused to catch his breath. His lungs burned from the effort it'd taken to reach Hope and the fear that had all but consumed him.

"You okay?" one of his coworkers asked, coming to stand at his side.

It was all Cade could do to nod. His entire body was trembling, not as much from the exertion, but the memory of another vehicle on fire in another place and time.

"I'm fine," he finally managed.

He'd opened up a little with his coworkers, Jason and Boyd, over the last few weeks, eating lunch with them and shooting the breeze. Since his split with Hope, he'd taken to eating in his truck or making an excuse to drive off to collect his meal from McDonald's. He wasn't in the mood to be friendly, and rather than alienate Jason and Boyd, he'd avoided them.

The fire truck arrived, forcing them all to move back toward the building so the firemen could work. The bell rang, dismissing classes. The students poured out of the building. Most stood around and stared at the scene, talking among themselves.

With the fire truck there, the entire area around the school was in chaos. Smoke and fire billowed upward, clouding the sky, and the scent of burning leather lingered in the air. The firemen quickly put out the flames; all that remained was the thick water hose snaking from the truck and the smoking cavernous vehicle with the blackened interior. The fire chief broke away to speak to one of the school officials.

More sirens blared in the distance as law enforcement rushed to the scene. Several students had their phones out, filming the event: no doubt to post on social media.

They'd had a lucky escape. Cade had so much he wanted to say to Hope. She stood by the two students and he reached for her, pressing her against his dirty coveralls and his hurting heart. Pinned against his chest, she lifted her face to his, her eyes full of questions.

Rooted in the spot, Cade couldn't have let her go had it meant life or death. He was starving for the sight of her. His need was so great, he remained frozen in place. Silently he pleaded, begging her to look away, to release him. In the same breath, he prayed she'd never let him go.

With her gaze holding his captive, she gave him a gentle smile.

"Hey," she said, her voice husky as she broke contact and stepped back.

Her actions shook him.

For more than ten days he'd been fighting, angry with life, the world, and mostly himself. He'd been in a battle he knew he was destined to lose. His pride was all that had kept them apart. But pride was lonely and unrelenting in its demands, never comforting.

The instant he'd held Hope again, peace flooded through him like a spring swollen creek. He'd been wrong, so wrong.

Once he was willing to own up to what he'd done, he realized he didn't care what it cost, he needed Hope in his life.

"You're not hurt?" he asked again, needing her to say the words to reassure him.

"I'm fine," she said, keeping her arms crossed, shutting him out.

"It was reckless of you to run to a burning car."

"I had to do something," she said. The distance between them was killing him.

"I know." Although he wanted to reprimand her, he couldn't. He would have reacted the same way. In fact, he had, racing toward the burning vehicle for fear she would be burned. Seeing that she wasn't exactly falling into his arms, he asked, "Can we talk later?"

She hesitated before answering, and it felt like an eternity. His pulse pounded loud enough to echo in his ears.

"I think we should," she finally said.

Before another minute passed, he needed to tell her of his regret. "I'm so sorry, Hope."

A simple nod was her only acknowledgment.

Although he didn't want to leave her, he had no choice. She was needed at the school, and he had a job to finish.

"I'll stop by the cottage after work," he said.

"Okay."

Because he felt the need to say more, he added, "I've missed you."

How foolish he'd been, unwilling to listen, unwilling to accept that she had been innocent. He'd wanted to hurt her the way she'd hurt him, only to discover the only one he'd punished had been himself.

"Me, too," she said. Hope turned away and headed toward the school. Cade's heart sunk and he prayed with everything in him that he could repair the damage he'd done to their relationship.

As soon as Cade was back, his boss hit him with questions.

"Your girl okay? How's the school? What happened?" Cliff asked, exiting his office and leaning against the doorframe.

"Looks like a car fire."

Cliff frowned, and Cade noticed the other two mechanics exchanging glances.

"A car fire," Cliff commented, shaking his head as if to say nothing shocked him any longer when it came to the happenings around the high school. "It's a good thing the fire department got there when they did, otherwise the vehicle could have exploded."

Although his thoughts remained on Hope and their upcoming conversation, Cade worked the rest of the afternoon. As soon as he finished, he rushed to his apartment, showered, changed clothes, and then headed to the cottage by the sea. He was headed to see Hope.

Hope.

She'd been accurately named. He'd been penalizing himself by staying away. His pride made for miserable company. He chose to be alone, telling himself he was an island and needed no one. More fool he. The car fire had sent that theory flying out the window.

When he feared Hope might have been in danger or hurt,

his pride had died a sudden death. He didn't care if Hope had collaborated against him with his mother. Cade needed her for the light she brought into his life. Whatever had passed between her and his mother they would sort out together.

Shadow was in the fenced yard when Cade arrived at the cottage. When he climbed out of the truck, he saw Mellie Young in the house across the way. She'd pulled aside the curtain and stared at him from the kitchen window. Even from this distance, Cade could see that Mellie was frowning. It seemed he would need to make amends to her right along with Hope. He'd been warned. He was sure to face the landlord's ire if he hurt Hope. It encouraged him to know Preston and Mellie had Hope's back.

When Shadow revealed no excitement at seeing him, Cade hesitated. The mixed-breed shepherd regarded him warily, as if his absence had destroyed Shadow's trust in him.

"I've come in peace," he told the dog.

Hope opened the door and stood on the small porch. "Shadow, it's Cade."

At her voice, his tail wagged and he approached Cade, who paused long enough to scratch his ears before heading into the cottage with Hope.

Once inside, they stood facing each other. For several awkward seconds neither spoke. They remained several feet apart. Hope had her arms about herself as a shield, as if unsure what to expect.

Seeing that he'd been the one to suggest that they talk, he

felt an obligation to begin. He hardly knew where to start. All he knew was that he was willing to do or say anything that would bring her back into his arms.

"I've been an idiot."

Hope didn't argue.

"I have to believe if you sought out my mother—"

Hope cut him off with a shake of her head. "If you'd given me the chance to explain, you'd know she came to the high school and asked to speak to me."

"How did she know about you?" He'd reviewed a number of scenarios and could think of no way his mother would know about his relationship with Hope.

"She saw us that day on the beach when you bought us hot dogs."

"She was there?" he asked, unable to hide his surprise. "What reason would she have to be in Oceanside?" Although he asked, he didn't expect Hope to have an answer.

"You really are oblivious, aren't you?" she said, shaking her head as if it should be obvious. "She told me she's driven into town several times, looking for you." She continued to tell him what she'd learned about his mother being in the courtroom and how she'd guessed he lived in Oceanside.

"Why?" he asked.

"Several reasons," Hope said. "She deeply cares about you and wanted to be sure you were doing okay."

As much as he wanted to believe his mother cared about him, Cade found it hard. Especially after the way she'd deserted him six years earlier. "Why didn't she talk to me?"

"She tried but was afraid after you turned your back on her in the courtroom that you'd do it again."

It was difficult to wrap his head around what Hope was telling him. He ran his fingers through his hair as he paced her compact living room. Hard as it was to imagine, there might actually be a path that would restore his relationship with his parents.

His mother, he corrected himself. Cade was convinced his father knew nothing of his mother's attempts to reconnect. Without question, John Senior would never have allowed it.

"I jumped to conclusions when I saw the two of you together," he was willing to admit. He had no excuse other than what experience had taught him. "I'm sorry, Hope. Can we get past this and start again?" He held his breath, awaiting her answer. "Please," he added, recognizing how much she meant to him, and how badly he needed her.

"You refused to listen. You blocked me and immediately sought out another woman."

"It isn't like it sounds, I swear. Yes, I blocked you, and yes, I was stupid enough not to give you a chance to explain. But I swear by all I hold holy that there was no one else. That woman was all over me. I had to be rude to get rid of her. She meant nothing to me. The only woman I want is you, Hope."

"I wanted to believe that; I really did. When I told you about Hunter, you said I wasn't alone any longer, that you weren't going anywhere. Remember that? Your words were empty, Cade. The instant you had a single doubt you walked away and didn't look back."

"I was a fool. Have I lost you?" His heart was in his throat, waiting for her answer.

"Can I trust you, Cade?"

With everything in him, he wanted to give her the reassurance she needed. He couldn't lie, couldn't lead her on. It would be far too easy to tell her what she wanted to hear, and then disappoint and hurt her again. He refused to do that.

"I don't know, Hope. I'd like to say I'm all in with this relationship. It's the way I feel and what I want more than anything. The biggest problem is me. I'm a work in progress. The future is unknown. I can say this. I will do everything within my power to be as forthright and honest with you as I can."

Hope listened and appeared to understand.

"Is that enough?"

Her sigh seemed to empty her chest and she nodded. "I have my own issues to work out. When I talked to Willa, which I've done several times now, she's helped me understand a lot of things about myself. I thought, wrongly, as it turned out, that because I had you in my life I wasn't alone any longer. She had Sean and the rest of her family. I had no one else until I met you, and . . ." She hesitated and looked away before looking back. "The truth is, I had to deal with the fact I am alone with no family. That was painful for me when I realized I couldn't count on you."

Her words cut him. She seemed to realize it because she quickly added, "To have put you in that position was wrong. I had to search deep within myself, to find the peace that I would be all right. I think we might be able to help each other, Cade. In answer to your question, being truthful with each other is enough. The trust will come in time."

"Thank you," he whispered, and because he couldn't bear not to hold her for another moment, he reached for her.

Weaving his fingers into her hair, he leaned forward and

kissed her with relief and need, unable to get enough of her taste, of the lemon scent that was her. He breathed it in like it was life itself.

They continued to hold each other for several minutes before sitting down on the sofa, side by side. Needing to maintain contact, Cade kept his arm around her shoulders. It was sheer joy when Hope leaned against his strength. Shadow settled down on the floor in front of them, his chin resting on Hope's foot.

"Does anyone know what caused the car fire?" he asked. He hadn't been able to stay long enough to hear what had led up to the car fire.

"Not yet, although I have my suspicions. Callie was upset earlier in the day. She'd had some differences with Spencer and just needed someone to talk to about what was happening in her life. While we spoke, she said she'd been stressed over her brother and felt certain he was on drugs. She also seemed to believe she knew who was responsible for selling Ben the drugs. I immediately went to Dean Wilcox, and he sent for the coach. Coach had a lot of questions for me. I answered him as best I could. Callie had already left the school. She's the one Coach and the dean really needed to talk to about all this."

"And?"

"The three of us spent a good thirty minutes going over the information. Coach is convinced he'd know if any of his players were stupid enough to take drugs, let alone sell them."

Cade paused as if to absorb this. "What was Dean Wilcox's reaction?"

Hope released an irritated sigh. "He said he would personally talk to Scott about it, but then Coach reminded him that Callie had recently broken up with Scott, and this was likely a lie she'd invented to discredit Scott and get him kicked off the team."

"And since you didn't have any evidence other than what Callie said, they were inclined to let the matter drop."

"Exactly. The thing is, I believe Callie. I don't think she'd do anything that underhanded to retaliate against Scott."

Hope grew quiet and intense. "The school has a no-tolerance drug policy and I'm afraid that pointing the finger at the school's top athlete is going to be ignored by both Dean Wilcox and the coach. I did my due diligence and reported what Callie told me. I don't know that I can do anything more."

"What about talking to Sheriff Terrance?"

"I considered it, but going behind the administrative staff at the school would be professional suicide. All I can do at this point is wait it out. If what Callie said is true, and I don't doubt that it is, then it will all come out in time."

"You know how I feel about you putting yourself in danger."

"I'll be careful," she promised. "I won't do anything to make myself a target."

"Did anyone see you when you went to talk to Dean Wilcox?" he pried.

Hope looked away.

"Hope?"

"Scott saw me talking to Callie and then followed me when I went to the dean's office. I'm hoping he assumes this has to do with the car fire. By the time I left, Scott wasn't anywhere around that I could see."

"What about the car fire?" Cade asked.

"It's under investigation, but my gut tells me Scott is the one behind it." She broke away enough to look Cade in the eye. "Spencer believes he's responsible, too. Soon after you left, he lost it. Before anyone could stop him, he went after Scott, shouting and shoving him."

Cade knew the football player had a good forty pounds of muscle on Spencer. The kid was bound to lose in any physical confrontation. "That wasn't even close to a fair fight."

She bit her lower lip before speaking. "It was awful, Cade. Scott retaliated and hit Spencer. Then Callie jumped on Scott's back. He tossed her off like she weighed nothing, and then Scott and Spencer went at it with fists. It took both Dean Wilcox and another teacher to break it up."

"Was anyone hurt?"

"Spencer has a split lip, Callie had cuts and bruises. I don't think Scott was hurt at all."

"Why did Callie get involved?" The girl should have known better than to interfere in a physical altercation. She could have been badly hurt.

"Callie blames herself. It all goes back to the deal she made with Spencer regarding the homecoming dance. She needed him to find out who was responsible for getting Ben drugs and enlisted Spencer's help."

"You did what you could to help," Cade said. Seeing her put herself in danger had nearly been his undoing. The terror was all too fresh in his mind.

"I tried. The one who really lost it, though, is Callie. She feels dreadful and blames herself for everything that happened."

Cade's mind was buzzing, all the dots coming together at once.

"As soon as Callie told me Scott was the one giving Ben drugs, I took it seriously and asked several questions. I trust Dean Wilcox to get to the bottom of this."

"Even when Scott's a key member of the winning football team?"

Hope mulled over his question. "I trust him. If drugs are being dealt at the school, Dean Wilcox will put an end to it, and it won't matter to him what position Scott plays on the football team. Coach knows that, and I believe he's cooperating."

"Hope, listen, this is important." He firmly took hold of both her shoulders and held her eyes. "I don't know what's going on here, but you've got to stay out of it."

She blinked, as if she didn't understand. "I don't know that I can."

"Hope, please. Whoever is responsible is sending Spencer a message. You already got one, and if you ignore it, then these sorts of incidents will only escalate. You can't allow yourself to be put in harm's way."

She considered his words and then shook her head. "I wish I could, Cade. If what Callie told me is true and there are drugs being sold on school grounds, I had a legal obligation to involve the school. If Dean Wilcox and Coach Simmons need my help, I can't refuse."

"Hope, you need to think this through," he begged. "This isn't a game. You've put yourself in danger."

"You're overreacting."

"Maybe. Maybe not. If for nothing else than my peace of mind, stay out of this." Cade feared she was in denial and had no clue what she was getting herself into.

"At least I know Spencer is safe for now." Hope sighed.

"How's that?"

"After the fight, Spencer, Scott, and Callie were escorted to Dean Wilcox's office. Spencer and Callie have been suspended from school for the remainder of the week."

"And Scott?"

"A slap on the wrist. Scott, the precious football star, got off with nothing more than an extra study period because he wasn't the one who started the fight. He claimed it was self-defense."

Cade was relieved both Spencer and Callie wouldn't be on school grounds, at least for now. A lot could happen before the end of the week.

"Spencer left the school with his dad," Hope added. "He was devastated, and who could blame him? That car was more than his transportation. Spencer and his dad spent countless hours working on the engine, getting it to run again."

"The poor kid." Cade hated the possibility that Hope might be targeted next. "These people don't take interference lightly. Just look at what happened to Spencer."

Frustration ate at him. He wanted to argue, explain that whoever was behind her slashed tire and the car fire wasn't going to idly sit back and do nothing. He didn't want to start their reconciliation with another argument. Cade could tell: Hope's mind was set.

"Promise me you'll watch your back," he said with feeling.

"I promise."

That was all he could ask of her. It would have to be enough.

Chapter 21

Spencer heard the doorbell ring and turned up the volume on his headphones. He hoped it wasn't someone for him. He was in no mood for company. The bell was pressed a second time, and his mother left the kitchen to answer the door.

A minute later, she found him in his bedroom, in the dark with his blinds shut. He was sprawled out on his bed with his eyes closed, music blaring in his ears. His mother waited until he removed the headphones. "Callie's here," she told him.

Callie was the last person he had any desire to see, let alone talk to.

Now or ever.

"Send her away," he said, glaring up at his mother to be sure she understood he wasn't willing to compromise, no matter how good of friends their parents were.

"The least you can do is hear her out," his mother insisted.

He stubbornly disagreed. "Tell her to leave."

"I know you're upset, sweetie, but I think you should listen to her. She's upset and—"

"Mom, no."

"It's all right, Mrs. Brown," Callie said. She'd apparently followed his mother down the hallway leading to his bedroom. "I can understand why Spencer wants nothing to do with me."

Spencer groaned and yearned to cover his face with his pillow and block out the world. If not the world, then at least Callie.

"I promise this will only take a minute," Callie assured his mother, but the message was for him as well.

As far as he was concerned, even one second with Callie was more than he could tolerate.

"Spencer," his mother said, chastising him. "The least you can do is give her a chance to speak, seeing as she came all this way."

All this way? What? A mile, maybe two? His mother didn't get it. Callie had literally ruined his life.

"Please," Callie whispered, standing next to his mother, crowding the doorway.

"Fine." He sat up, but refused to look at Callie. He feared once he did, he'd lose the fragile hold he had on his temper. The urge to verbally rip into her hovered on his lips. One wrong word and he was going to lose it.

Callie remained standing in the doorway after his mother left. Spencer kept his gaze focused on her shoes. He'd listen; not that he expected anything she said would be worthwhile. Polite or not, he intended for her to leave as soon as possible.

"I came to tell you how horribly sorry I am about your car," Callie said, barely sounding like herself.

"Fine. You're sorry. So am I. Good-bye." All he wanted was to get this apology over with so he could continue blocking out the world with his music.

"I blame myself."

As she very well should. Callie was the one who'd dragged him into this mess. Furthermore, she'd set him up by telling Scott that he was on to the fact the football player was dealing drugs.

"I know how important that car is to you."

He had nothing to add. That car was a classic. He could only imagine how much the repairs would tally. Money he didn't have, unless it came out of his college fund.

Sheriff Terrance had questioned him about who Spencer thought might be responsible. It was on the tip of his tongue to name Scott Pender. He didn't, though, sensing that there would be further retribution if he did. Besides, he had no real proof.

Scott getting away with this left a bitter taste in Spencer's mouth. He ended up telling Sheriff Terrance he had no idea who might have set fire to his car. The deed was done. Naming Scott would cause the entire school, and the entire city of Oceanside, to hate him for pointing a finger at the most important member of the football team. In their eyes, Scott Pender could do no wrong.

Undoubtedly there would be an investigation, but in the end, it would be impossible to prove. Spencer had watched enough crime shows to know how highly unlikely it was to find those responsible in arson cases.

"I have three thousand dollars saved from my summer job, and birthday, and Christmas money," Callie said, as she came all the way into his bedroom. "I know it probably isn't enough, but it's all I have. It's yours with my apology."

Spencer didn't want her money.

"I . . . don't have a clue how much it'll cost to replace the interior. If you'll let me know, I'll do whatever is necessary to make up the difference. I don't know that much about that sort of thing, so I'll need you to tell me."

"Don't worry about it," he said, reaching for his headphones. He didn't want to be rude, but he wanted her to leave. Leave his room. Leave his life. Just leave.

Despite his lack of welcome, Callie sat on the bed as far away as she could from him.

"What do you want me to say?" he asked, perplexed at her blatant attempt to ignore his wishes.

"I . . . I don't know. I suppose I'm looking for forgiveness."

"You'll get it at some point," he said, "just not now."

"I don't blame you for hating me."

He didn't hate her. It might be easier if he did. What he needed, what he wanted, was time to absorb what had happened and figure out how best to move forward. "Callie, please just go."

She sniffled. "I don't think I can."

He turned to face her, meeting her gaze for the first time.

The sight shocked him. Callie, who'd always been perfectly put together, was anything but. Her eyes were swollen and red from tears. Her eye makeup had left black meandering streaks down her cheeks. Her hair was a mess. She looked worse than

Spencer could ever remember seeing her. Whatever he was about to say died before he could utter the words.

For a long moment all he could do was stare.

The envelope, with the cash inside, rested on the mattress between them. Spencer handed it back to her. "Keep your money."

"I can't do that. It's yours. I should have gone to my parents the way you suggested, and I would now, except they're in Hawaii, celebrating their anniversary. They won't be back until Sunday afternoon."

He had nothing to say.

"I'll go to the police and tell them everything I know."

"I doubt it will do much good without proof," he said, discouraged and disgruntled. Spencer didn't have the strength to fight her. If this was what she needed to do to make up for what she'd done, then he'd accept her guilt offering. He needed his car for his job and for when he left for college.

"Did you get suspended for attacking Scott?" she asked. She sat with her shoulders slumped forward, and her hands clenched in her lap.

He nodded.

"Me, too."

Spencer didn't know what possessed Callie to leap on Scott's back. It'd been a crazy thing to do. It infuriated him when Scott tossed her off him like a sack of potatoes. "Were you hurt . . . you know, when Scott threw you?"

Callie shrugged.

"You shouldn't have gotten involved."

"I had to," she admitted, her hands white with how tight

they were clenched. "Scott was going to pulverize you if I hadn't done something."

Callie didn't understand that her fighting his battle only made him look weak, which, admittedly, he was compared to Scott.

"How many days are you suspended?" she asked.

"Three. You?"

"The same," she told him. "The rest of the week."

"What about Scott?" Spencer had been with Dean Wilcox, and because of the volatile situation, Scott had gone to Principal Wentz's office.

"He claimed he was only defending himself and so he wasn't suspended."

"It figures."

All the more proof Scott remained invincible. Without Scott on the football field Friday night, the Oceanside Eagles would suffer their first defeat of the season. And no one at the school, or likely the entire community, would let that happen. Too much was at stake. The football team was the pride of everyone in Oceanside.

Silence rested between them. The tension had left, but the mood was somber.

"Scott's going to get away with this," Callie whispered.

"I expect he will, even if you talk to Sheriff Terrance," Spencer agreed. He understood far better the dilemma Callie faced when she'd confronted Scott. No one would want to believe her. Little wonder Scott had laughed at her. He knew better than anyone, dealing drugs or anything else: He was untouchable.

"Do you think . . . I mean, would you be willing . . ." Callie hesitated.

"What?" he asked, almost afraid of what she might want next.

"Could you not hate me?" she asked in a trembling voice.

Spencer could see she was on the verge of fresh tears.

"I could never hate you," he admitted.

"In time, do you think you could find a way to forgive me?"

Spencer saw the pleading in her eyes.

"Yeah." He exhaled a slow breath. "I can."

"Thank you," Callie whispered. "I don't deserve that."

Not that long ago, Callie was all he could think about. At night his dreams were full of her. When she'd agreed to attend homecoming with him, he was on a high no drug could deliver. Holding Callie, dancing with her, was all he'd ever wanted. All he'd ever hoped for.

"Could I ask you something?" She sounded tentative and unsure.

"Okay."

She looked down at her folded hands. "Would you mind very much if I came back here tomorrow?"

"Back here? Why?"

She slowly released her breath. "We can't be at school, so I thought, you know, that we could hang out. Maybe play video games."

"You want to play video games?" He wasn't sure he'd heard her correctly. That was something they'd done quite a bit when they were younger. Callie was good, but then so was he, often evenly matched. He assumed her gaming days were long over.

"Yes, a lot. I haven't gotten my class assignments yet. Whatever they are won't take me long. My parents are out of town, so I'll be home alone and bored. I'd like to spend time with you, Spencer."

"Sure."

"I mean it," she insisted, as if she thought he was being sarcastic.

"What games do you play?"

It didn't take her long to answer. "Actually, I haven't played that much lately. What about you?"

"Mario Cart and Call of Duty."

"I know those games. I'll be by at ten tomorrow, if that works."

Spencer grinned "Be ready for me to kick your butt."

Callie smiled then and reached for his hand, squeezing it. "We'll see about that."

Chapter 22

Spencer had purposely let Callie win. Excited, she threw her head back and laughed when she outscored him in Mario Cart. For the last three days they'd spent nearly every minute together. They'd been the best days of his life, and that included the time he was named the junior high state chess champion. It was reminiscent of a time years before when they'd been the best of friends. They laughed and joked just as they once had.

"I finally beat you," Callie said, leaning back on the family room sofa. "And to think it only took me three days."

"You were always good at video games," he said, playing along.

Callie scoffed. "Yeah, right. I'll admit I was rusty, but it didn't take me long to find my groove. By the way, where's your mom?"

"It's my aunt's birthday, so Mom and Dad left for a surprise birthday party for her in Spokane." Spencer had originally planned to travel with them. He'd begged off because he'd been enjoying his time with Callie and didn't want to lose out on their last day together.

"So both our parents are out of town for the weekend."

He hadn't realized that until she mentioned it.

Spencer set aside his controller. "You hungry?"

"A little." They'd played three hours straight, and it was just past eleven, their normal lunch hour at school.

Spencer went into the kitchen. "A sandwich okay?"

"Sure." Callie joined him and jumped up on the countertop, letting her feet dangle over the edge.

"You like tunafish?"

"Hate it, sorry," Callie said.

He should have remembered that. "Peanut butter?"

"With grape jelly?"

Spencer checked the refrigerator. "You're in luck. Peanut butter and jelly it is."

"Do you have any chips?"

Spencer rolled his eyes. "Mom's on another one of her health kicks. Chips aren't allowed in the house." He didn't know why it was that the entire family had to suffer because his mother wanted to lose five pounds.

"No problem."

"Milk or soda?" he asked.

"Milk goes better with peanut butter," Callie said.

Spencer agreed.

"Did I tell you Ben didn't go to school this morning?" Callie mentioned this casually. "Which means he shouldn't be allowed to play, but we both know that Coach will let him."

Spencer paused from removing the carton of milk from the refrigerator. *Ben not at school? Coach Simmons must be freaking out.*

As a wide receiver, Ben was Scott's favorite target. Ben had the ability to catch almost every pass from Scott. With him out sick, the team might lose the game.

"It's Friday. The game's tonight," Spencer said, thinking out loud.

"Yeah, I know." Callie's legs continued to swing, as if this news was insignificant.

"Ben must really be sick. What's the problem?"

Callie gestured weakly with her hands to suggest she wasn't sure. "I don't know, I'm mad at him."

"Why, what did he do?"

She hesitated before answering, as if she wasn't sure she wanted to explain. "We got into it this morning before I left. I told him I blamed him as much as I blamed myself for what happened to your car. He might not have personally started the fire, but he might as well have." Spencer focused his attention on Callie. She hadn't mentioned any of this earlier, although when she'd first arrived, she had seemed preoccupied and out of sorts. It was only when they became wrapped up in the video games that she became herself.

"Did Ben say anything?" he asked. Although he'd never said anything to Callie, he was convinced Ben was somehow involved in the car fire.

Callie frowned, as though perplexed. "He told me to stay

out of this and to leave him alone. Funny, you know. Ben's always had a quick temper, and even more so lately. I was surprised when after a couple minutes, he just stood there and let me go off on him. Exasperated, I walked away in a huff, and then a few minutes later he came into the kitchen and said he wouldn't be going to school because he had stomach cramps."

Spencer hadn't been friends with Ben in a long time. But the thought that Ben would skip the game out of any sense of guilt troubled him. "The team needs Ben."

Callie appeared unconcerned. "I gave him something to think about. My guess is he'll have a miraculous recovery before the game tonight."

"So it's not because you pointed the finger at him and he feels guilty?"

"I doubt it. If I gave my brother something to think about, then all the better. He needs to own up to his part in all this. Besides, knowing Ben, he could be staying home to avoid taking a test."

Spencer intuitively felt Ben missing school was far more than stomach cramps, especially on a game day. Something was up, something they couldn't ignore.

With his mind buzzing over Callie's one-sided fight with Ben, Spencer brought out the bread and peanut butter.

"We should call him," he said.

"Why would I do that? He's the last person I want to talk to right now."

"I think there's more going on here than the football game."

In response, Callie tossed him an exasperated look.

"Just text him," Spencer pressed, more adamantly this time.

"He's perfectly fine," she groused. "I wish I'd never said anything."

"Fine, if you won't text him, then I will." Reaching into his back pocket, he retrieved his phone.

"All right. You win." Callie grabbed her own phone, unlocked her screen, and then dialed before holding the phone to her ear.

Spencer could hear it ringing. No one answered.

"See," she said with a pout. "He's most likely at school. I knew he'd have a miraculous recovery in time for the game tonight."

"Try texting."

"If you insist," she said.

Reading over her shoulder, Spencer watched as she typed. *Call me ASAP. Important.*

"There, are you satisfied?"

Spencer nodded.

"You know if he's at school, he won't be able to respond."

"School or not, if you say it's important, he'll find a way to answer."

She reluctantly agreed with a short nod. "I think you're making much more of this than necessary."

"Maybe, but I don't think so, Callie. The Ben I remember has a conscience, drugs or not. I can't imagine him standing by and seeing other people hurt. Your fight with him this morning might have triggered something inside him."

"Are you saying you are more familiar with my brother than I am?"

"What I'm saying," Spencer said, quickly losing his patience, "is that you're making assumptions. I don't know Ben the way I once did, I'll admit, but my gut tells me something is up and that we need to find out what it is."

"You're overreacting. Ben's at school."

"Do any of your friends have first lunch?"

"Yeah, why?"

"Call and ask if anyone has seen Ben at school."

With a huff, Callie reached for her phone a second time. She went into her contact list and then held the phone to her ear once again.

Standing this close to her, he could hear Alyse pick up. "Callie, dance team is going nuts without you. Is there any way you can stop by after school to review the routine?"

"Maybe," Callie said. "I'm not calling about the dance team. Any chance you've seen Ben? He stayed home from school this morning and—"

"He's not sick, is he?"

Alyse sounded alarmed, recognizing that if a key member of the football team was absent, it might mean a loss, and a loss at a home game would be devastating.

"He said he wasn't feeling well when I left him earlier," Callie explained.

"You left him? Where did you go?"

"To Spencer's house."

"You went to Spencer's house?"

Even standing this far away, Spencer could feel the shock waves.

"Spencer and I are longtime friends," Callie insisted.

"Since when?" Alyse asked, laughing.

"Since forever," she muttered, clearly unamused. "Have you seen Ben or not?"

"I haven't, but let me ask around. Give me five minutes and I'll call you back."

"Thanks."

Spencer had the impression the first four minutes would be Alyse telling all their gal pals the shocking news that Callie and he were together.

Five minutes passed and then ten with no call.

"He's at school," Callie reiterated, although she didn't sound nearly as confident as she had earlier.

"You're probably right." He stuffed the tips of his fingers into his rear pockets, lunch forgotten.

"But what if he isn't?" she asked, her eyes wide, and seeking what looked like reassurance.

"We'll cross that bridge when we need to."

"Right," she said, nodding.

When Callie's phone finally did ring, it came so unexpectedly that they both jumped.

She answered right away. "What did you find out?" she asked, without giving the normal greeting.

"No one's seen him, so I asked Scott, figuring he would know," Alyse said, and then hesitated.

"And?" Callie pressed.

"And . . . he acted sort of weird. Cagey."

Callie's eyes connected with Spencer's. "Cagey? In what way?"

"W . . . e . . . l . . . l," Alyse said, dragging out the word. "It's hard to describe. I mean, you'd think he'd be concerned if Ben was home sick, about the game and all."

"Right," Callie agreed.

"Instead, he said something about Ben being stupid. If Ben

is sick, it isn't because he lacks intelligence. When I said as much, Scott glared at me and said I didn't know what I was talking about. Then he said Ben was about to ruin everything, but that probably has to do with him missing the game."

"You're probably right," Callie said. And then to reiterate, asked again, "So no one's seen Ben around the school, then?"

"Not anyone I asked."

"Okay, thanks, Alyse."

"No problem. Be sure and stop by the field this afternoon, if you can," Alyse said. "The dance team needs you."

"I'll try."

Callie ended the conversation and looked to Spencer. "Now what?"

"We check your house. Maybe Ben was genuinely sick and is asleep."

They left together. Thankfully, Callie had a car. As soon as they arrived, they rushed into the house and up the stairs to Ben's room, which was empty. A quick search through the rest of the house showed no signs of Callie's twin.

Standing in the middle of the family room, Callie looked to Spencer. "Now I'm concerned. Where could he be?"

Her phone dinged, indicating she'd received a text. Callie snatched her phone. It was from Alyse.

Genny said Ben came to the school and then must have left. No one has seen him since.

"We need to go to the school," Callie said.

"We can't. In case you've forgotten, we've been suspended."

"But this is important."

"I agree. Before we do, I think we should check out anywhere he would go."

Callie automatically shook her head. "There's no place. School and football are Ben's life."

"What about when we were kids? He liked . . ."

"Eagle Rock," Callie finished for him. As kids they'd spent countless hours at the small creek that led to the beach and the huge rock that had named the area. Spencer remembered watching the salmon fighting their way up the creek to their spawning grounds. The sight of those fish had fascinated him and Ben.

The drive took only a few minutes. Although they looked all around and called his name several times, Ben was nowhere to be seen.

"Where to now?" Spencer asked, ready to head out. Standing at the edge of the creek bed, Callie remained still.

"Callie," he said, urging her to come.

Holding up her hand, she stopped him. "Ben was here," she whispered, her face somber and intent. "I can feel it. Laugh if you want, but I know my brother came here. Something is wrong, Spencer. Something is very wrong."

Chapter 23

As planned, Cade stopped by the cottage to pick up Hope for the game. Her day had been hectic, as was common on days the football team played. It'd been even more so this Friday, as rumors about Ben Rhodes had been speeding through the school faster than a flu bug. Because he was such an important member of the football team, to have him home sick had created quite a buzz.

Then she'd heard someone claimed to have seen Ben at the school arguing with Scott Pender. If that was the case, then it was unlikely he'd stayed away because he was sick. Speculation ran rampant. One of her students claimed they'd overheard Ben and Scott in a verbal confrontation about the fire that destroyed Spencer's car. Another said the argument had nothing to do with that but over the fact that Scott wanted all the glory.

Another rumor claimed a scout for one of the college teams

would be attending the game. Scholarships to major universities hung in the balance. It could be the scouts were coming to look at more than the players. With one state championship under Coach Simmons's belt, and another likely, it could be an opportunity for Coach was in the works as well.

With the information Hope had given Dean Wilcox and Coach Simmons, Hope was surprised Scott hadn't been suspended from the team. She suspected that without proof, the accusation that Scott was involved in selling drugs was considered conjecture and speculation. Because Callie was on suspension, she hadn't been questioned yet. Any action against Scott would likely need to wait until the following week.

What surprised Hope was Coach. With all that hung in the balance, he didn't appear overly concerned about Ben's absence. As soon as classes were dismissed for the day, the team had assembled to go over the game plan the same way they did before every game.

"You about ready to head out?" Cade asked.

"In a minute. I'll need to stop by the school before the game." With everything that had been going on, Hope had inadvertently left her phone behind.

"Sure, no problem."

It wasn't until then that Hope noticed how quiet Cade had been ever since he'd arrived. "Everything okay?" she asked, reaching for her jacket. Evenings were chilly these days, and sitting in the stands with the wind made it all the colder. She knew he and Silas were back on good terms and things seemed to be going well at work.

"Sure . . ."

Hope focused her attention on him. "You don't sound it."

Cade's face tightened, and Hope knew then something was definitely off.

"My mother showed up at the shop this afternoon."

So that was it. Making a big deal of it would probably be the wrong thing to do. She remained silent, waiting for him to voluntarily give her the details.

Cade rubbed his hand down his face. "I blew it, Hope."

Oh dear, this was the last thing she wanted to hear. "How? Tell me what happened."

He looked down at the carpet where Shadow had curled up and slept. "Mom wanted to talk, and I told her I was working and now wasn't a good time."

That wasn't so bad. "I'm sure she understood."

"But then I told her, seeing that it'd taken her six years to contact me, that there probably wasn't a lot she had to say that I wanted to hear."

"Cade!"

"I know, I know."

"So what happened?"

"She got all weepy and said both she and my father were available any time I was ready to reconcile. All I needed to do was let them know. Before I could respond, she returned to her car and drove away."

"Oh Cade." Hope wasn't going to berate him, seeing how miserable he was.

"I was embarrassed," Cade said, as if he needed to defend himself. "Cliff was there, and a couple of the other guys. They could hear every word. I didn't need them listening in on my business."

Knowing how hard it was for Cade to open up to others,

Hope understood. "The one good thing is that you know the door's wide open for you whenever you're ready."

He shrugged. "After what I said, I doubt Mom will want to hear from me."

"I think you're wrong about that. Give it some thought."

He nodded and then smiled. "I feel better. Thanks for listening."

Wrapping her arm around his, she smiled up at him. "Come on, soldier boy, we have a football game to attend." Before she left the cottage, Hope made sure Shadow's food and water bowls were filled.

Cade parked his truck in the school parking lot. The front door was locked, but the alarm hadn't been set because the team would be using the facility. Luckily, because as a school counselor she often stayed late, she had been given a key to the building. Cade came inside with her.

"This will only take a minute," she assured him. They had plenty of time before the game, so there wasn't any rush.

Cade followed her down the hallway toward the counseling office when the sound of someone pounding against the outside glass door attracted their attention.

"Who's that?" Cade asked.

"I don't have any idea."

The pounding continued, becoming even more frantic. Hope retrieved her phone and then stepped into the hallway to see Spencer and Callie standing outside the main door, both looking excited and more than a little panicky.

Walking toward the school entrance, keeping Hope behind him, Cade opened the door, but not wide enough to allow them inside.

"What's up?" he asked.

"It's Ben," Callie said, her eyes looking past Cade and pleading with Hope. "I got a call from my parents. Mom is freaking out. Ben contacted them and told them everything and now they can't reach him."

"What do you mean Ben told your parents everything?" Hope asked.

Both Spencer and Callie started talking at once.

"Stop," Hope said, holding up both hands to get their attention. "One at a time. I can't make sense of what you're saying."

Breathless, Spencer motioned toward Callie. "You go first."

Callie drew in a deep breath, and tears filled her eyes. "Ben stayed home from school, but then we heard he showed up and was seen arguing with Scott."

Spencer interrupted her. "We haven't been able to find Ben anywhere. He was missing and wasn't answering his phone or texts. Then Callie remembered the Find My iPhone app."

Callie cut in next. "Ben must be somewhere in the school. He's never without his phone, so if it pings here, then this is where he is. We need to find him." Callie paused and bit into her lip. "I have this feeling something is terribly wrong. I can't shake it. Please, Ms. Goodwin, let me in so I can find Ben."

Being a twin herself, Hope didn't doubt the teenager's intuition.

Callie hurriedly spoke again when Hope didn't respond right away. "I know you might find this hard to believe, but there's this thing between Ben and me. I guess it has something to do with being twins. You have to believe me, Ms. Goodwin."

"All right. Show me where his cell phone pinged, and we'll go from there."

"Thank you," Spencer said. He held Callie's hand, and Hope noticed the teen girl was fighting tears.

"No way," Cade said, stopping them. "I'm not going to let you put yourself in any danger. I'll go with Spencer. You two stay here."

"You can't do that," Hope countered. "If you get caught in the school you'll be arrested for trespassing. I have to be the one to go."

"All right," he agreed, with obvious reluctance, "but I'm going with you."

"Can we please just find Ben," Callie pleaded.

Using Callie's phone, the four continued down the hallway until they stood in front of Coach Simmons's office. When Cade turned the doorknob, it was locked.

"Try your key," Cade suggested.

"That isn't going to work on this door."

"Try it anyway," he said.

Hope handed him the key, and to her shock, with a bit of jiggling, the door opened.

Sure enough, Ben's phone was on top of Coach's desk. The phone was there, but Ben wasn't.

"Where's my brother?" Callie cried, her voice wobbling with emotion.

A muffled sound came from inside the closet. Cade hurried over to the door and found it was also locked. This time, no matter how hard they tried, her key wouldn't work.

"Hold on," Cade said, searching the top of the coach's desk until he found what he wanted. Kneeling down in front of the door, he took a paperclip and tried to release the lock, to no avail.

"Try this," Hope said, and handed him a fingernail file.

All the while they worked to open the closet, they could hear kicking and muffled sounds coming from the other side.

After several tries, Cade managed to unlock the door. Once open, they discovered Ben tied up inside, duct tape across his mouth. Cade removed it first before undoing the binding around his arms and legs.

"It's Coach." Those were the first words out of Ben's mouth. "He's the one giving us the drugs."

"Coach Simmons?" Hope asked, stunned, finding it hard to believe. She gulped as her brain assimilated what Ben was saying. It wasn't a student who'd been dealing drugs. It was the coach. In that moment, it felt as if all the oxygen in the room had been sucked out.

"What a mess," Coach Simmons said, shocking them all as he strolled into the office. "Let me assure you this isn't what it looks like."

"You've been drugging your players?" Hope asked, before she could stop herself.

Coach's demeanor changed immediately. He glared at Callie and Spencer before turning his attention to Ben and Cade. "I don't know what lies these kids are telling you. I trust you are smart enough not to take their word over mine."

"He's lying," Ben cried. "Coach is giving the whole team enhancement drugs."

"The boy lies," Coach insisted.

"If that's the case, why was he tied up in your closet?" Cade demanded. He'd placed himself in front of the teens and

Hope, facing the coach. Spencer was having none of it and stepped around Cade to stand at his side, wanting answers as badly as Hope did.

"Ben gave me no choice," Coach said, with a deep sigh of regret. "This is the biggest game of the season. If Ben were to go to Dean Wilcox or Principal Wentz with his lies, they would call off the game. I couldn't let that happen with scholarships on the line. I realize I might have overreacted by tying him up," he conceded, "but I didn't feel I had any choice."

"Perhaps the authorities should be the ones to sort all this out," Cade suggested.

"Yes," Spencer insisted. "We need to call the sheriff. What you did was wrong."

"That's unnecessary." Coach immediately rejected the idea.

"I'm not lying," Ben shouted.

"You're blowing this all out of proportion," Coach Simmons continued, making light of the accusation. "It's not drugs like heroin, or meth, or anything like that. There's no way I'd endanger any member of my team by giving them illegal drugs."

"Then what are these?" Ben asked, holding out his hand with a number of different-sized pills. "There're several bags of them in the closet. Look for yourself if you don't believe me."

"Those are the same pills I found in Ben's backpack," Callie said, glaring at Coach.

Coach Simmons frowned, as if to say this was all a simple misunderstanding that would easily be cleared away. "Those tablets are harmless."

"Steroids?" Hope asked.

"And a few others . . . nothing that would do the team any physical harm, let me assure you."

"My brother doesn't believe that, and neither do I." Callie wasn't letting up. "You should be in jail for what you're doing. Ben hasn't been the same person since you started giving him those drugs. Scott, either. My brother never had a temper like this. He's aggressive and unreasonable. Scott, too."

"Callie's right," Spencer added angrily.

"Why would you feel you had to give the team anything?" Hope was probably naïve to ask. For Coach to take such a huge professional risk was beyond her comprehension.

Coach looked as if it were the stupidest question he'd ever heard. "Why do you think?"

"You're undefeated," Cade said, "and now we know why."

"He's a cheat," Spencer said with disgust.

Coach sent them a smug look. "We win and that's all that matters. If you think I'm going to let you ruin that for me, then you're wrong."

"You didn't win those games," Hope said, growing angry now. "Yes, the Eagles scored more points, but you did it at the physical and emotional risk of teenage boys."

Coach snickered, as if to suggest she was completely unaware of how things worked. "Do you seriously think other coaches don't give their players performance enhancers?"

"Yes," Hope insisted, finding it hard to accept this was a common practice.

"Then you're wrong."

Hope refused to believe him. "Have you no conscience?" she asked.

Coach seemed to find her questions amusing. "You have to know I never forced these kids to take enhancers. They asked for them. They know a good thing when they see it."

"I don't care what you call them. Enhancers or drugs, it's wrong and harmful," Hope insisted.

"Tomato, tomahto," he returned flippantly. "I was helping these boys get scholarships. They're grateful and so are their parents."

"Their families would be outraged if they knew," Cade said.

Hope could tell he was as angry as she was. What he said was right. From what she knew of both Ben's and Scott's parents, they would be horrified. They had no choice other than to report Coach Simmons to the authorities.

"I doubt the parents would care," Coach insisted. "They want the best for their sons, and I'm giving them the chance of a lifetime."

"You said if we told our parents we were off the team," Ben inserted.

"It was for your own good. Do you seriously believe there'd be college scouts out there looking at you if I hadn't helped you?" Coach's eyes narrowed as he focused on Ben.

Hope shook her head and realized that Simmons had rationalized his behavior to the point that he had lost all sense of decency. "Don't you understand how dangerous this is?"

"I know what I'm doing," he countered stiffly. "No one is at risk. I'm careful never to give them more than what they need."

It occurred to Hope that this wasn't the first time Coach had done something like this. "Are you admitting you've done this with other teams?"

He brushed off the question. "Not your concern."

"It is my concern."

Coach sighed, as if losing patience. "Let me say this as plain and simply as I can. I'm not about to let some outsider step in and ruin me."

He didn't seem to recognize that it was too late. Hope wasn't the only one who knew what he'd done. Cade knew now, too. And once the truth was out, there would be no stopping it. Ben had been brave enough to step forward, and Hope was convinced that would lead others on the team to do the same. There was no way Coach Simmons would be able to brush this off as common practice.

Coach's eyes became like steel points as he glared at Hope and Cade. "You won't tell anyone, and neither will Ben and these other two."

Callie joined Spencer and glared at Simmons. "You kidnapped my brother, tied him up, and put him in a closet."

"He did that because I told Scott I was quitting the team," Ben explained.

Coach's face hardened. "You should have kept your mouth shut."

"I couldn't," Ben cried, "not after you set Spencer's car on fire."

"That was you?" Spencer yelled, his face red with anger.

Coach shrugged, as if it was a small thing. "I didn't want you snooping where you had no business."

It wasn't only Spencer's Dodge Dart that had been vandalized, Hope realized. "You're responsible for my slashed tire, too, aren't you?"

Coach Simmons smiled and gave a half-shrug. "That was Scott. He got carried away with that, and I told him so."

"You won't get away with this," Hope said, praying the coach would listen to reason. This had gone too far; there was no turning back.

"All your threats end right here. Right now," Coach shouted, loud enough for his voice to echo off the walls.

"I don't think so," Cade shouted.

Hope grabbed her phone, but before she could connect, Coach leaped forward and wrestled the phone out of her hand.

Raising his fist, he grabbed Hope hard enough to fling her back, slamming her head against the edge of the desk before she crumpled onto the floor.

Callie hurried to help Hope to her feet, while Cade struggled with Coach. Spencer raced from the room, phone in hand. Desperately reaching out, Hope grabbed hold of Callie as the room tilted at an awkward angle. Blood ran down from her forehead and into her eyes.

Seconds later, a siren could be heard in the distance. That didn't seem possible. The authorities had no way of knowing what was happening. Her head was spinning, and then all at once everything went black.

Chapter 24

⚜

Red and blue lights flashed outside the windows of Coach's office as Sheriff Terrance arrived, followed closely behind by the paramedics in the aid car.

Cade had been horrified and frantic when he realized Hope had been injured. As soon as he realized she was unconscious he'd nearly lost it. Fortunately, Sheriff Terrance had arrived when he did, otherwise Cade didn't know what might have happened. The urge to hurt Coach for what he'd done to Hope had been close to overwhelming him. His biggest concern, however, was for her. Somehow, Spencer had been able to call 911 for help during the confrontation, as the medical team arrived shortly after with law enforcement.

With his hands behind his back, Coach Simmons didn't go silently. He struggled against the restraints, all the while shouting obscenities.

"I'm going to sue your department for every penny it's worth. You won't get away with this," he snarled at the officer as he was led down the hall and outside, where a large crowd of students and parents had gathered in anticipation of the football game. "I have done nothing!" Simmons shouted to anyone who would listen. "This is an outrage."

Unconcerned about anything else, Cade focused his attention on Hope. She was sitting up as the paramedics worked on her. When he tried to get close, they shooed Cade away.

"Is she going to be all right?" he demanded.

"Cade, I'm fine," she insisted. "It's only a cut."

"You're not fine."

She laughed at his insistence that she was unwell.

"You lost consciousness."

"It was only for a few seconds."

"We're going to transport her to the hospital," the paramedic said, "as a precautionary measure."

"See," Cade said, grateful Hope would receive the medical attention she needed.

Although Hope protested, a gurney was brought in and she was placed on it. She held out her hand to Cade, and he walked alongside her.

"Thank you," she said. "I'm so grateful you came inside with me. Your fast thinking saved us."

He was quick to dismiss her appreciation and set out to follow her to the hospital, only to be held up by Sheriff Terrance, who asked that he and the three teenagers stay behind to answer a few questions.

Now that the deputy had taken Coach Simmons into custody and Hope had been transported to the hospital, the crowd had started to break up. The air was humming with speculation as to what had happened.

While they waited for the sheriff, Cade turned to the three teens. "How did the sheriff know where we were?" he asked. It seemed like a miracle.

Looking completely drained emotionally, Spencer explained. "When I ran into the hallway, I called nine-one-one and they connected me with Sheriff Terrance, who was headed to the game. Thankfully, he was close enough to respond quickly. I told him Ms. Goodwin might have been hurt."

Ben added, "I'd called my parents and told them everything. They urged me to go directly to Sheriff Terrance, but I wanted to talk to the rest of the team first. I felt we needed to stand united. Dad urged me not to risk it, but I wasn't sure anyone would believe me if I came forward alone."

"You should have listened to Dad," Callie said.

Ben's face fell as he nodded. "I thought I could trust Scott, but he was the one who tricked me and then handed me over to Coach Simmons."

Callie stood next to her twin, her face tight with suppressed anger. "Scott cared more about keeping his scholarship and reputation than worrying what might happen to Ben."

Cade couldn't help wondering what Coach had intended to do to Ben after the game. Once the truth was out, everything would fall apart. Simmons couldn't allow that to happen. Too much was at stake. He'd lose the right to compete at the state championship, and possibly lose the title Oceanside had won the previous year. And that was only the beginning of the fallout that was sure to follow. Once word got out, the accolades and possible career advancements would all come tumbling down.

One thing was certain: Simmons couldn't let Ben go free. Coach was backed into a corner, and there was no telling what the man was capable of. Cade didn't like to think what might have happened if they hadn't arrived when they did.

Cade couldn't stop thinking about what Hope had said as the paramedics wheeled her toward the aid car. She'd claimed he'd saved them. The words echoed in his mind with the memories of those he hadn't been able to save. This was vindication, a release. A heavy weight had been lifted from his shoulders and from his heart. It was as if Jeremy and Luke were standing next to him and giving him high fives. Then he recalled how badly he'd blown it with his mother earlier that day. Time was on his side. As Hope had reminded him, the door was open. The next move was up to him. As soon as he learned Hope wasn't badly hurt, he intended to connect with his family.

"How'd you know something was wrong?" Ben directed the question to his sister.

"Eagle rock," Callie told him. "When we couldn't reach you, Spencer and I went to the creek. You went there, didn't you?"

Ben nodded. "I needed to think things through. It was hard with both Mom and Dad out of town. What you said this morning about me being responsible as well for what happened to Spencer's car hit home. I knew Coach giving us those performance enhancers was wrong and the way we had been pledged to secrecy said as much."

"Spencer and I went there, and I could feel something was really wrong," Callie said.

Spencer placed his arm around her shoulders, holding her protectively against his side.

Ben smiled, studying the two of them standing side by side. "So you and Spence are an item now?"

Callie looked to Spencer, who only seemed to have eyes for her. "Yeah," she whispered. "We are."

Spencer cleared his throat. "We are? I mean, we are. Yes, we most definitely are."

Cade had to hand it to Ben. It'd taken courage to stand up to Coach, knowing there would be a price to pay.

The sheriff returned, and they were all questioned for what seemed like hours. As soon as Cade could, he broke away and hurried to the hospital where Hope had been taken. By the time he arrived, she had been checked over, given a CT scan to be sure there was no internal bleeding, and released. She sat in the waiting area outside of the emergency room and leaped to her feet, then walked directly into his arms. "I don't know what would have happened if not for you," she said, hugging him close.

"I'm no hero," he said, embarrassed to have what seemed like half the hospital staff watching them.

"You are to me," she said.

Closing his eyes, he rested his chin on the top of her head. "You're the only one who thinks so and the only one whose opinion matters to me."

Then, hand in hand, they headed home.

Chapter 25

The fallout from the drug scandal was the talk of Oceanside for the next few days as shock waves rolled through the tight-knit community. Two of the Seattle television stations sent reporters to town. In an effort to put a positive spin on things, Mayor Dudley claimed any publicity was good for the community. Hope prayed he was right.

A lot of the focus fell on Hope, as she had been in the center of the drama, along with Cade and the three high school students who had stood up against Coach. Channel 13 had specifically asked to interview her. She declined and recommended the reporter talk to Cade, who was the real hero in her eyes. He declined as well, uncomfortable with the attention.

As she entered her U.S. History class and saw the two teenagers who'd been with her that fateful day with Coach Simmons, she couldn't help but smile. Spencer and Callie were almost always together these days. Where one was, she was sure to find the other. They sat together in the two classes they shared and at the same table in the cafeteria.

It did Hope's heart good to see them both happy. The way she saw it, the two nicely balanced each other out. From what she'd heard, Spencer had decided against Yale, and they were both planning to attend Washington State University in Pullman following graduation.

As for Scott Pender, with the football program suspended for the rest of the season, his chance at a scholarship was gone. Although he'd played an explicit role in Ben's kidnapping, he was given a light sentence of community service hours that would take him well into the new year. That and his fall from glory were punishment enough.

Ben Rhodes had been praised by the local newspaper for his willingness to stand up against what he knew was wrong. Even with Coach's threats hanging over his head, Ben had made a courageous decision to come forward.

Despite declaring it all a misunderstanding, Coach Simmons had been charged on a number of counts and was currently awaiting trial. He hadn't been able to make bail, and sat in his cell, which Hope personally felt was the best place for him. He'd been smug and delusional to believe he could get away with what he did. His arrogance had led him to believe he was invincible, and no one would dare to stand up against him.

The high school halls were filled with milling students and chatter as they made their way to the last class. Hope had waited for this day for a long time. She had special guests visiting this afternoon. Cade, Silas, Ricardo, Dean, and Shelley were in the school, ready to speak to her class.

The bell rang and her students automatically took to their seats. Hope waited until the room quieted down before she stepped in front of her students.

"Instead of the lesson today . . ."

"Ah, come on Ms. Goodwin, you're not giving us a pop quiz, are you?"

A groan echoed through the room. This was a Friday before a holiday weekend, and everyone was more eager than usual to get out and get going.

Hope waved her hand dismissively. "No pop quiz, I promise."

Sighs of appreciation followed.

"Can anyone tell me what we're celebrating on Monday?" Hope asked.

"No school day."

"Very funny," she said, shaking her head at their lack of knowledge and appreciation for the meaning of this holiday.

"Veterans Day," Spencer supplied. If anyone knew, it would be him.

"That's right. Can anyone tell me why the holiday is celebrated on November eleventh?"

No one seemed to know. "That's the day the armistice was signed ending the First World War," she explained. "Which was also called the War to End All Wars, but did it?" She left the question open-ended.

"My dad's older brother, my uncle Bill, was in the first Gulf War," Brooke mentioned.

"Anyone else know someone who served in the military during wartime?"

Several hands shot up, and a few students shared their own friends and family members who served.

As the conversations slowed, Hope suggested, "If you have the chance, thank each one for their service."

Walking toward the door, Hope turned back to her class. "As it happens, I have had the opportunity to meet a few veterans recently. I've invited them to speak to our class. Before I introduce them, I want to encourage you to carefully listen to their stories. These are valiant individuals who have sacrificed a great deal for the freedoms we enjoy. I would ask that you give them the respect and gratitude they deserve." She had the full attention of her class.

She paused and then added, "I can't say this strongly enough. Be worthy of the sacrifices they have made."

Hope opened the door, and Cade walked in first, followed behind by Silas, Ricardo, Shelley, and Dean.

"I'd like to introduce my friend Cade Lincoln first. Cade served in Afghanistan and was honorably discharged after being injured in an IED explosion."

"I saw you with Ms. Goodwin earlier," Carter said.

"Yes, your teacher has been a good friend to me," Cade said, as he moved to the front of the class. "You may have noticed that I walk with a slight limp. It was a lot worse when I first came home, but it's better now." He hesitated before he continued. "You see, not all injuries in war are visible or physical. Compared to my friends here, my physical injuries are minor. You wouldn't have been able to see all the damage that was going on in my head, or the way I looked at the world. Two of my best friends were killed, and for a long time I regretted that I hadn't died with them."

For the next forty minutes each man spoke in turn, telling of their experiences. Shelley spoke last. Hope was proud of her class, proud of the attention they paid and how intently they listened to each veteran's story. Shelley got the most questions from the female students in the class. When the bell rang, calling for the end of class and the end of the school day, not a single student got up to leave.

"Do we have to go?" Angela pleaded. "I have another question."

"Me, too," several others called out.

For the following thirty minutes, those who didn't need to catch a bus remained in their seats, their curiosity and wonder apparent. They would have stayed longer if Hope hadn't put an end to the discussion. Groans of disappointment followed.

"I'll invite them back another time," Hope promised.

It was obvious by the reluctant way her class got up from their desks how much they wanted to continue. Even then, they lingered in the classroom, gathering around the men and Shelley with more questions. With respect and awe. With an understanding and appreciation of what it meant to be a veteran and to sacrifice for honor and freedom.

Before Cade's friends left, Hope personally thanked each one. She didn't need to tell them the impact their stories, their sacrifices, had made on her U.S. History class. Until that afternoon, the teenagers had viewed Veterans Day as a holiday. A day they didn't need to attend classes. A morning to sleep in and not worry about homework or pop quizzes. Their under-standing now went much deeper, thanks to the bravery of the stories they'd heard.

Cade silently stayed behind to accompany Hope to the teachers' parking lot. Hope could tell something was on his mind. She wondered if it'd been talking about the loss of his two closest friends.

"Cade?"

He shuffled his feet back and forth and placed his hands inside his pockets before blurting out, "I reached out to my mother."

So that was it. She had thought he would, especially after the regret he felt when she'd sought him out. Hope carefully weighed her reaction. She didn't want to appear overly ex-cited, although she was, for fear the conversation didn't go well. Nor did she want to downplay the significance of what he was telling her.

"How'd it go?"

He shrugged. "All right, I guess. I wanted to tell you earlier. I guess I probably should have."

"It's fine, Cade."

"I didn't want you to think I was doing this behind your back."

He didn't owe her any explanation.

"I just wasn't sure how it would go. Naturally, I was hope-ful. We talked a lot about my dad. We've both been angry and bitter, not that it's done either of us any good."

"It's a step in the right direction."

Cade nodded. "Mom read about what happened with

Coach Simmons in the paper and was proud of the role I played. She asked about you, and I assured her we were good." He lifted his head so he could look into her eyes. "We're good, aren't we?" he asked.

Hope smiled. "Very good."

His smile broadened. "I think so, too, which brings up something else."

"Oh?"

"Mom asked us to come to dinner on Monday. She made sure I understood that the invitation came from my father, too."

Veterans Day. That had significance, as if his parents were telling Cade, as best they could, they were proud of the fact that he'd served his country.

He exhaled a long sigh. "I don't know what to expect. Would you be willing to come with me?"

"Of course."

"Not as a crutch," he was quick to explain. "I want you with me because Mom invited you and because you mean everything to me. Any healing between me and my parents would never have happened without you."

Hope could tell he meant every word. "I'd be honored."

Monday afternoon, Hope didn't know who was more nervous as they approached the beautiful hilltop home that overlooked the Tacoma Narrows. The neighborhood was affluent, and the view of the water was spectacular, even in the rain. The twin bridges spanned the waterway and captured Hope's attention. The scene was like something out of a travel magazine. Cade parked in the driveway, cut the engine, and then turned to Hope.

"You ready?" he asked, and reached for her hand.

"That's the question I should be asking you."

He drew in a deep breath and appeared to be holding it before releasing it, as if mentally preparing himself. "I think so. Mom insists the invitation is from my father, too, but I wonder if that is wishful thinking on her part."

"It's going to be fine." She had faith, even if Cade remained skeptical.

"Be prepared if we need to leave on short notice. My dad's . . . well, you'll know once you meet him."

"I'm not worried." Hope had to believe his mother wouldn't bring Cade back into the family home without first having laid the groundwork for a reconciliation between Cade and his father.

Cade escorted Hope to the front door under the porch covering and out of the rain. He hesitated for only a second before ringing the doorbell. His mother must have been standing in the entry awaiting their arrival because almost immediately they were welcomed inside.

Sara looked at her son and blinked back tears as she pressed her hands on either side of his face. She gave him a watery smile before the two hugged.

"I've dreamed of this day," she said, and turned to greet Hope. "Welcome, welcome. Please come inside."

Cade reached for Hope's hand, as if gaining strength and resolve by the connection. He seemed to be filled with nervous energy, and frankly, so was she.

Cade's father sat in the formal living room in a wing-backed chair in front of the fireplace, which had a gentle fire flickering. He was reading the newspaper. He looked up when Cade and Hope entered the room and lowered the paper.

"Cade," he said with a curt nod.

"John." Cade's returning one was equally brusque.

John frowned. "I'm your father, son, and that's what you should call me."

Silence filled the room before Cade said, "Dad." His voice cracked and he cleared his throat.

Coming out of his chair, his father stood. There appeared to be a thin sheen of moisture in the older man's eyes as he gripped Cade by the shoulders and hugged him close. "Good to have you home, son." He blinked a few times before he turned his attention to Hope. "Seeing that my son hasn't seen fit to introduce you, I'm John Cade Senior."

"I'm Hope Goodwin," she said, as the tension eased from between her shoulder blades.

"Your mother has been fretting over this meal for a week." He directed the comment to Cade, as he shook Hope's hand. He led them into the dining room. "She wanted to be sure she remembered all your favorites."

"Tacos and fried chicken?" Cade asked, smiling.

"It seems both are on the menu. I insisted on mashed potatoes and gravy to go with the chicken." As he spoke, he pulled out a chair for Hope, silently inviting her to take a seat.

"I'd like to help in the kitchen, if I may," she said.

"We appreciate the offer, but Sara's got everything under control."

Hope took the seat and Cade sat down beside her. He

reached for her hand and released a sigh as his father made an excuse to go into the kitchen. He returned in quick fashion to deliver the serving dishes.

"That's new," Cade whispered, as his father headed back into the other room.

"What is?"

"My father lifting a hand to help Mom with dinner. It appears things have changed in the last six years."

The meal was delicious, and as it progressed the tension left the room. Conversation flowed freely with a lot of discussion revolving around the recent events in Oceanside. Neither man spoke of the past. What amazed Hope was how Cade and his father pretended this split in their relationship had never happened. Perhaps it was easier that way. The closest it came to being the least bit uncomfortable was when the subject of Cade's job arose.

"I understand from your mother you work at a tire store as a mechanic. Is that right?" his father commented, and although it sounded casual, Hope knew it wasn't an idle question.

"I do," Cade said, without elaboration.

"And you enjoy that work?"

"Very much."

It seemed everyone at the table held their breath for his father's reaction. They didn't need to wait long.

"You always were good with your hands. Even as a kid you enjoyed taking things apart. Cars these days are complicated machines. It takes someone who knows what they're doing to figure out their inner workings."

—

After dessert was served and enjoyed—lemon meringue pie, another of Cade's favorites—he made their excuses. They had a two-hour drive to Oceanside ahead of them. After words of appreciation from Cade and Hope, both parents walked them to the front door.

"It was good to see you, son," John said.

"You too, Dad."

His mother hugged them both. With the rain coming down hard, Cade placed his hand at the small of Hope's back as they raced toward his truck.

Once out of the weather, Cade reached for Hope. He placed his hand around the back of her neck and dragged her mouth to his for a lengthy kiss. She was breathless when he released her, blinking several times at the passion behind the unexpected kiss.

"What was that about?" she asked, her hand over the rapid beat of her heart.

"A thank-you for coming with me today. For sharing your heart with me. For helping me to bridge the gap between my parents and me. In case you haven't figured it out, I'm in love with you, Hope."

Smiling, she leaned her head against his shoulder. "I sorta figured. Guess you know I feel the same way about you."

"Yup," he said, and started the engine. He put the car in reverse, ready to back out of the long driveway when Hope placed her hand on his forearm, stopping him.

Cade reverted his attention to her. "Treasure your family, Cade."

Her words deeply touched him, seeing Hope had none of her own. "I do," he assured her.

Her smile was wide as she gave his arm a gentle squeeze.

"Ready?" he asked.

"Ready," she told him.

They were headed home.

Chapter 26

As much as he'd first hated the thought of counseling and group therapy, Cade had come to look forward to his weekly sessions with Harry. The man was wise beyond his years.

Cade had come a long way from the angry, bitter man who'd stood before Judge Walters. He never would have believed serving his community with the court-ordered hours would have such a profound effect upon his life. Meeting Hope had changed everything for him. She was his light. His hope. Watching her patience and care for Shadow changed him. When he'd left the courtroom to do the community service hours required by the judge, his head had been messed up. He found it hard to believe that anyone really cared. Not for returning veterans, or for discarded animals. From the moment he'd met Hope, he'd been drawn to her. The attraction had gotten stronger, week by week, until she was all he thought about. Meeting with Harry and the others had helped him see he had the will and the power to move beyond the pain and loss of Jeremy and Luke, and the war in general. Hope gave him the incentive to be more, to work hard, to let go of the mental and physical agonies of war—to be the man she deserved. As was his practice, Harry waited for Cade to start the conversation. Eager to talk, Cade leaned forward. "The dinner with my parents went far better than I hoped."

"Wonderful, Cade. I felt that it would." These weren't words of platitude. Harry had never been one to speak anything but truth, whether Cade wanted to hear it or not. What Cade found amazing was how little Harry talked during their sessions. He let Cade find the truth with a few leading questions that subtly pointed him to the answers he needed.

"Dad didn't bring up our fight all those years ago, and I didn't, either." Cade had been prepared if his father had been determined to dig up the past. The bitterness between them could explode with only a few misspoken words. Cade had decided he would politely listen, more for Hope's sake than for his own, apologize if that was what was needed, and ask if they could find a way to forgive each other. He had everything he'd planned to say prepared in his mind.

Yet neither of them said a word about that horrible day when Cade had walked away from his family. Not a single word.

A smile teased the edges of Harry's mouth.

"You find that humorous?"

"Not exactly. I find it refreshing. You referred to him as Dad now instead of John."

It had been the most telling moment of the evening. As

soon as his father spoke, Cade knew they were both ready to move forward and leave that final scene buried. He never would have thought it possible until then.

They both had regrets. Both had misgivings. And it seemed neither one was willing to review their mistakes. There was no need when they were willing to let bygones be bygones. His dad preferred it that way, and frankly so did Cade. Right away the atmosphere had relaxed, and they were able to enjoy the dinner. Some awkwardness had remained, but only in the beginning. As the meal progressed it was almost as if no time had passed.

Cade had been grateful for Hope's presence. She was exactly the buffer they had all needed. He could tell that his mother was fond of her, and it wouldn't surprise him if he learned the two had talked a couple times before this dinner. It was important to Cade that Hope feel comfortable with his parents. His desire was that one day she would be his wife and they would become her family.

"This is our final session," Harry reminded him.

"The time went fast."

"It always does. I'm proud of you, Cade, and the work you've done."

"Thank you." Harry wasn't one to hand out easy compliments. His words of praise warmed him from the inside out.

"What are your plans for the future?" Harry asked.

"I'm a good mechanic," Cade said. The grease under his fingernails proved it. "I've always enjoyed solving puzzles and using my brain. When I first went to college, I squandered my time with parties, giving my studies the bare minimum of effort. I'd like to go back, and this time apply myself."

"Don't you already have one degree?"

"I do, in political science. It was a degree my father thought would be an advantage before I entered law school."

"And what would your studies be now?" Harry asked.

"Engineering. I believe I can make a success of it. It won't take nearly as long this time, as I've fulfilled all my prerequisites. I've talked it over with Hope, and she's all for it. We both know it won't be easy to manage both school and work, plus our relationship. She's my encouragement. I thank God every single day for sending her into my life."

"An attitude of gratitude," Harry said. "That, young man, will take you far."

"The VA will help me with tuition costs, and hopefully I'll be able to work enough hours to pay for my basic living expenses." His budget would be tight, leaving little room for entertainment and unexpected costs. Sacrifices would need to be made. He was willing, and with Hope at his side, he felt confident of success.

"Have you talked to your parents about this?"

Cade hadn't. Their relationship was fragile, and he didn't want to risk upsetting it until they were on firmer ground. "Not yet."

"Why not?"

Leave it to Harry to ask.

"Guess I'm afraid they'll be disappointed. Not my mother so much as my father." There, he'd said it out loud. He couldn't bear to destroy the delicate relationship they had started to rebuild.

Harry nodded, as though he understood.

"I'll tell them in time."

"I can't speak for your parents, Cade, but I believe they've learned their lesson and are willing to give you the support and encouragement you need to follow your own path."

"From your lips to God's ear." Cade sincerely hoped his counselor was right.

"Will I see you Wednesday night?" Harry asked at the end of their session.

"I wouldn't miss it," he said.

They both stood and exchanged handshakes. Cade owed this man a great deal. He'd never forget Harry and the work he had done for him and countless other returning veterans. The counselor had been on the battlefield himself. He, too, had struggled with demons and found his way back, and in doing so helped to lead others on the same path to wholeness, despite their experiences and losses.

The Wednesday before Thanksgiving, Harry and his wife, Penny, had invited the group session attendees to a potluck dinner at their home. They were to have their own celebration together.

Over the weeks since they'd first started meeting, these men and Shelley had become his closest friends. They had shared a piece of themselves with one another, the deepest, darkest moments of loss. Together, they had held one another up with understanding, compassion, and encouragement. Cade knew that although the group wouldn't meet again formally, they would all remain in touch as friends. Good friends. The kind of friends one could call in the middle of the night and not worry about being a bother.

Cade picked up Hope and had to wait for her corn casserole to finish cooking before they could leave. The recipe was one she got from her grandmother, and a Thanksgiving tradition. They gave Shadow lots of love and attention before heading out.

Because Hope had gotten delayed at school and hadn't been able to get the casserole into the oven when she'd originally planned to, they were the last to arrive.

Penny invited them into the house, and Hope disappeared into the kitchen with her, carting the casserole with thick oven mitts.

Silas greeted Cade with a slap across his back. "About time you got here."

"Glad to hear I was missed." Silas had brought Jada, who was chatting with Dean's wife on the sofa.

Shelley and Ricardo were on the other side of the room, sitting next to each other, holding hands. Romance was brewing between those two. Cade hadn't noticed what was right under his nose until the day the group had gone to the high school to speak to Hope's U.S. History class and they arrived together. It was the first time he'd seen them outside of their sessions. The way they looked at each other that day spoke volumes.

As they gathered at the table, Cade noticed it was a crisscross of cultural delights, each person sharing their family favorites. Silas brought sweet potato pie, but he was quick to credit Jada for baking it. Ricardo contributed homemade tamales and Dean and his wife added potato casserole. Harry and Penny provided a ham.

Before they dished up, Harry paused and offered a simple prayer.

As he looked around at those seated at the table, Cade felt good. Bowing his head, he silently thanked God for His many blessings.

When Harry finished the prayer, Cade looked up and knew this was only the beginning. The very best was yet to come.

Epilogue

After politely knocking, Cade waited for permission to enter Judge Walters's chamber.

"Come in." Her voice came from the other side of the door.

The judge sat at her desk, her glasses perched on the tip of her nose as she reviewed the papers in front of her.

"Thank you for agreeing to see me," Cade said, as he came into the room.

When she looked up, Cade could tell by her expression that she didn't remember him. With literally hundreds of defendants parading through her courtroom week after week, it was little wonder.

"I'm John Cade Lincoln Junior. I stood before you a little over a year ago with a list of charges as long as your arm." He reminded her of the circumstances and the orders he'd been given.

Recognition lit up her face when he mentioned the physical therapy. "Soldier boy."

"Yes, Your Honor."

"What can I do for you, young man?"

"I wanted to thank you. By all that was right and fair, I should have spent the last year behind bars. But you gave me a second chance, and I wanted to tell you how much I appreciate your faith in me."

Leaning back, the judge removed her glasses and set them on her desktop. "As I recall, you needed to make restitution."

It'd taken longer than Cade had hoped to pay off the cost of those damages. As it happened, Silas was working in an upholstery shop. Together they had reupholstered all the booths. Cade had paid for the fabric. The bar owner had deducted the cost of the booth against what he owed in damages, and that had helped considerably. Silas had refused to accept any compensation for his time.

"You aren't paying me, man. This is what friends do," Silas had grumbled, as if Cade's offer had insulted him.

"Need another favor," Cade told him. He had no intention of abusing the other man's friendship.

"You name it."

That was the kind of friend Silas was. "I'm going to need a best man, and I can't think of anyone who has been a better friend than you."

Silas had laughed. "You want this ugly face standing next to you while you wait for your bride?"

"No one I'd rather have."

"You got it, with the stipulation that if Jada decides she'll be my wife, you'll stand up for me."

"Soldier," the judge said, bringing Cade back to the present.

"Paid in full, Your Honor."

She nodded approvingly.

"All my community service hours are completed, as are the counseling sessions," he told her, and then, because he thought he should tell her, he added, "I didn't go into it with a good attitude. I'm here to tell you it was the best thing I could have done. It would never have happened if it hadn't been ordered by you."

Her smile told him she appreciated his truth.

"I can see by the way you waltzed in here that the physical therapy helped, too."

The pain in his leg came and went. It would always be part of him, just as the loss of his two friends would. The pain was a constant reminder that he had been left alive for a reason.

"Your limp is barely noticeable," she commented.

"I'll admit there were days when I was cursing your name while doing those exercises. In the end they helped. I still limp, especially at the end of a long day, but not nearly as much as before."

The judge reached for her glasses. "So, what's next for you, Soldier?"

"I'm returning to college for an engineering degree. I was prepared to become a starving student, take on the loans, and do whatever was necessary to get my degree."

"You can manage working and school?"

"I can now, thanks to my parents. They had money set aside for me to attend law school and offered to pay my school expenses for this next degree. I wasn't going to let them, thinking they'd already paid for one, but I changed my mind."

Hope had helped him to see he was being stubborn. This offer was his father's way of apologizing for pressuring Cade to enter law school. It didn't take much of an argument to convince Cade to accept, especially since it meant he'd be able to marry Hope much sooner than he would if he had to pay all his expenses himself.

"Good."

"I wanted to pay them back at some point, and they said the only way I could do that was by giving them grandchildren to spoil." Cade was back on an even keel with his parents. They were overjoyed when he announced he'd asked Hope to marry him, and she'd agreed. While he and Hope talked wedding plans, his parents were a couple years ahead, planning for the arrival of grandchildren. It never failed to amuse him how anxious his dad was to hold a grandchild. That was what he expected from his mother, though she was equally enthused. His father's eagerness was what had surprised him.

"I told my daughter I'd pay her a hundred thousand dollars for a grandchild," the judge told him with a straight face.

Cade's eyes flared. "You were teasing, right?"

"Yes, unfortunately. I'm tired of waiting, and I wanted my daughter and her husband to know I'm not getting any younger."

Cade held back a laugh. It seemed his parents were on the same wavelength.

"I'd like to send you a wedding invitation," Cade said. "Hope and I are planning a January wedding. I'd be honored if you could attend."

"I'd be more than happy to come if I can," Judge Walters

assured him. "Thank you for stopping by, Soldier. You made my day."

What the judge didn't seem to understand was that she'd saved his life. He owed her everything. He fully intended to live up to her expectations in gratitude for the second chance she'd given him.

"How did everything go?" Hope asked, when he joined her. He'd wanted her to come with him, but she'd refused, preferring to wait for him outside. This was something he needed to do on his own, she'd said.

"It went really well," he said, as he turned her into his arms and kissed her. This was the woman he loved, the very one who'd filled his life with her warmth and love, the one who had given him hope and a future.

ABOUT THE AUTHOR

DEBBIE MACOMBER, the author of *The Best Is Yet to Come, It's Better This Way, A Walk Along the Beach, Window on the Bay, Cottage by the Sea, Any Dream Will Do, If Not for You,* and the Rose Harbor Inn series, is a leading voice in women's fiction. Fifteen of her novels have reached #1 on the *New York Times* bestseller lists, and five of her beloved Christmas novels have been hit movies on the Hallmark Channel, including *Mrs. Miracle* and *Mr. Miracle.* Hallmark Channel also produced the original series *Debbie Macomber's Cedar Cove,* based on Macomber's Cedar Cove books. She is also the author of the cookbook *Debbie Macomber's Table.* There are more than 200 million copies of her books in print worldwide.

debbiemacomber.com
Facebook.com/debbiemacomberworld
Twitter: @debbiemacomber
Instagram: @debbiemacomber
Pinterest.com/macomberbooks

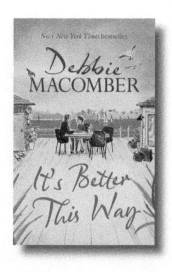

Will Julia get a second chance at her happy-ever-after?

It's been nearly six years since Julia Jones had her heart broken.
After her husband fell in love with another woman, Julia fought
to keep her family together, but now, recalling the words of her
beloved father, she realises it's time to move on: It's better this way.

Desperate for a fresh start, Julia sells the family home and
moves into an apartment complex, and she's delighted to
discover that her new abode comes with a gorgeous new
neighbour. Heath is a welcome change from the men Julia
usually dates, and as a divorcé himself he understands
the difficulties of a fractured family all too well.

As a relationship between Julia and Heath blossoms, Julia
dares to dream that her life is looking up - until a dramatic
revelation threatens their newfound happiness. Will Julia and
Heath find a way through – and will it be together?

Could a holiday romance save Everly's Christmas?

When the opportunity arises for work-obsessed Everly
Lancaster to take the whole of December off, she decides
it's time to go on the holiday of a lifetime. Little does
she know, there's more than one surprise in
store for her this Christmas . . .

Hoping to escape a snowstorm, Everly prepares for a
sunny, relaxing cruise – until a mix-up with her booking
lands her somewhere she never expected. At first, not
even the handsome tour guide Asher can improve
her mood, but soon the spectacular sights open
Everly's eyes to all she's been missing out on.

As Christmas approaches and the tour comes to an end,
will Everly finally realise there's more to life than work?
And could Asher be the person to help her see it?

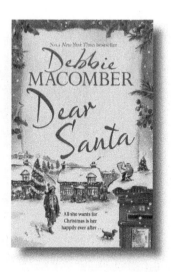

There's no place like home for the holidays . . .

Lindy Carmichael isn't feeling particularly joyful as she returns to her childhood home for Christmas with her family. Having just had her heart broken, it seems that nothing can reignite her in festive spirit. That is, until her mother uncovers a box of childhood letters to Santa in the hope of restoring her faith.

Reminiscing about what she'd wished for as a child sparks the inspiration Lindy needs to get her life back on track. With her mother's encouragement, she decides to write a new letter to Santa, filled with her hopes for the future – and little does she know, her wishes are about to unfold in the most unexpected of ways . . .

With a little Christmas magic – and a surprising connection with a handsome former classmate – will Lindy realise that there truly is no place like home for the holidays?

Will they find their happy-ever-after this Christmas?

Peter and Hank are lifelong friends, but when it comes
to their jobs they couldn't be more different. Peter is a small-
town pastor while Hank runs the local pub, and neither of
them ever settled down, believing their demanding jobs are
keeping them from finding love. Convinced that the other has it
easier, they hatch a plan to swap places the week before
Christmas to put their theories to the test.

But as Hank quickly becomes overwhelmed by nativity plans,
and Peter struggles to control the rowdy festive pub-goers, they
each begin to worry they're in over their heads . . .

This Christmas, will Peter and Hank's stunt fall flat, or will it
open their eyes to the possibility of love at last?

Join us at

The Little Book Café

For competitions galore,
exclusive interviews with our lovely
Sphere authors, chat about
all the latest books
and much, much more.

Follow us on Twitter at
🐦 @littlebookcafe
Subscribe to our newsletter and
Like us at 🄵/thelittlebookcafe

Read. Love. Share.